JOHN STURGLON

BURN MARKS

Black Rose Writing | Texas

ISBN: 978-1-68513-053-4
PUBLISHED BY BLACK ROSE WRITING
www.blackrosewriting.com

Printed in the United States of America
Suggested Retail Price (SRP) $22.95

Burn Marks is printed in Chaparral Pro

*As a planet-friendly publisher, Black Rose Writing does its best to
eliminate unnecessary waste to reduce paper usage and energy
costs, while never compromising the reading experience. As a result,
the final word count vs. page count may not meet common
expectations.

To Mary, my love, thanks for all you do and pictures that make me look good.

BURN
MARKS

Siesta Key, Florida

It was the last day of their trip, the last of ten days they had spent sitting in the sun, eating raw oysters and drinking silly drinks with tiny umbrellas stuck in them. It was a Thursday and Siesta Key Beach was not as crowded as it would be the next day. There were still people, but most of the noise in the air came from the waves of the Gulf and the constant wind from the south. The sun was hot as the clock neared four o'clock; they had about twenty minutes before their rental chairs and umbrella were due back. There would be one more dinner, one more night of drinks and oysters and love making. One more night and then back to Milton.

Steve Marks had hoped that the trip would bring him clarity. He didn't need clarity with Tori. None was needed. He wanted to get married and have children; she didn't. He still loved her and wasn't going anywhere. That wasn't the problem. Marks had been on the Milton Police Department the last twelve years; he had been a detective for the last eight. With the exception of the Fatty Fuller mystery the past fall, most of the cases that Marks dealt with were domestic disturbances or a fight in one of the bars, strip clubs or the Trips Aces casino. There was very little police work and less detection.

Most of what he did was closer to managing a high school detention class.

There was little hope for Marks when it came to promotion. His former high school classmate, Lou Katz, was the Chief of Police. He was the same age as Marks. Unless Lou decided to run for some political office, it didn't look like he was going anywhere. Why would he? He had a nice, cushy job, nice pension, beautiful wife and great family. No, Lou would be the Chief for some time and Marks would be his lead detective when someone stole a lawn ornament, or two drunks went at each other in Lifers.

He had heard about the offer from a friend that lived up in Chicago. They were looking for qualified detectives and Marks had applied. His friend had helped push the application along. The ZOOM interview had gone well. He got the letter before they had left for Florida. Chicago had offered him the job. They gave him two weeks to decide. He had four days left to respond. It would give Marks the opportunity to get out of Milton, up to Chicago, and do some real police work. It would give Marks the opportunity to do what he wanted. Tori was all for it. She told Marks to take the offer and get an apartment up in Chicago. For the time being, she would rent out the condo overlooking the Mississippi and then follow Marks to Chicago. She was an artist. She could work anywhere.

Marks rubbed the stubble of his chin. His beard never came in evenly and he rarely went a day without shaving, but he had let it go for a few. The bristles were tough. He'd shave before dinner. The thoughts of leaving nagged him. He couldn't decide. He wanted to get out, away from Milton, and the Milton PD, but he had lived his entire life in Milton. There was also the issue with his mother. Sixty-five years old with dementia and now suffering from cancer. The outlook for her was not good. What kind of son would leave his mother behind and move one hundred and fifty miles away? It wasn't that far, but it bothered Marks. He shook his head.

He looked to the water just as Tori was making her way out of the Gulf and walking towards him. The sun was directly behind her, providing a glare which silhouetted her body. It didn't matter. Marks knew how beautiful she was and how lucky he was. She got back to the umbrella and leaned over to kiss Marks on the cheek. He smiled.

"You look extremely lost in thought," she said as she toweled herself off.

"Just thinking," he said.

"Chicago or Milton?"

"You should have been a cop."

She laughed. "The decision doesn't sound that tough to me. You are bored with the work you do and there's no place to move up. I understand about your mom, but she's in a good home and it's only a two-hour drive. If there's an emergency, we can get back here in a hurry."

He looked out at all of the vast water of the Gulf. "There's just something about leaving Milton that keeps gnawing at me."

"Lou Katz?"

"No, not Lou. He'd be mad I'm sure, but he'd understand, I think."

"So what is it?"

"I've been in Milton my whole life. It's all I know. Maybe I'm a little scared."

"Of what? Failing in Chicago?"

"Not failing, Tor. Just maybe not fitting in. You leave a town of twenty thousand to go to a city of six million it's a little daunting."

"Maybe," she said, "but what about the chance of you doing some real police work and possible promotion?"

"That's what I give up if I stay."

"Well," she said, "you've got four days before you've got to let them know. We still have tonight. What do you say we try and make the best of our time?"

He looked over at her, her face tanned from the days in the sun, the long auburn hair and her brown eyes shining brightly. "Tonight is for you. Tomorrow we get back and in a couple of days I'll make a decision."

She reached out and touched his hand. "You'll make a great Chicago detective. The city can give me a lot of inspiration. It also has some of the best restaurants in the world."

He nodded. "Guess we'll know in four days."

ONE

The phone on the bedside table rang. Marks was in a deep sleep and thought for a moment the ringing was coming from a dream. He tried hard to avoid the phone, but Tori nudged him. The poke in the ribs made him realize that the phone that was ringing was the one next to him. He reached across and grabbed it. "Marks," he said.

"Stevie, Lou. You've got to get over to the Aces," Lou Katz said.

Marks checked the alarm clock on the same table as the phone. It said five-forty. "I said I'd be in by eight."

"Sorry about the early wake-up call, but somebody killed a homeless man behind the casino."

"Homeless man? Behind the casino?"

"That's what I said, but maybe I wasn't clear. Somebody stabbed the poor guy in the throat."

Now Marks was fully awake. "Anybody see anything?"

"Just the janitor throwing out bags of trash. The body was leaning up against a Dumpster. Can you be ready in twenty? I'll swing by and get you?"

"Do I have a choice?"

"See you in twenty."

Marks hung up the phone and lay back on his pillow, staring at the ceiling.

"That didn't sound good," Tori said.

"Somebody killed a homeless guy in back of the casino. Not too much to go on, but the guy was stabbed in the throat."

"So much for boring old Milton." Tori rolled on her side away from Marks.

Boring old Milton thought Marks. He got out of bed and headed for the shower.

. . .

It was a late March morning, and it was cold. There was frost on the cars and a thin layer of ice-covered spots in the driveway. After the ten days in Florida, Marks was sure his blood had thinned. He shivered as he saw Lou Katz pull up in the department sedan. Marks gladly got in.

"Not like Siesta Key, I bet?" Lou said.

"Sure. Twenty-four and foggy every day. Perfect for your tan."

"Brought you this." Lou handed Marks a Styrofoam cup with a lid on it. "Mary made it for you. I didn't think I'd be able to stop."

Marks took the lid off the cup and smelled the coffee. He took a generous sip. "Mary is too good for you."

Lou laughed. "Sorry to give you the shock treatment upon your return."

Marks sipped the hot coffee again. "I'm sure you didn't plan on this."

"We went from a town with no murders to one that gets one every month or so."

The Fatty Fuller murder had exposed a torrent of corruption and violence. Now this homeless guy's murder. Maybe Milton wasn't so boring, Marks thought. "So, what do you think about this one?"

"Not much, yet. Let's get out there and see what we've got."

The Dumpsters where the Trips Aces Casino piled their garbage were located about a hundred yards behind the main casino building. Behind the canisters was the Mississippi. The fog that rose off the river was thick, but the area was well lighted. This didn't keep the rats away. Some, many said, were as big as a small dog. Tonight, the area was flooded with Milton uniformed cops, probably the entire graveyard shift. One portion had been roped off with yellow crime scene tape. Marks thought it looked like something out of a movie or a TV show.

The gathered cops, who were mostly gawking as Lou Katz and Marks walked up, parted so that the Chief and lead detective could pass through to the dead body. Near the Dumpster at the far end of the row was a tall light tower. At the base of this tower lay the body.

Marks stepped under the crime tape and approached the body; Lou was close behind him. For some reason, Marks was nervous. Was it okay to feel this way when dealing with a homicide? How could he go to Chicago if he couldn't handle this? He took a deep breath. There was enough light under the tower for them to see everything clearly. The dead man wore old, rumpled clothes. His hair was a mixture of gray and black. There was a smell around the man, but Marks couldn't tell if it was from the man or the garbage bins. Next to the man were two large, black plastic bags, the man's life possessions. Marks noted a small dish. He stepped closer. The dish held some sort of dried dog food. Lastly Marks noted the severe puncture wound at the base of the man's neck. That and the amount of blood that had spurted down the front of the man and onto the ground.

"Fuck," he said.

"Looks like somebody just walked up to him and stabbed him in the throat," Lou said.

"Yeah. Looks like his dog got away," Marks said, pointing at the dish. "Who's the guy that called this in?"

"Guy's name is Martin. Johnny Martin. He's a custodian. They are holding him inside. Say he's pretty shook up."

"Yeah, me too, but there isn't much for us to do here. Guess John Mack can bag this poor guy. Let's go have a chat with Johnny Martin."

Before they could step back under the crime tape, a younger man in a suit and raincoat stepped under it. The man was in his mid- twenties, his longer blonde hair hanging down over his forehead. He looked up at Marks and Lou. "Sorry I'm late, Chief," he said.

"Who the hell are you?" Marks said.

"This is Anders Hedberg," Katz said. "He's on loan to us from Sterling, a cross training project. He'll be riding with you for the time being."

"That's refreshing," Marks said.

"Do I need to do anything?" Anders Hedberg asked.

Marks threw a thumb over his shoulder. "Go take a look at your first client."

Anders walked past the two of them and took a look at the dead man. "Oh my god," he said. He took about ten steps to the right and quickly threw up in a small stand of bushes.

"This out to be fun," Marks said. "Thanks for the help."

• • • •

Johnny Martin was a thick-bodied, middle- aged black guy. He had a short Afro and wore big glasses that covered his eyes. He was sitting at a table in the employees' lunchroom, sipping on a cup of coffee. A patrolman was sitting near him, but the two were not talking. Johnny Martin looked like he had seen a ghost.

Marks approached the table with Anders Hedberg. Lou had left in his car; Marks would return in Hedberg's car. Johnny Martin barely looked up when Marks stood by him.

"Sorry it had to be you that saw that, Johnny," Marks said. "I'm Detective Marks. I'd like to ask you a couple of questions."

Johnny took a sip of the coffee and looked up at Marks. "The only dead bodies I ever seen was in a casket," he said.

Marks laughed. "It's not the best thing to see."

"Ain't really too funny. I was out there about an hour before and seen nothing. I went back out and that's when I seen Herbert."

"You knew the victim?" Anders asked loudly.

Marks thought to shush him but said nothing. Johnny looked at Anders. "You look like a boy scout."

Anders had a very young-looking face and little facial hair. He did look about twenty, Marks thought.

"Did you know him?" Marks asked.

"You know, I'd see him about every night. Him and that dog. Sometimes I would bring him food if I could. He was harmless, man, and he didn't have nothing. Why would somebody do that to him?"

"How long was Herbert coming around the casino?" Marks asked.

"I dunno. Maybe a couple of years I seen him back there. Him and that dirty old dog."

"Know much about him?"

"Him? He just a bum. He told me his name. That was it. Told me his dog's name, Buster. That's all I know. Some old bum, with his dog, and somebody stabbed that man in the throat."

"You ever see any other homeless men out here?"

"By the casino? There's a bunch. Herbert, he come all the time, but there's others. They look for food or sleep by the building heat vents when it is cold. Might be ten, fifteen I see here and there."

Marks nodded. "See any of the others tonight?"

Johnny shook his head. "Nope. Just Herbert and that was enough."

"What do you think?" Anders asked. They were walking towards the car Anders was using.

"What do I think?" Mark stopped and lit a cigarette; he offered one to Anders who declined. "I think I'm pretty dumb. I guess I knew we had some homeless people, but never imagined fifteen. That was enough to surprise me, but when one of them gets stabbed in the throat in our nice little town it kind of shocks me."

"Yeah, I read one of Milton's visitor's guides. Said that crime was almost non-existent," Anders said. "Maybe it's time for an update."

"Don't try and be funny," Marks said. "You asked me what I thought. What do you think?"'

"I'm thinking not too many regular people knew Herbert. The only ones who might know anything about him are probably the other homeless types. They might be able to tell us something about Herbert. Maybe he pissed somebody off and that's how they dealt with it. That, and maybe somebody stole his dog."

"So, we've got to talk with the other homeless crowd for leads on Herbert or look for somebody who now owns a scruffy dog named Buster?"

"You got any other ideas, boss?"

"None and cut the boss shit. It's Marks or Stevie. Let's get into the station and get some more coffee.

When it gets a little lighter, we can start hunting up the homeless folks of Milton."

"I didn't think my first case was going to be a murder and talking with the homeless and looking for clues."

"Usually, it's one of the wives trying to kill one of the husbands with a kitchen utensil."

Anders rubbed at his jaw. "Damn tooth is killing me."

"Can't help you there. Try a dentist."

• • •

Tammy Glaser was working at her desk in her small cubicle when Steve Marks entered the Records Department. She gave Marks a big smile and took off her reading glasses; she waved a few loose red hairs off of her face. "Early morning for you, Detective Marks."

"Very early. It wasn't my idea."

"Looks like your little trip to Florida did you good. You've got a nice tan. When I go out in the sun, I get major freckles and I fry up.

"Ten days in the sun and eighty degrees will do a lot for you. Coming back here was a bit of a shock."

"Not just the weather. I heard about what happened out at Aces. That's terrible, some poor homeless guy. Any reason why somebody would kill this guy?"

Marks felt that he was distracted by her pretty face. "That's what I'm trying to figure out."

"And is there some way that I may be of service to you?" She showed a full, toothy smile.

"I still owe you a drink from the last time I came for help."

"Don't think I've forgotten," she said. "What can I do for you today?"

"Like I said, we don't have much of anything on why this guy was killed. We figure talking to some of the homeless in the area will be the only way we can learn anything about the victim and who might have killed him and why. It might be a silly question, but does the department do any tracking of these people and know who they are and where they can be found?"

"Nothing like that, I'm afraid. Once in a while one will get pinched for trespassing or stealing something. Then they might have a record and some prints, but that would be about it. Like this guy this morning, Herbert. I checked our data base and came up with zilch. I'd need a lot more to figure out anything about him."

Marks ran his hand through his dark hair. "That's what I thought. The best way to find out about these people are to talk to some of their own."

"Probably," she said. "You could also check out St. John's Lutheran tomorrow night."

'What happens there?"

"Every Tuesday at six the church prepares a free meal for the homeless. It gets pretty crowded. You might learn something."

Just then Anders walked up behind Marks. Marks was right. He looked about twenty years old. He smiled broadly. "Hello," he said to Tammy.

She blushed and smiled. "A friend of yours, Detective?"

"This is Anders Hedberg. He's on loan from Sterling. This is Tammy Glaser, our top researcher in records."

Anders stuck out his hand and shook Tammy's. Her hand was warm. "I'll have to remember that," Anders said.

Another smile. "Please do," she said.

"Lou is looking for you in his office," Anders said. "Somebody said you might be down here."

"Well, the boss is calling," Marks said.

"Don't forget me," Tammy said to both of the men.

"Oh, I won't," Anders answered.

Walking up the stairs, Anders said, "She seems like a friendly one."

Marks laughed. "If you like the man eater type."

•   •   •

"So, your next move is to try and interview other homeless people to see what they know?" Lou Katz said.

"Unless you have any other ideas," Mark responded.

"What do you think, Anders?" Lou asked.

Anders cleared his throat and blushed. "I agree with Detective Marks. The maintenance man, Johnny Martin, knew nothing. All he did was find him. We have to get out on the street and see if anybody knew anything about Herbert or who might have done this to him.'

Lou rubbed the back of his neck. Up since four-thirty, he was already tired. "The mayor is going to go nuts over this news. You know, Milton, the town with no crime."

"Maybe that slogan is getting a little tired," Marks said.

"Tired or not, I'll hear about it. What's your plan?"

"There's a couple of spots along Brewster that I know some of the homeless hang out by. We can run by them. Tammy down in records says that St. John's Lutheran hosts a dinner for the homeless on Tuesday nights. We'll run by there tomorrow."

Just then there was a knock on Lou's office door. He waved his secretary, Millie, into the room. Millie was in her mid-fifties and had been in the department for over twenty-five years. "Sorry to interrupt," she said, "but somebody left a dog tied to the fence by the animal hospital. Small and scruffy was the description I got."

"The animal hospital is at least two miles from Aces," Marks said. "Somebody drove that dog there. Wasn't some homeless person."

"Maybe the killer just let the dog go," Anders said. "Maybe somebody just picked him up if he was stray and took him over there."

"And just left him?" Lou said.

Anders shrugged.

"Could have happened that way," Marks said. "We don't know. We really don't know shit."

• • •

11

The Milton Animal Hospital was located on the north side of town on Route 20. It was an old, converted house. The place had a good reputation. Marks wondered how many animals actually got treated there and whether the business was profitable. Then he hoped they could find something out about Herbert, the dead homeless guy, from the dog that had been left there.

The young woman that greeted them was not the veterinarian. Her name was Susie, and she was a little past college age. She was short, cute blonde who smiled a lot. "Yeah," she said. "The dog was tied to one of the fence posts when I got here. I almost didn't see it when I drove up. He didn't bark or anything."

"Can we see him?" Marks asked.

She smiled again. "Sure. Doc wasn't too happy I took him in. That's why I called the police. Doc thought the dog might have some disease or something. He wanted to try and find the owner if we could."

Susie led the two of them to the back room where there were some holding cages. In one lay a medium-sized, mangy looking dog who was sleeping peacefully. "I gave him some food and water," Susie said. "He fell asleep soon after."

Marks looked in on the sleeping dog. "Buster," he said loudly. The dog's eyes popped open, and Buster stood and wagged his tail.

"You know his name?" Susie asked.

"He's been missing for a while," Marks said. "Find anything else with him?"

"Just a leash. No tags or anything like that. He needs a bath. He really stinks."

Marks noticed the smell and it wasn't an understatement.

"Will the owner come get him soon?" Susie asked. "Doc wasn't happy, like I said. If the owner can come soon, I would be really happy."

"Owner can't come soon," Marks said. He'd never really known or seen a homeless dog, but he kind of liked this one. Buster's tale was still wagging wildly.

"But if you know the owner, why can't he come get his dog?" she asked.

"Because the owner is dead. Right now, Buster doesn't have a home."

"Oh my," she said.

"I'm going to need you to hold onto Buster for a while. Tell the Doc that I will pay any bills that occur. Give him a bath and a checkup. Feed him and make sure he's okay." Marks took out a card and gave it to her. "Anybody asks about Buster I want to know. Do you understand?"

Susie looked really suspicious. "Is Buster a drug dog?"

Marks laughed. He didn't know what a drug dog was. "Look, Buster is just a dog whose owner died. We need to try and find him a home. That's all there is to it."

"Then why do you care if anybody asks about him?"

Good question. "Somebody took Buster from his owner's place and took him here. We are trying to find that person."

Susie smiled. "I got it."

"Think she's got it?" Anders asked on the walk to the car.

"Fifty-fifty."

"Think anyone is going to ask about the dog."

"Don't think so, but you never know. I think we can head over to Brewster Way."

"What's on Brewster Way?"

"All of the night life of Milton and presumably all of the homeless people who reside in our fine town."

• • •

Brewster Way was a stretch of road that ran the width of Milton. The street contained a vast number of bars, poker rooms, vape shops and strip clubs. You would think this was a perfect environment for crime, but over the years, under Teddy Brown's rule, there was a no tolerance program in the town. People knew that if you broke the law in Milton you could pay with a severe penalty. Sometimes people who broke the law never came back to Milton.

"I've seen some homeless behind Satan's Palace," Marks said as Anders drove along Brewster, eyeing the different venues.

"This is quite the street," Anders said.

"You can find whatever level of adult entertainment that you are looking for on Brewster."

"But no prostitution?"

"Who said that?" Marks answered. "It's illegal, but it happens now and then. You've got grown men with cash looking at girls with no clothes on. Sometimes things go a little further, but not often."

Satan's Palace was a good-sized strip joint in the middle of Brewster. There was an alley that ran behind the place and Marks directed Anders to drive back there. "There's a couple of storage buildings back there and I've seen some bums hanging out back there," he said.

"Bums?" Anders asked.

"Sorry. A little insensitive. Teddy Brown would call them bums all the time. Couldn't tolerate them hanging around anywhere."

"I heard he was something else."

Marks thought of the culmination of the Fatty Fuller case. "That's one way to describe Teddy."

Behind Satan's there were three unused storage sheds. They were wooden and not much to look at, but they provided some cover and warmth from the winter cold. Doors that once had locks on them just hung open now. Anders parked the car and the two men got out and approached the sheds. Marks banged loudly on the first one. Nothing happened. On the second building he banged his hand again on the door. This time there was some commotion inside and two straggly, worn looking men stumbled out of the small building. It was hard to tell their ages from their appearance, but Marks had them between thirty and fifty. The dirty clothes, straggly beards and long hair did nothing to help him figure this out.

"We didn't do anything," the first man said. "We're just trying to keep warm and get some rest." He was the taller of the two, skinny and hunched over. There was twitching at his left eye.

Marks showed his badge. "We don't think you did anything wrong. We're just looking for a little information."

The first man turned to look at his partner who just shrugged. "Information about what?" the first asked.

"We're trying to find out some information on a guy named Herbert. Hangs out by the Aces casino. Travels with a small, scruffy dog named Buster."

The first man got this quizzical look on his face, scrunching his nose. "Don't think I know him."

"You sure? You're not going to get in trouble if you tell us what you know."

"What did Herbert do?" the second man asked.

"He didn't do anything," Marks answered. "Somebody did something to him."

"Like what?" the second asked.

"Killed him," Marks said. "Stabbed him in the throat and took his dog."

"Don't know nothing about that," the first man blurted. "Don't know anything about a stabbing."

Marks could see he was getting nowhere with this one. He turned to the second. "How about you?"

"I knew Herbert. I mean I saw him around a few times. I saw him with that dog. He never said too much, just him and that dog."

"You don't know where he came from, his hometown, his family, anything like that?"

The second man laughed. "Home? Family? What's that shit? Think we'd be out here freezing and hungry if there was such a thing as family and home? That's not real, man."

Marks felt stupid. "Sorry. We're just trying to figure out something about this guy. Trying to figure out who might have done this to him."

"You gotta find Big Tony," the first man said. "I think he got into a fight with Herbert because his dog peed by where Tony was trying to sleep, threatened him pretty bad."

"I thought you said you didn't know Herbert. How'd you figure this out?"

The face scrunching again. "I remembered. I was there. Tony said he would kill Herbert if his fuckin dog came anywhere near him again."

"Where can we find this Big Tony?"

Both men laughed. "Where it's warm. Where there's food," the second man answered. "Sometimes here, sometimes Dubuque, Gilberts, Savannah, who knows?"

"Do you remember the last time you saw him around here?"

Both men shook their heads.

"Why is he called Big Tony?" Anders spoke for the first time.

"Well, he's big," the first said. "Bout six-five, bout three hundred pounds."

"That's big," Marks said.

"Gotta watch him," the second said. "Got a bad temper and he carries a big fucking hunting knife."

17

"You don't say," Marks said. "Any chance he'll be at the dinner at St. John's Lutheran tomorrow?"

"Never know," the second answered. "Sometimes there's ten people there, sometimes fifty."

"Huh," Marks said. "I didn't realize there were that many homeless people around Milton."

"That's because you cops aren't really paying attention to us," the second said.

Marks couldn't argue with the man. Of all of the social plagues that were present in Milton, homelessness was one that he knew the least about.

•   •   •

They drove up and down the alleys behind the buildings along Brewster but failed to locate any other homeless people. Marks thought about the comment the one man had made about the police not paying attention to the homeless. He hadn't been a patrolman for a long time but remembered coming upon a homeless person or two and just thinking they were a nuisance. Now it was a bit of an epidemic. He felt out of the loop. He also felt tired and hungry. They headed for The Start of the Day Café. More coffee and breakfast were needed.

"What made you want to be a cop?" Marks asked Anders. They were seated in a back booth away from the door. The waitress had brought them coffee and dropped off menus.

Anders blew on his coffee and took a sip. He rubbed at his bad tooth. "My dad was a Sterling cop. When I got out of school, I had no idea what I wanted to do. Somebody suggested the police force and I went in. They hired me right away."

"Your dad was a career Sterling cop?"

"A long time."

In the light of the restaurant, Marks could tell how young Anders looked. He thought about how long he wanted to remain a Milton cop and the big city of Chicago. "Did he retire or is he still at it?"

Anders took another sip of coffee and wiped his lips with a napkin. "No, nothing like that. Some nut shot him on Route 84. Just a routine traffic stop. Shot him right in the face. He was looking to get out in a year or two, do some private security stuff. He was DOA at the hospital."

Marks felt his stomach plummet. "Jesus. I'm sorry. I had no idea."

Anders smiled. "It's okay. People ask if I joined the force to revenge my dad or something heroic like that, but that had nothing to do with it. I needed a job, they were hiring, and I took the job. Nothing more than that."

"Well, welcome aboard. I don't know if it's fortunate or unfortunate that the first thing you get is a homeless guy murdered out by the casino."

Anders laughed. "I didn't expect that. Sorry I got sick out there. The only dead people I've ever seen were in a funeral home."

"It's okay. I've seen some bad stuff. I hate to say you get used to it, but the first time is the worst."

"What about you? Your dad a career cop around here?"

Now Marks laughed. "Not close. I guess if I had to categorize my father, I would say he is a professional gambler. That's what he's done his whole life. I've never known him to have a job, like a nine to five thing. Just hits the poker tables wherever there's a game and somehow, he survives. Moves around a lot. I haven't seen him in years."

"Mom and dad divorced?"

"Long time now. Mom is sick with cancer and dementia. She's in Parkview. It's a long-term care place."

"Sorry to hear that," Anders said. "Talking about families can sure brighten the mood."

The waitress came by, filled their coffee cups and took their orders.

"How do we find this Big Tony?" Anders asked.

"Good question. If we see him would be the best way, but we can inquire with the other towns. Based on his size, he can't stay hidden that long."

"Do you buy any of that stuff those guys told us about why Tony might have killed Herbert?

"First, we don't know that he did, but some of these homeless folks are desperate. They might kill somebody over five bucks."

"So, a dinner date tomorrow at St. John's Lutheran?"

"Sounds like it."

•   •   •

Chicago, November 2008

The crime scene was behind Allegretti's, a popular Italian place on State Street a little west of the Gold Coast area. The area had been taped off and the two detectives from the 2nd Precinct had just arrived; the guys from the Medical Examiner's office were milling about. Two were smoking cigarettes.

"What do we know?" Detective Mike Burke asked. He was a twenty-five-year vet of the force, hated winter, and was already counting days until his thirtieth year when he could retire and move somewhere south. Of course, this decision rested with his wife. Their daughter was due to have a baby and his wife wanted to be around for the grandchild. Mike did, too, but this fucking Chicago cold.

The M.E. named Laskey, a smart aleck, whose dad got him the job in the department, flicked his smoke away and cleared his throat. "Somebody stabbed this dude in the throat. Didn't cut it. Looks like they plunged a pretty long knife in just below the Adam's apple. You can tell from all of the blood that the dude just bled out."

Mike Burke grunted. The "dude" was lying in the alley near some trash bins. The lighting wasn't great, but Mike could tell that the dead man looked homeless. He was wearing a heavy coat and a knit cap. On his hand he wore tattered gloves. He had a straggly beard and Mike could make out pieces of debris in the beard. The guy looked pretty peaceful, maybe sleeping, except for the gash under his neck and the blood that had spilled out everywhere."

"Who found this guy?" Mike asked.

"One of the Mexican busboys. Came out for a smoke, half an hour ago," Laskey said. "The patrolmen who answered the call talked to the guy, but he didn't know shit. Just some homeless dude."

"And of course, nobody has any idea who this guy is?" Mike asked.

There was no answer from any of the cops or coroner's team to the question.

"Let's get him out of this alley and try and figure out something," Mike said. "Who murders a homeless guy? What were they trying to get?"

It took a while, but the victim was Richard Archer, twenty-eight years old. Richard had been a theatre student, had done a few plays, and had given up on society a couple of years ago. He decided that the only way to discover the true meaning of life was to live it without many of the comforts he was used to. He became a minimalist and decided to try and live life on the street. His homelessness was voluntary. He was going to keep a journal, found in an old backpack by his body. His family, as outraged as they were by his decision to drop everything, insisted he keep a cell phone. He did, but this phone was missing from the backpack, but the holder was there. The holder was checked for prints, but there was no match in any data base.

"So, who killed this guy, Mike?" Eli Roach asked. He had been Mike Burke's partner for nine years.

"Who fucking knows," Mike said. They were in McGuire's On Rush having a drink. "Somebody who learned that Richard had a cell phone? Most homeless people don't have anything that anyone would want. Somebody heard he had a phone and went to get it."

"Not much negotiation involved,"

"Doesn't look like it. Looks like whoever did this stabbed Richard and then went through his backpack."

"So now we are looking for somebody with a five-year-old Motorola cell phone."

"That's our clue. Nobody saw anything or heard anything. We don't have a weapon and we don't have any prints. All of the blood at the scene was from Richard. Hair samples were numerous, but useless. We are as you said, looking for somebody with a used Motorola."

"Piece of fucking cake," Eli said.

They looked and they asked. Any homeless people in the area were grilled about what they might know. They were all asked if they knew anyone who recently came in possession of a cell phone. There was nothing. Nobody heard, saw, or knew anything about Richard Archer's murder. He was buried about a week after his death. His file, like a lot of others in Chicago, was buried with all of the other unsolved murders in the city.

CHAPTER 2

It was the first of April, April Fool's Day, and Marks owed the City of Chicago an answer about the job offer. Marks was sitting on the condo's balcony overlooking the Mississippi, drinking his morning coffee. He wanted a cigarette but was trying to stop. It was cold and it was going to be a cloudy day, but his thoughts took him away from being chilled.

He had complained about the simplicity of his job for months. That was what had led him to apply for the position in Chicago. Now, with the decision time near, a vicious murder had overtaken his brain and his thoughts were far from leaving the town of Milton. They had one lead on who might have killed Herbert, the homeless man, a big guy going by the name of Big Tony. The rest of the day before they had looked for other homeless people to talk with and they had come up with nothing. Several people knew of Big Tony, but no one had seen him in a while, and nobody had any idea where you could find him. Marks was frustrated and twirled a cigarette in his fingers. He put it back in the pack and put the pack back in his pocket.

The sliding glass door opened, and Tori came out on the balcony. She had taken a large blanket and wrapped herself in it. "What the hell are you doing sitting out here? It's freezing."

"Good morning to you, too," he said. "Right now, just thinking a bit."

"Decision day for Chicago," she said, taking the seat next to him.

"Don't think so."

"Don't think it's the day? I thought they said by April one."

"They did. I don't think I can take that job with an open murder case looming. I can't do that to Lou."

"Do you think Lou would do that for you?"

Marks laughed. Lou Katz was an ambitious man and didn't let much stand in the way of his rise up the department ladder. "I'm not Lou," he said. "I don't want to walk out on something this bad that just started. We've barely started to try and figure out what happened out at Aces, and I just can't pick up and leave."

She placed her hand over the top of his that was resting on the chair arm. "You're a good man, Marks. Not many people would do that."

He smiled and took her hand and kissed it. "What about the move where I ask you to marry me?"

"Maybe not that one."

He squeezed her hand and looked out over the clouds above the big river. "I may never quit asking."

"That's fair," she said. "Tell me about the guy who was killed."

"Some homeless guy named Herbert. That's what we know. Owned a dog that somebody, we think the killer, brought into the animal hospital in town."

"Well, that was nice of him."

"Who said it was a him?"

"You told me that the dead man had been stabbed in the throat. No woman would do anything like that?"

"You don't think? History says that women can do some awful things. Think of Lorena Bobbitt."

"Forgot about her. Point made. What else do you know?"

"Not much. The homeless community, those that we have found, know very little. There's a big guy, Big Tony, who runs around with a big knife. He's the only lead we have right now. We're looking for him."

"No idea why Herbert was killed?"

"Somebody didn't like him."

She shivered and punched Marks lightly in the shoulder. "Don't be a smart ass," she said. "I'm freezing and headed inside."

"Don't think I'll be home for dinner. Anders and I have a date at St. John's Lutheran for dinner with the homeless."

"Anders?"

"My new partner on loan from Sterling. Looks like a Boy Scout but seems okay."

"Well, I don't think you can get in much trouble at the homeless dinner. Try and relax. Things will work out." She got up and went back inside of the unit.

Sure, Marks thought. Things will work out. One way or the other.

• • •

Across town, Anders Hedberg was staring up at the ceiling, eyes wide awake. He wasn't sure what he was looking for and wasn't sure how he'd ended up in this bed. His first day on the Milton police force had started with a murder of a homeless guy behind the casino. He had expected nothing like that. After spending much of the day talking with other homeless people, they had one lead, a big guy called Big Tony. Nobody knew where he was or where he could be found, but it was something.

He had heard a bit about Steve Marks before he came over to Milton. Marks was supposed to be a straight shooter and he seemed to be. He had treated Anders fine. Anders was okay with that. Anders had also heard that Lou Katz was intense and hard driving. He hadn't seen that yet.

After the long first day, Anders made his way down to the records department. The cute redhead, Tammy Glaser, was still in her cubicle with a number of windows opened on the screen in front of her. She smiled as Anders came up to her work area. "Are you lost, Detective Hedberg? Maybe I can help you."

"I don't think I'm a detective yet, but I need all the help I can get."

They went to Lifers, which Tammy described as kind of a government worker's bar. They had a couple of drinks and played three games of darts. Tammy won two. Anders said that he was hungry, and Tammy invited him back to her place for leftover pasta. The food was great and so were the two bottles of red wine. One thing led to another, and they ended up in the bedroom and here was Anders looking up at the ceiling. Tammy rolled over and kissed him on the cheek.

Anders smiled. "What was that for?"

"A very nice evening. I enjoyed it very much."

"I did as well.

"And it's not just a one nighter?"

"Oh no. Not at all. I had a lot of fun. I wouldn't do that."

She poked him in the ribs. "Don't get defensive," she said. "What were you looking for on my ceiling?"

"Don't really know. I was thinking about this dead guy, homeless, with nothing more than his little dog, and somebody comes up to him and stabs him in the throat."

"Doesn't seem random."

"Not at all. Somebody killed this guy for a reason. Maybe they stole something from him."

"Stole something and then stabbed him?"

"Could be. I was thinking about this guy, Herbert. Living outside like that in the cold, barely living, no family, nobody knows anything about him."

She ran a finger up Ander's ribs. "Somebody does. What was the name of your lead again?"

"Some guy named Big Tony. We've already sent out alerts to all of the neighboring towns for any leads on this guy."

"Well, if he killed this Herbert guy, I doubt if he's still in Milton."

"I wouldn't be," Anders said. "Then there's this thing with the dog. The animal hospital is a couple of miles from the casino. There's no way the killer walked this dog over there and tied him up. Had to be driven in a car."

"Maybe the dog got loose and got out to the parking lot and a gambler drove him over there. An act of kindness."

"After a long night of losing at the tables or slots?"

"Maybe. Look I can send out some feelers for you. I know you guys handled all of the official channels, but I can ask some favors. Maybe I can find this Big Tony for you."

Anders put his arm around Tammy's shoulders and pulled her close. "That would be awfully nice of you."

"Help you get some brownie points with Detective Marks."

Anders shook his head. "Not really what I'm after. I just keep thinking about Herbert, dying like that. It pisses me off. I'd like to find who did this to him." He glanced at the digital clock on the bedside table. "I've got to get moving soon."

"But you have a little time left for me?"

He glanced at the clock again. "I do," he said.

•   •   •

Before heading into headquarters, Marks stopped by the Parkview Home to visit his mother. He hadn't been there to see her in over two weeks. He did make regular calls to the staff to see how she was doing. They always said she was about the same, moody at times, but generally in an okay mood. The biggest thing, they said, was that her memory was failing rapidly. She couldn't remember the staffer's names from one day to the next. As far as her cancer went, there was no improvement. It was still there and not getting any better, but currently not getting much worse. Once it did completely take over, this was what was likely to kill her.

Janet Marks was sixty-five years old. When Marks entered her room, she was lying on the bed watching a television show. She looked closer to eighty years old. She had lost a lot of weight and her skin color looked close to a light shade of gray. She didn't turn to look at Marks when he came into her room.

"Hi, mom," he said.

Her head moved slightly towards the sound of his voice. She squinted and stared for a moment, looking for clarification. Her eyes told of some vacancy in the thought process. "Is that you, Thomas?"

Marks had no idea who Thomas was. Maybe one of the staff. "It's Stevie, mom."

"Stevie?" The mention of his name wasn't getting through to her.

"Stevie, your son." Marks felt his stomach tighten.

"Stevie, oh Stevie," she said. "How are you, Stevie?"

"I'm good, mom. How are you? Are they taking good care of you?"

Janet Marks smiled. "Sure they are. These are wonderful people. You'll never guess who I saw yesterday."

"Who was that, mom?"

She smiled. "I ran into Uncle Dan and Aunt Martie on the bus. They were on their way to get groceries. It was so good to see them. I hadn't seen them in a while."

Uncle Dan and Aunt Martie were from Marks' grandparent's generation. They had both been dead for quite a while. "That's nice, mom. What were you watching on the TV?"

She stared blankly at him. "I wasn't watching the TV."

He nodded and looked closely at her. She was there, but she wasn't. He felt tears forming in his eyes. Murder case or not, there was no way that he could leave Milton. He couldn't leave his mother alone now. He should have known this before he even contemplated going to Chicago. He was ashamed of himself. Her sight had turned back to the TV. Marks noticed it was a morning news channel. She didn't say anything further. He turned and left the room.

. . .

Kyle James felt very lucky today. He was feeling this way every Tuesday and Thursday, especially recently. Tuesday and Thursday were the days that Kyle worked the afternoon shift at Mercury Auto Repairs. He had worked there for eight years; it was a great job. On those two days, Kyle usually went to the gym around eight in the morning, grabbed some breakfast and relaxed until his shift began. These days, things had changed. They had changed because he had met Lisa Burnett at the club. She had been taking yoga classes on those days, but now they had met, and they hit it off right away. Soon after they met, they got some breakfast together. Kyle was ecstatic. Lisa was beautiful and she had a fantastic body. The only real problem was that Lisa was married. She had been married to Ricky Burnett for five years. Ricky's family had owned Burnett Furniture for decades.

For the past couple of months, Lisa had begun to skip the yoga classes and come straight to Kyle's apartment on Tuesday and Thursday mornings. Not only could Kyle still get in his workout, but he could start the day with some marvelous sex. He felt a little guilty about sleeping with Ricky's wife, but Lisa had told him how bored she was with Ricky. She said that Ricky was becoming a bit of a workaholic, staying at the store for all hours. She hardly ever saw him and when she did, he was too tired to do much of anything. Lisa had a lot of pent-up energy.

That was good for Kyle, because she had plenty of energy when they got into his bed.

Kyle and Ricky Burnett had both gone to Milton High. They ran in different circles. Kyle had played football and wrestled; Ricky had been on the golf team. Like Kyle, his father had been a mechanic; his mother worked at the Trips Aces Casino. Ricky's family owned five furniture stores in the area. Kyle didn't know Ricky's mom, but he was pretty sure she'd never worked a day in her life. Kyle hadn't known Lisa until they met at the club. She had attended the parochial schools. Kyle was glad he had finally met her. It brought excitement to his life. That made Kyle feel really good. He just didn't know how long this would last. He smiled. He didn't mean to hurt Ricky Burnett, but he wasn't going to pass up such a good thing as Lisa.

• • •

Marks was looking at the internet when Anders showed up in his office. It was a little after nine. Anders' hair looked a little messed up and the young cop definitely wore a tired look. "Tough night, Anders?"

Anders blushed. He wondered if Marks knew something. "Just a few cocktails. Didn't sleep that well."

"Seeing people stabbed in the throat may do that to you."

"It wasn't the prettiest thing I've ever seen."

"How's the tooth?"

The damn thing ached all the time. "About the same."

Jeff Blakely, the night shift watch commander, entered the office. He was a tall, skinny man with pale skin. The skin at his neck was loose. Blakely was almost sixty, approaching retirement. Marks always thought that Blakely was a man of little talent, a department holdover, but at least he showed up every day and did the best he could.

"Hey, Jeff. What did your boys find last night?" Marks asked.

"Who's this?' Blakely asked, pointing at Anders.

"This is Anders Hedberg, on loan from Sterling. He's going to be working with me for a while."

Blakely's look showed disinterest. "We didn't find much of anything, and I had the boys looking. They scoured Brewster Way pretty well and made several runs at the grounds around the casino. They talked to a few people, but no one seemed to know much about Herbert, the dead guy. Fewer had any idea where we might find this Big Tony fella. It seemed like we were spinning wheels a bit."

"Spinning wheels?" Marks asked.

"Well, you know what I mean, Steve. We had a lot of manpower out there doing a search on this dead guy."

Anders shifted nervously in his chair, sensing the mood change.

"Were there more important things that the shift guys needed to be doing?" Marks asked. "It was a Monday night after all."

"Oh, I didn't mean more important. I just meant..."

"I think I know what you meant. The dead guy, as you call him, what a homeless guy, a bum. He's gone now so that's one less homeless guy we need to worry about, but I want you to think about this for a minute. Somewhere that guy has a family, I think. Somewhere his life got all fucked up. He was all alone with his little dog, trying to stay warm. Think about that and then think that somebody stabbed Herbert in the throat and left him near the trash dumpsters to die. Don't minimize the victim. This was a murder of a person, a human being."

Blakely's face was frozen. He swallowed hard. "I didn't mean to minimize anything, Steve."

"Just make sure your guys don't share your attitude. There's a murderer out there and I'd really like to find the son of a bitch."

Blakely nodded but said nothing. He left the office.

"I think you got his attention," Anders said.

"Too much country bumpkin in some of these guys. When a real crime comes along, they have no idea what they are supposed to do."

"And what are we supposed to do?"

Marks laughed. "That's a damn good question, Anders. I suppose we are back on the street looking for more homeless people to talk with. That should make for an exciting day until our dinner date tonight."

Anders nodded glumly. "Do I have a little time to grab some coffee?"

"Yeah, sure. I have a call I need to make. Close the door on the way out."

When Anders had left, Marks turned his chair and looked out of his window. It was the same view he'd seen for years. Milton didn't change much and wreaked of sameness, but he was electing to stay. He picked up the phone and dialed the number that he had for Chicago.

• • •

Lisa Burnett got out of the shower and spent longer than usual drying and brushing her hair. Several times while she sat on the chair in front of the mirror she caught herself looking at her face and thinking. She wasn't daydreaming. She was contemplating what she was doing. It had been a couple of months that she had spent mornings with Kyle. She liked him. He was funny, had a great body and he made her feel good, but he wasn't the sharpest tool in the shed. He really wasn't very smart at all. She had heard somewhere that he was a great car mechanic but might be slightly smarter than a rock. She never really talked to him that much. Their whole relationship, if it was one, was based on sex. That part was great. Everything else was way below what she was looking for. The problem was she had no idea what she was looking for.

She had married Ricky five years before. He was a decent looking guy from a wealthy family. Once they were married, they immediately bought a house on the ninth fairway of the Milton Country Club. She joined the best health club in the area, the one with the top spa. They only ate at the top restaurants. Ricky never said anything about the money that she spent. Every year they took fantastic vacations. She never had to work; she had all the free time in the world. Life was great. People would sell their souls for the life Lisa had. And then it all stopped. It all stopped when she got pregnant and nine months later she had Henry. Henry, now almost two and a half, was great. That wasn't the issue. The issue was the life that she was enjoying, and could have existed with, ended.

Once she had a life of unlimited free time and unlimited finances. That all changed. Her pregnancy had been difficult, morning sickness for three months, gestational diabetes, some irregular spotting and zero sleep. She was miserable. The birth would be by C-section. She thought some of this would end when Henry was born, but a new set of problems occurred. Henry was a fussy baby, colic they said. Sleep was in shifts of an hour or two. Lisa was losing her baby weight, but in a wrong way. She wasn't eating right. She noticed some of her hair falling out. She had to get some help. Her mother was in Cincinnati. She couldn't stand Ricky's mother. Ricky agreed to get her some help. She hired Marguerite Lopez.

Once she hired Marguerite, things got better in a hurry. The woman was great with Henry. He suddenly settled down, ate better, slept better, and got bigger and stronger. Lisa had time for herself. She started to eat better and she felt better. She started going to yoga classes and workouts at the club. Marguerite was looking for money; she would work any hours that Lisa asked her to. This gave Lisa more free time. While Ricky worked from eight until nine six days a week, Lisa started to go out with some friends and to shop more often. She was getting her old life back. The two days that changed the most were Tuesday and Thursdays, her usual yoga days. Now they were days she saw Kyle and came home and spent the day with Henry; Marguerite would leave when she got home from the class (Kyle's). It was perfect for her. She would return from Kyle's and Marguerite would lay Henry down for his nap. Lisa would have two to three hours to herself. Thursday nights she would meet up with her girlfriends.

As she thought of this her attention turned to the baby monitor that she kept in the bathroom on the vanity. The green light was lit up; the unit was working. Lisa listened closely. Usually, she could hear Henry murmuring to himself. This usually made her smile, but today she could hear no sounds at all. Normally, this wouldn't bother her. Henry wasn't always jabbering, but today felt different. She got up from her chair and left the bathroom. Henry's room was the smallest in the house located only fifteen feet from her own room. The door was slightly ajar as always. She opened the door and peered in. From the hall it was hard to see into the crib.

She stepped forward and looked into it. Her heart jumped. The crib was empty. Lisa screamed.

•   •   •

The morning was cold; Marks and Anders were a little reluctant to head outdoors in search of any homeless people who knew anything about Herbert or Big Tony. Marks was slowly drinking his coffee; Anders was hoping he could sneak a couple of aspirin before they did go out. They both knew they had to head out shortly. They both knew they had absolutely nothing worthwhile on the murder. Their little break was interrupted when Lou Katz walked into the office.

"Can you tell me anything more about Herbert the homeless guy?"

Anders sat up straight in his chair; Marks stifled a yawn. "You know that somebody stabbed him in the throat and somehow his dog, Buster, ended up at the animal hospital. We got a lead that there's a big homeless guy, real big, goes by the name of Big Tony. We heard he always has a big knife on him. We're looking for him. We've notified all of the surrounding area's departments."

"You don't say?"

"That's what we've got. The night shift did some canvassing but came up with nothing. Speaking of nothing, our night watch commander, fits that bill."

Katz put up both hands to quiet Marks. "It's only a little while and he's gone. Relax."

"If you say so."

"I've got another problem that I need you to look into right away."

Now it was Marks who leaned back in his chair. "Right away?"

"Remember Ricky Burnett from school?"

"You can't buy any furniture around here without remembering Ricky."

"Well, we got a call not long ago. Ricky's two-year-old son Henry is missing."

"Missing? What do you mean missing?"

"Looks like he might have been kidnapped. There's a patrol car there now. They say everyone is freaking out."

Marks knew a little about Ricky Burnett. They all went to the same high school. "Rich kid," he said to Anders. They were on their way to the Burnett house. "His family owns a furniture store in every town around here. Good stuff. Ricky didn't hang out with us. He played golf. I was on the baseball team. He was driving a BMW in his junior year. I had an old Ford. He went away to college. I did, too, but going to school in Dubuque is not the same thing."

"Sounds like you're a little envious."

Marks gave him the death stare. "Maybe. The guy about had everything given to him. I guess he's one of those guys that you don't know, but you don't like."

"Know anything about his wife?"

"Her name is Lisa. She was with Ricky at a charitable event for the department. I didn't speak to them, but I saw her. Looks like something out of a magazine. When you hear somebody say drop dead gorgeous, she fits the bill."

"Is this Ricky some sort of studly type?"

"Not at all. Very average. Not ugly or anything like that. Tall, skinny, and always looked a little hunched over."

"She didn't go after Ricky for his looks?"

Marks laughed. "She went after Ricky for his money, maybe some love, but money was the starter."

• • •

The house was a good-sized, brick ranch. The early April morning was cold, but there were signs of grass growth and budding plants. Behind the house, you could see the golf course fairway, not in use this morning. There was a Milton cop standing guard by the front door. He waved Marks and Anders into the house.

They walked into a large living room with a full glass background. The golf course was clearly visible out of the large windows. The sun was starting to peak through some heavy clouds. In the living room, Marks recognized Ricky Burnett. He was sitting on a couch, holding the hands of a beautiful blonde who was dressed only in a bathrobe. To Ricky's left was an older man who resembled Ricky, but with less hair. Had to be his father, Marks thought. An attractive older woman sat nearby in a chair, wiping tears from her eyes. A small, slightly overweight, Hispanic woman sat in a chair across the way. Two Milton cops stood nearby, quietly, their hands behind their backs.

The older man walked over to Marks as he entered the room. He extended a long, bony looking hand. "Detective, I am Richard Burnett, Ricky's father." He was wearing brown, tweed trousers and a light white sweater.

Marks took the hand and shook it. "I'm Steve Marks. This is Anders Hedberg. He is working with me."

The older Burnett seemed to avoid Anders. "This is a terrible tragedy, a nightmare."

"Yes, sir," Marks said. "I understand Mrs. Burnett was home alone with the child..."

"Henry," Burnett said. "Named after my grandfather."

"Yes, sir, Henry. Was Mrs. Burnett the only one home with Henry when he was taken?"

"Yes. She was in the shower. When she came out, she checked on Henry and his bed was empty."

"Can we talk with her now? I'd like to hear the story from her."

"Sure, sure. Let me take you over there."

Lisa Burnett looked up as the two detectives approached her. It was obvious that she had been crying. Her eyes were red and swollen. Her hair looked like it had just started to be dried and set. It was mostly just combed back. Her face bore no makeup, but she didn't need much. She was clearly beautiful.

"Lisa," Burnett said, "these are detectives with the Milton Police Department. They would like to ask you some questions."

With that, Ricky Burnett stood up. "Hey, Steve." He wore a goofy smile that seemed out of place.

"Ricky," Marks said. "Haven't seen you for a while."

"Don't we need to call in the FBI or something like that?" Ricky asked.

"Not just yet," Marks answered. He wasn't really sure what the protocol was for calling in the Federal agency. "Let us get some of the preliminary questions out of the way."

"Yeah, sure. Lisa wants to talk about it. She wants to find Henry right away."

That seemed obvious, Marks thought. Ricky sat back down and Marks took a step forward and faced Lisa Burnett. She looked up into his eyes and Marks felt her pain. She looked devastated. "I'm sorry about this, Mrs. Burnett. We are going to do our best to get Henry back to you as soon as we can."

She nodded. "Why did this happen? Why would someone want to take Henry?"

Marks wasn't sure he could answer those questions. "Can you tell us what happened, what led up to you finding out that Henry had been taken?"

Those couple of words caused Lisa to sob and a single tear ran down her face. She wiped it with a sodden handkerchief. "I just got out of the shower," she said. "I had started to do my hair when I realized I couldn't hear Henry on the baby monitor. Usually, I can her him making noises. He usually makes a lot of little noises when he sleeps. He was very quiet, and I went to check on him and he was gone." Another big sob.

"You were home with Henry all morning long, before you went into the shower?"

She paused before answering. She was clearly thinking before answering. "I was out early in the morning for a bit. Marguerite was with Henry until I got home."

Marks looked across the room at the Hispanic woman sitting in the chair. She had been crying as well. "She is your babysitter?"

"Our nanny," Lisa said. "She was here the whole time that I was out."

"What time did you get home?" Anders asked.

Marks looked at him but backed off stopping him.

"Who is this?" Ricky asked abruptly.

"This is Anders Hedberg, on loan from Sterling," Marks said. "He will be working with me to find Henry."

"He looks like he just got out of high school," Ricky said.

"A few years removed from that, Mr. Burnett," Anders said. "Back to my question. When did you arrive home?"

"Somewhere after ten," she said. "I'm not sure of the exact time, but it's about the same time every Tuesday and Thursday."

"You go somewhere every Tuesday and Thursday morning?" Marks asked.

Again, a pause before answering. "Yes, I do," she said.

"Where would that be?" Marks said.

"I go to a yoga class on those days," Lisa answered quietly.

"We are not trying to be invasive. We are simply trying to see if there is a pattern of yours that someone could follow. If someone knows your patterns, it might be easier to plan a kidnapping of this nature."

She nodded. "I see. I understand."

"Do you always come home and take a shower after your class?"

"Yes, almost always. Sometimes I don't shower right away if Henry is awake. Sometimes I play with him for a while."

"But Henry went down right away when you got home today, and you went into the shower?"

She looked across the room at her nanny. "When I got home, Marguerite told me she had put Henry down and he was sleeping."

Marks turned toward the Hispanic woman. She wore a look of fear more than anything. "You put Henry down for his nap?"

She wiped her eyes. "Yes, I did," she said.

"Was he asleep when you left?"

She thought for a moment. "He lay right down, and he looked tired. I thought he would go to sleep right away." She spoke with a slight Hispanic accent.

"And then you left the room?"

"Yes. Mrs. Burnett always tells me to turn on the monitor and leave the door a little open. I said goodbye to her, and I left."

"What about the front door?" Anders asked. "Was it locked when you left?"

Marguerite's eyes went wide. "I think so. I pulled it closed behind me. I think it was locked."

"But you're not sure?" Anders persisted.

Again, the moments of thought. "Not sure, but I think."

"And you went straight home?" Marks said.

"Yes, sir," she said. "I went home until Mrs. Burnett called me and told me that Henry was not in his crib. I came back here right away."

"What do we do?" the senior Mr. Burnett asked.

Good question thought Marks. "My initial thought, due to your known prominence in the area, is that someone took Henry for financial gain."

"Meaning what?" Mr. Burnett asked.

"Meaning, I think we'll hear something soon from the kidnappers in regard to a ransom. Whoever took Henry knows you have money. I don't think they just took him. I think they will make a monetary demand."

"Oh, my God," Ricky Burnett said.

"Are we not going to look at the biggest suspect in the room?" Ricky's mother said loudly.

Marks and Anders turned towards her. "What are you saying, Mrs. Burnett?" Marks asked.

She stood up from her chair, smoothing out her clothes as she rose. "I'm saying check out where Lisa has been. She is the one who is always out and about, leaving Henry with this woman. It wouldn't be too hard for someone to figure out the patterns of her day to know that Henry was alone in his room while she was showering."

"Mother, please!" Ricky said loudly.

"This is not the time for this," Ricky's father said.

"She never wanted Henry in the first place," Ricky's mom continued.

"That's not true," Lisa said. "That's not true at all."

"That is not true," Ricky said, glaring at his mother.

"Let's try and control ourselves," Marks said. "This is a time of high emotions and anxiety. Not a great time for finger pointing and accusations."

Ricky's mother sat back down and crossed her arms over her chest.

"What do we do?" Ricky's father said.

"What you do is wait. You wait until you are contacted by the kidnappers. I'm sure they don't want to keep Henry. I'm sure they are looking for money. They will contact you soon."

"And if they don't?"

"Mr. Burnett, one thing at a time. While we wait for the kidnappers to contact you, I want to start interviewing each of you individually to develop your daily patterns. This may hopefully lead us to the kidnappers."

"All of us?" the father asked.

"Yes. Ricky, Lisa, and Mrs. Lopez first," Marks said. "We'll start with Mrs. Lopez. She was the last person to see Henry before he disappeared. She can follow us back to the station and we'll start our questioning. We'll come back here later to talk with Ricky and Lisa."

"Do we need our lawyer present?" the father asked.

Marks thought for a moment. Regardless of Ricky's mother's comments, he didn't think any of them were suspects. "That's at your discretion," he said. "Mrs. Lopez, you will follow us into the station."

"Yes, sir," Marguerite said.

"In the meantime, I'm going to have the officers that are here canvass all of the neighbors to see if anyone saw anything suspicious. You contact us right away if anyone contacts you for money."

This comment drew nods from everyone in the room. Mark and Anders headed for the door. Marks stopped to tell the remaining officers what he wanted from them. They got in their car and headed for the station making sure Marguerite Lopez was following them.

"You're convinced that this is a kidnapping for money?" Anders asked.

"Not convinced, but that is my first thought?"

"And the comments that Ricky's mother made?"

"Emotional, anti-daughter-in law, comments. A little ludicrous don't you think?"

"But we'll ask her what she meant?"

"Absolutely. They might be ludicrous, but we have to ask."

· · ·

The Milton Police Department had a large and a small conference room. Since Marguerite Lopez was not under arrest or officially a suspect, Marks decided to just talk to her in his office. He noticed how nervous and scared she looked at the Burnett house. Now he wanted her to relax and tell them what she knew. She took the seat nearest the door. Marks had offered her coffee or water but she declined. She looked nervous.

"How long have you worked for the Burnetts?" Marks asked.

"I would say a little over two years," she answered quietly. "I think Henry was about six months old."

"And they are good people?"

The question seemed to catch her off guard. "How do you mean?"

"How do they treat you?"

She had to think for a moment. "They treat me good. They are nice."

"Do you know them very well? I mean, I know you work for them, but do you know them? Did they ever discuss things with you?"

She was wringing her hands together. Anders had a good look at them. She was squeezing the life out of them. "I never talked much with Mr. Burnett. He is very quiet. Sometimes I talk with Mrs. Burnett. She is always nice to me."

"How often do you work for them?" Anders asked.

"I always work Tuesday and Thursday mornings from about seven-thirty until about ten. I work on Saturday mornings when Mrs. Burnett gets her hair done and does her shopping. I also work whenever Mrs.

Burnett needs me to. She goes out sometimes and I will come over and watch Henry."

This puzzled Marks. "Where does she go?"

"I don't know, sir. She goes out at night for a couple of hours after dinner, usually on Thursday. I don't ask where she goes. It is easy for me as Henry goes to sleep at this time."

"And where is Mr. Burnett?"

"He always at his stores from eight in the morning until eight or nine at night. The only day he doesn't work is Sunday. I never work on Sunday for the Burnetts."

Marks made a few notes on a sheet of paper. "So, let's get back to today. Can you tell me what happened?"

Marguerite thought he meant what happened with the kidnapping. "I don't know anything about what happened with Henry?"

"I don't mean that," Marks said. "Tell me how the day went."

She shrugged. "It went like most days. I got there about seven-thirty. Henry was just getting up. I made him his breakfast while Mrs. Burnett got ready to go out."

"She goes to yoga class?" Anders asked.

"Yes, she goes to yoga on Tuesdays and Thursdays."

"When you say gets ready," Marks said, "you mean she changes her clothes."

She shook her head. "No. She takes a shower before she goes and when she comes home. She spends time on her hair, too."

Both Marks and Anders looked at each other. "Something wrong with that?" Marguerite said.

"She showers before and after a workout class?" Marks said.

"And does her hair?" Anders added.

She smiled. "You can see. Mrs. Burnett is a very beautiful woman. I think she likes to look her best when she goes out."

"You ever see her where she didn't look her best?" Marks said.

She laughed. "No, sir."

"What else happened?"

"I fed Henry and then we played for a while, and I read him two books. They don't like it if I put on the TV too much."

"And when Mrs. Burnett came home?"

"She will play with Henry for a bit, but today he was already napping. She went in to take her shower. That is when I left."

"You always put him to bed?"

"Mostly. He goes down easier if I do it. I tuck him in, put on the monitor and I go home."

Marks made more notes and thought carefully about his next words. "You ever tell anyone outside of the Burnetts and us what your routine is?"

Her eyes widened. "What do you mean?"

"I mean did you ever tell anyone that you put Henry down for a nap while Mrs. Burnett is in the shower at roughly the same time on Tuesday and Thursday. Would someone know that Henry is alone in his room while his mother is showering and unlikely to hear any intrusion?"

They could see that this question immediately upset her. Her lip began to quiver; a tear rolled out of her left eye. Anders handed her a fresh Kleenex. "I never did that, and I would never do that. I am always careful with Henry. I make sure the monitor is on. I check it all the time. I would never do anything to harm the Burnetts and Henry."

When she had left, Marks and Anders compared notes. There was nothing too startling. "She just seems like a woman trying to do her little job and make some money," Anders said. "Seems like she genuinely likes Henry and doesn't want any harm to come to him."

Marks was twirling his pen in his fingers. "I agree, but there does seem to be something just a little weird about Lisa Burnett."

"Like where she goes all the time?"

"That would be a big part of it."

• • •

The Eyes West café was a nice little place, open only for breakfast and lunch that had a magnificent view of the Mississippi from atop an eroding bluff. The café had been warned by the county and the state that if the erosion got worse they might have to close down. Other than that, they had incredible crepes and offered unlimited mimosas. Tori Rooks was sipping on one as she looked across the table at her agent, Betty Palmer. Betty had been her agent for the past five years. She was older and some of her ideas seemed archaic, but she had gotten Tori into several great shows and had helped build her brand.

"You look nice and tanned and relaxed," Betty said. She was drinking a jasmine tea; she didn't drink alcohol before five o'clock PM.

"The trip was great; the weather was perfect," Tori said. She took a sip of her drink.

"You don't seem like you are in a particularly good mood."

Tori looked out over the great river. It looked like the sun might poke through the clouds, but it was still cold. She could still see ice on some of the trees. "I'm fine," she said. "It would be a lot better if it wasn't cloudy and freezing."

"But that's not all?"

"I suppose not."

"Does it have to do with Steve?"

Did it have to do with Steve, or did it have to do with her? She thought the move to Chicago would have been great for both of their careers. She thought that staying in Milton and small-town America was not the best thing for them. "Steve had a chance to move to Chicago. He would have been a detective there. It would have been a great move for his career. Here he is stuck behind Lou Katz. They are the same age. Lou could be the Chief of Police forever and Steve would be the head of investigations."

"That's not such a bad position, probably good for the future."

Tori shrugged. "He has been in a terrible rut for a bit now. It would have been the right move for him. It wouldn't have hurt me either."

"So why didn't he take the job?"

"There's been a murder. Some poor homeless guy was killed behind Aces. Steve thought it would be wrong to leave Lou with an unsolved murder. I think he was calling Chicago today to tell them that he isn't going to take the job."

"But wasn't that the right thing to do, not leaving with a large case pending?"

Tori smiled weakly. "Probably, but there are a lot of ramifications staying here."

Betty placed her hand over Tori's. "You do love Steve?"

Love? What a fucked-up concept. "I love him to death, but it's maddening with him sometimes. He says he wants to get out, but his loyalty to the Milton Police Department and Lou Katz trump everything else."

"Including you?"

Tori thought for a moment before answering. She wasn't sure. She knew Steve loved her, but in what order of things. She didn't get a chance to answer the question as the waitress came to take their orders.

• • •

Chicago, April 2009

Wacker Drive runs from near the Sears Tower north, turns abruptly east and ends up at Lake Michigan. Underneath Wacker is a road that runs along the same path with a few split-offs. This road is called Lower Wacker. It provides a quick short cut from the Eisenhower to Michigan Avenue. Since it is below the street level it has numerous building vents where heat from all of the high rises escapes. This makes it an ideal place for members of the homeless community to huddle near the vents and keep warm on a cold night. This is where Mike Burke and Eli Roach found themselves on an early April morning. The temperature was below freezing, but on Lower Wacker, near the heat vents, it wasn't that bad.

"Same as the last one?" Eli asked. He lit a cigarette and walked around Burke to get a look at the victim.

"Pretty much. Homeless guy of an undetermined age stabbed in the throat. Looks like he bled out."

"Did they steal his cell phone this time?" Eli exhaled a large plume of smoke.

"Don't know. Don't know shit. This guy appears to have been sleeping near his grocery cart of belongings, when somebody came up to him and rammed a good - sized knife into his throat."

Eli stepped closer to get a better look. "The throat is not really cut."

"No. The son of a bitch that killed this guy just seems to ram the knife into the throat as far as it will go. We'll need the ME to confirm that, but that's what I see."

Eli walked around the body and looked at the cart. It looked like it was undisturbed. "Doesn't look like the killer touched his stuff."

"Like I said, looks like somebody just walked up and jabbed the knife in and took off.'

"Sure he walked up?"

Mike looked behind him. There was an opening where a car could have pulled in, the driver could have done the deed, and then drove off. "Not sure of anything. I know a lot of bums sleep down here. It seems when the squad showed up with the flashing lights everybody made for the hills."

"Who called it in?"

"Guy named Meyers. Said he pulled into the opening to take a leak. Traffic was bad on the Ike, and he wasn't going to make it to his office before he wet his pants."

Eli laughed. "Been there. Coffee and beer."

"Yeah. Poor way to start your day. Stop to take a piss behind a pillar and stumble over a dead homeless guy."

"Did he ever get to pee?"

"Have to ask him."

"What next, Mikey?"

Mike looked down Lower Wacker. Morning traffic was gliding past, stopping to stare at the cop lights flashing. "We've got a dead guy behind an Italian restaurant and one on Lower Wacker, several miles apart. Both killed in about the same way. One had their cell phone stolen. The other looks like nothing taken at all. Is there a connection between these two?"

"Who the fuck knows?"

"Exactly. Maybe we can ID this guy and learn something."

Eli flicked his cigarette butt away. "Big maybe."

Mike's stomach hurt suddenly. It wasn't hunger. His hands were getting cold. He longed for warm air and retirement. He took a look at the dead guy. Would he retire first or find this guy's killer? He shook his head and headed for his car.

CHAPTER 3

Back at the Burnett house, Marks and Anders were greeted by Ricky's father. He wore a tired and agitated look. This was certainly understandable. Ricky's mother was seated in the same spot that she had been in earlier, looking out at the golf fairway. There was no sight of Ricky or Lisa.

"Ricky and Lisa?" Marks asked.

"Ricky had to go into one of the stores for a bit; he trusted me to watch Lisa and keep an eye on the phone if anyone called about Henry."

"How about Lisa?"

"In her room. I'm not quite sure what she is doing."

Marks noted all of this. He wasn't sure if his baby had been kidnapped, he would have run off to check on his business. After hearing Ricky's mother's snide remark about Lisa earlier, he could understand why she had retreated to the solitude of her bedroom.

"Did the officers that were checking on the neighbors hear or see anything?" Ricky's father asked.

"They checked all of the houses on both sides of the street. One woman remembers Mrs. Lopez arriving around seven-thirty. Another woman saw Ricky leave for work. Other than that, nothing. No one saw or heard anything that looked suspicious. To be more direct, no one saw anyone leave the house with Henry or saw any strange vehicles around the house."

He nodded. "That seems almost impossible."

"That's what he know so far. That doesn't mean someone won't remember something later on. We'll keep pressing," Marks said. He thought his answer sounded like an apology.

"I suppose you want to talk with Lisa now?"

"She was the one that was home when Henry was taken. We have to start there. We would like to speak with her in private if that is possible."

"She knows something," Ricky's mother said loudly.

All three men looked in her direction. "She's very upset right now," Ricky's father said. "Let me get Lisa. You can talk to her in Ricky's den."

"Should we have a chat with mom about why she keeps making these comments about Lisa?" Anders asked quietly.

"Not just yet. I agree with the father. I think she might not like her daughter-in- law and she is just upset. We'll get to her in due time."

Ricky's father returned with Lisa a moment later. She had dressed in a nice pair of jeans and a light beige sweater. Her golden hair hung loosely about her shoulders. She had applied a light amount of makeup. She was beautiful.

"Lisa will take you down to Ricky's den," the father said.

Lisa turned and walked towards the back of the house. Marks and Anders, a little like two puppies, followed quickly behind her. They both were a little transfixed by her looks and her athletic shape. The door to the den was closed. Lisa opened it and stepped in before the two cops. She took a seat behind Ricky's desk. There were two other chairs in the room. Marks and Anders took these. Marks closed the door behind them.

"I don't need a lawyer, do I?" Lisa said at once.

Marks cleared his throat. "I don't believe so. We are just trying to gather some basic information, trying to develop patterns of everyone involved. The kidnappers knew your routine and jumped on it."

"I think maybe only Ricky and Marguerite knew my routine. They are probably the only ones that know that I come home from my class and go into the shower when Marguerite puts Henry down for his nap," she said. She spoke with authority and no signs of being nervous. She seemed emotionless.

"That may be," Marks said, "but let's review it one more time." He was surprised how calm she was in contrast to their first visit to the house; she seemed composed.

She let out a deep breath. "My routine on Tuesday and Thursday is to go to my yoga class. I come home and visit with Henry for a bit and then Marguerite lays him down for his nap. That is when I take my shower."

"Why don't you lay Henry down for his nap?" Anders said. Marks shifted nervously on his chair.

The question caught her off guard and she sagged a bit in her chair. "Well, Marguerite is here. She always does that. I think Henry is used to it. He never complains when she puts him down."

"Does Henry complain when you put him down?" Anders persisted.

"What? No, of course not. I put Henry down for a lot of naps. He doesn't complain about it. Why would he?" She had regained her initial composure.

"Detective Hedberg didn't mean anything offensive. We are, again, just trying to develop patterns. It is important to know that Mrs. Lopez always puts Henry down for his naps on Tuesday and Thursday mornings."

Her eyes widened. "You don't think Marguerite is a suspect, do you?"

"No one is a suspect yet, but I suppose everyone is a prospect."

Her Adams apple bobbed, a few times. "What does that mean?"

"That means we are going to question everyone that we can think of to determine who might have known that Henry was alone in his crib while you were in the shower."

She nodded. She seemed to understand where Marks was going with this. "I will tell you everything I know. I just want to get Henry back."

"That is our number one goal. Anything and everything you tell us could be important. Please try not to leave out anything."

Again she nodded but said nothing.

"How long has Mrs. Lopez worked for you?" Marks asked.

She pushed a few strands of hair out of her eyes. "She came to work for us when Henry was about six months old, I think."

"What do you know about her?"

"Well," she paused. "She is a good worker, always on time, always does what I ask her to do."

"But what do you know about her?" Marks repeated.

"I know that she is married. I know that she has two children. She also cleans some houses and offices in town to make some extra money."

"So she probably comes in contact with a number of different people?"

She thought for a moment. "I would imagine she knows the people that she cleans houses for. I guess she runs into some people in the offices she cleans."

"Would you say that you know her well enough to say that she wouldn't tell anyone what your routine is on Tuesday and Thursday?"

"I can't say that for sure," she said. "You don't think that Marguerite is behind Henry being taken?"

"I didn't say that," Marks said. "I'm just trying to line things up."

"Where do you take your yoga classes?" Anders said.

Again she seemed surprised by this question. "My yoga classes?"

"Yes," Anders said. "Where do you go to take your classes?"

She bit down on her lower lip. "I don't like your attitude," she said. "You are very forward."

Anders smiled. "Mrs. Burnett, I am not trying to be rude. Like Detective Marks stated, we are just trying to find who could be behind taking Henry."

She looked over at Marks, but he said nothing. "I go to The River Club to take my classes." The River Club was a very nice private health club and spa located down by the river, about a mile from Aces.

"Do you remember ever telling anyone at The River Club what your routine was on the days that you went to classes?" Anders asked.

She really didn't care for this young cop. "I don't think I ever explained that to anyone. Why would I? They see me at class, but they don't know that I come home and shower while Marguerite puts Henry down for his nap."

"Of course," Marks said, trying to cool the situation. "What about Ricky?"

"Ricky? I think Ricky knows my routine. Why wouldn't he? If you're asking me if Ricky tells everyone at the store what I do, I don't know. You'd have to ask him."

Marks made a few notes and scratched his head. "Again, Mrs. Burnett, we are not trying to upset you. We are just trying to figure this out."

Her face turned red. "You both sound so accusational, especially this one." She pointed at Anders.

Anders' face never changed. "What about your in-laws?" he asked.

63

She turned her head and looked out the window at the golf course. "I don't think they know much about me at all. My mother-in-law clearly doesn't like me; my father-in-law is oblivious to most things, but his golf and poker games."

"Any friends you might have told what you do on these two days?" Marks asked.

She gave Marks another stern look. "They know I take classes; I don't think they know everything else."

Marks made a few additional notes and couldn't think of anything else to ask. This was all preliminary stuff and nothing substantial had come out of it. They were no further along than before they heard the name of Henry Burnett.

"You are going to be able to find Henry?" Lisa Burnett asked. For the first time since the morning visit it looked like she had tears in her eyes; her lips quivered.

"We are going to her do our best to find Henry," Marks said. "In the meantime, we have to ask a lot of questions. I know it may seem intrusive, but we may ask the right question and get an answer that leads us somewhere."

"What do you think we'll likely happen?" she asked. She was getting close to tears. "What do we do?"

"What you do is sit tight and hope someone calls with a ransom demand. I think that is what is going to happen, and I think it will happen soon. Watch out for prank calls, too. Unfortunately today, we live in a crazy society. So just sit tight and wait. We will do the poking around."

"Where are you going next?" she asked.

"We are going to talk to Ricky. He seems to be the most logical of anyone that knows your morning routine. We understand he went back to one of his stores."

She bit her lip again. "He loves those fucking stores."

• • •

They found Ricky in his store on Main Street. For a Tuesday, the store was doing a good business. Ricky was in his office going through a large pile of invoices on his desk. He was wearing a plain white shirt with a red tie. He looked like he would on a normal business day, Marks thought, not on a day his son had been kidnapped.

"You have time for us, Ricky?" Marks said, standing in the office door.

Ricky looked up quickly. "Sure. Sure, I do. Just trying to keep things in order."

The two cops entered the office, closing the door behind them. Marks noted all of the family pictures on the credenza behind Ricky's desk. Everyone in them was smiling.

"I remember that you were a pretty good ballplayer back in school," Ricky said. "You and TH Brown."

"We were pretty good," Marks said. He didn't really want to talk high school sports."

"Very wild what happened to old Chief Brown, Cindy Fuller and all of those old cops who got killed up in Iowa."

65

Marks nodded. What could he say? It had been wild. "We really need to focus today on what happened to Henry."

Ricky looked disappointed. "Of course. What did you find out so far?"

"So far, nothing. We have just started. We are trying to gather information on who would have known that Lisa was showering, and that Henry was left alone in his bedroom."

"Well, I'm sure Marguerite knew," he said a little quickly.

"We talked to Mrs. Lopez. She told us everything she knows. We are a little curious about what you knew."

"Me? What I knew?" Ricky's eyes widened.

"More like what you knew and what you may have told anyone else about Lisa's habits, especially when it came to Tuesday and Thursday mornings."

Ricky smiled, relaxed a bit. "I'm sure you've heard this all before. I go to work shortly after Marguerite arrives. Lisa gets ready for yoga and leaves Henry with her. When Lisa gets home she showers, and Marguerite puts Henry down for his nap. I'm pretty sure this is the same scene that plays out twice a week at our house."

"We did get all of that," Marks said. "Is there any possibility that you might have repeated this pattern of your wife's to anyone else?"

Ricky got a pensive look. "I can see telling someone that Marguerite watches Henry while Lisa goes to her class, but I don't think I ever told anyone the part about her putting Henry down while Lisa showers."

"Can you think of anyone you might have told the first part to?"

"That's just it, Steve. I might have mentioned it but I can't particularly remember saying it and certainly can't remember who I might have said it to."

Marks was thinking about writing some of this down but didn't. None of it seemed very pertinent.

"Your mother made some pretty damning statements when we were at your house," Anders said.

Ricky's eyes narrowed. "Who are you again?"

"My name is Anders Hedberg. I am on loan from the Sterling PD."

"You look like your sixteen."

"Sorry about that. Do you mind answering the question I asked about your mother?"

Ricky exhaled loudly. "My mother doesn't really like Lisa. She has said all along that Lisa was not the right one for me. She says Lisa spends too much time out of the house, leaving Henry in Marguerite's care. I am sure this is the reason that she is blaming Henry being taken on Lisa."

"Nothing else that you can think of?" Anders asked.

"My mother thinks Lisa is a gold digger."

Marks did write that down. "So there's nobody that you can explicitly say that you told about Lisa's daily routines?"

"Not that I can think of," Ricky said.

"Then I think you should be home," Marks said. "I think Lisa might need you. She's holed up in your bedroom. I also think that you should be the one answering the phone should the kidnappers or anyone else call your home. I'd rather they talk with you and not your father."

"There's just a few things I need to straighten up here," Ricky said.

"A bit of an asshole," Anders said on the drive back to headquarters.

"Seems oblivious," Marks said. "More concerned about invoices and inventory than little Henry being kidnapped."

"That makes him an asshole, doesn't it?"

Marks laughed. "I guess so, but I also wonder if that makes him a person of interest."

Anders turned to face Marks in his seat. "Really? You think?"

"Truth stranger than fiction sometimes."

Anders whistled and looked out the window. The clouds were starting to part.

• • •

When the police left her house, Lisa Burnett picked up the phone in the den and called Kyle James' cell phone number. She knew that Kyle went to the gym after they got together; she hoped he would pick up. He did after two rings.

"It's me," Lisa said.

"Oh. I didn't recognize the number," Kyle said.

Lisa realized she had only called Kyle from her own cell phone. "It's my house number. I'm at home."

Kyle paused for a moment. "Are you sure that's safe?"

Safe from what, Lisa thought? If the cops were going to find out about Kyle and her they'd find her cell phone number on his records. What was the difference? "I'm not sure it makes a big difference."

"Okay. What's going on?"

"Look, I want to tell you if the cops come around asking about me, I think you should say that you have not seen me."

"The cops? Why would the cops want to question me about anything?" Kyle felt suddenly nervous. He pictured himself losing his job at Mercury Auto Repair.

"Something has happened here that may lead the cops to question you about my whereabouts."

Now Kyle was full blown nervous. "What happened, Lisa?"

"Someone kidnapped Henry this morning after I got back from your place."

"Kidnapped? You mean like took your kid?"

"That's what I mean, Kyle. It's terrible. We are dealing with it now. I just don't want what you and I had together to get made into a bigger thing."

"A bigger thing? What do you mean?"

"Look, Kyle, I can't talk a lot now. I'll try and call later. Just remember, if the cops come, you haven't seen me."

Before he could respond the line went dead. Kyle stared at his cell for a moment. This wasn't something like Ricky Burnett getting mad at him. This was a kidnapping that happened after the child's mother had left his apartment. This wasn't going to go well. He could feel it. Why had he ever gotten involved with Lisa Burnett? Then he remembered how she looked and how she made him feel. He smiled.

• • • •

Ricky Burnett had used Micky Carter for private work since he had taken over the management of the stores several years before. Micky was a private investigator out of Dubuque. Micky had the reputation that said he would look into anything that needed looking into. A former boxer, Micky was known for administering some justice for his clients. Of course, this was done for an additional fee. Ricky called Micky before he headed back home from the store.

"Is there anything new you can tell me, Micky?" Ricky asked.

"Same thing as before. Same thing for five weeks now, Mr. B. Your wife leaves the house and goes by this mechanic's apartment for an hour or so and then returns to your house."

"And she was there this morning?"

"She got there a little before nine and left a little before ten."

Ricky's stomach tightened. He knew that Lisa was going through one of her "freedom" phases, but this one bothered him. To hear that Lisa was fooling around with Kyle James was a clear gut punch. Kyle James of all people. Would it make any difference if it was with someone of stature?

"You want me to make a visit to this little punk?" Micky asked.

Ricky considered this. What good would it do to have Micky rough up Kyle James? Beating the shit out of Kyle would certainly hurt him, but would it punish Lisa? He doubted it. "Leave him alone for now. It's Lisa who is the problem. Let me have a talk with her?"

"Whatever you say, Mr. B. By the way, I'm pretty sure I've got it nailed who's setting up the missing inventory in the West Dubuque store."

Ricky heard what Micky Carter said, but he was trying to figure out a way to approach Lisa. He was trying to get her back on track.

"Hear what I said, Mr. B?"

"I heard you Micky. Write that one up and email me. I'll have HR deal with it."

Micky heard the line go dead. "Spoiled kid," he mumbled to himself.

• • •

The dinner for the homeless at St. John's Lutheran Church was set up in the basement. There were two long tables set up in the front of the room for serving.

Volunteers dished out large helpings of salad, turkey, potatoes, and vegetables. There was bottled water to drink. In front of the food tables were four other long tables where the guests could eat their dinner. When Marks and Anders got to the church there were about twenty people eating their food.

"Good sized crowd," Marks said.

"Do you have to be homeless to eat here?" Anders asked. "That dinner looks way better than what I have been eating lately."

"Behave."

They had called ahead and spoken to the director of the dinner, Marion Campton, and told her they would be coming and what they wanted to accomplish. She told them they were more than welcome, that solving the murder of Herbert was extremely important, as long as they didn't upset any of the attendees. Marks had told her they would do their best.

As soon as they walked into the room, a tall woman with dark hair, wearing a navy suit approached them. Her smile showed perfect, white teeth. "Detective Marks, welcome to St. John's. "I am Marion Campton."

Marks returned the smile and shook Marion's hand. "How did you know who we were?"

"Most of our visitors don't wear suits and ties," she said.

He laughed. "This is Anders Hedberg. He is also investigating the case."

She nodded at Anders. "A terrible situation. I read about it in the Beacon."

"It truly is. Do you mind if we make our way around to the tables to talk with some of the people? We'll try not to upset anyone too much."

"That would be fine and thank you. These poor people have it tough enough without more emotional stress being dumped in their laps."

"I understand," Marks said.

They moved to the first table near them that had empty seats and sat down. Marks introduced them and told them why they were there. Then he asked if anyone at the table knew who Herbert was. Three of the four people at the table shook their heads and kept eating. The fourth, an older guy with a weather-beaten face, said he knew who Herbert was.

"How did you know him?" Marks asked.

"I read about him in the paper. He's the guy that got killed by the casino, the one where somebody took his dog."

"That's all you know about him?"

"Yeah, I guess so. I may have seen him, but if he always had that dog with him, I don't think so."

"Jesus," Anders muttered quietly.

"Did you try the turkey?" the lone woman at the table asked.

Marks smiled. "No. It looks great."

The woman didn't respond and continued after her meal. "Anybody know a Big Tony?" Marks said.

This time there were a couple of nods. The guy who said he read about Herbert spoke up again. "Kind of hard not to know of him. He's a big mean looking guy, not friendly at all."

"Anybody remember the last time they saw him around?"

Again, a bunch of head shaking and no response, they moved onto the second table. This one had five people eating at it. Marks and Anders stood near one end and explained their case. This table was less fruitful than the first. No one knew Herbert, but a couple had heard of the murder. A few knew who Big Tony was but hadn't seen him in a while.

"Do you think these people are being honest?" Anders asked. "I'm getting the feeling that they don't want to get involved in this case and are just clamming up."

"I thought that, too. Let's see what table three has to offer."

A big guy, healthier looking than most of the group, with long red hair and beard spoke up right away. "I knew Herbert. I'd see him out by the casino with his little dog. He never said a whole lot. He'd come in here once in a while, but not always. I'd say very private."

"When you say very private does that mean he didn't say much about himself or his past?"

The man laughed. "Most of us don't talk about our past. Most of us are trying to forget it. As you can see, not a whole lot went right. As for Herbert, I knew his name, not much more."

"He would steal some things," the lone woman at the table said.

"Jenny, you don't know if that's true," the man said.

"Quiet, Andrew. You know some people claimed he stole some clothes. That's why people didn't want him around. He was a thief."

Anders was fast taking notes. Marks addressed the woman. "You don't know much about his past or where he came from?"

"No, none of that. Just heard he was a thief. Most didn't want much to do with him."

"What about this guy Big Tony we keep hearing about?" Anders said.

The woman laughed. The big guy cleared his throat. "He is big, and he is mean. Carries a real big hunting knife. Not a nice person. Never comes here."

"Any of you remember the last time you saw Big Tony?" Marks said.

The whole table shook their heads in unison. The fourth table, like the first, had nothing to add to the discussion. They stopped by the desk that Marion Campton was sitting at. She flashed her big smile again. "I hope you found something useful," she said.

"Some," Marks said. "I was just wondering if Herbert ever came down here for dinner?"

"I tried to remember that, but I couldn't recall. Most people come here and eat and to stay warm. They are not always forthcoming with a lot of information. I just can't recall."

"Think she was telling the truth?" Anders said as they walked to the car. It was getting colder, and a light snow was falling.

"I think she was truthful. I also have no idea why she would lie to us."

"But now we know that Herbert has some history as a thief and Big Tony has got to be found."

"Yeah, he sounds promising for being a little dangerous, but the knife that got Herbert was a long, serrated type, not a hunting knife."

"You mean a kitchen type?" Anders had heard none of this.

"More like that. The ME called late today."

"Didn't know that."

Marks sensed Anders' mood. "Don't get all weepy, Anders. I was going to tell you, but with everything going crazy today, it slipped my mind?"

Anders let it go. "The Burnett parents in the morning?"

"Nine AM sharp."

• • •

Tori had made a pasta with olive oil and tomatoes for dinner. She also made a small salad. Both were waiting for Marks when he got home a little after eight-thirty. She wasn't sure he would eat, but she had kept everything for him.

"Would you like a glass of wine?" she asked. Marks had taken off his jacket and tie and taken a seat in front of the TV. The Celtics were badly beating the Bulls.

"I'm good," he said.

"Hungry?"

"Not really. Just need to sit for a bit."

"I take it things didn't go well with the Chicago call?"

Chicago, Marks thought. He hadn't thought about that since the call in the early morning. "They didn't seem too upset," he said.

"Something is bothering you."

"There was a kidnapping today. A little two-year-old boy. His dad is a guy that was in the same high school class as me. The family owns the Burnett Furniture stores."

"Oh," she said. "That's terrible."

"Yeah. A murder and a kidnapping all in one week. Suddenly, Milton isn't so boring."

"I didn't know," she said.

"It has nothing to do with you. Here I was talking about being a big detective in Chicago and now I've got two cases right here in Milton and I have no idea what the hell I'm doing."

She sat down next to him and took his hand. "I'm sure it's not that bad."

He looked over at her. "We're picking up little pieces on the homeless guy, Herbert, like tidbits. I'm not sure the other homeless types are telling us all they know. It's like they just don't want to be involved. It's a little frustrating. As for the kidnapping, we have nothing. Kid was taken while the mom was in the shower. They are a wealthy family so I'm expecting a ransom demand at some point, hopefully soon."

"The parents must be devastated."

"You would think so, but they both seemed like they were more interested in other things than the kidnapping. It was a little weird."

"I would be going nuts if that ever happened to me."

"You mean like if you ever got married and decided to have kids?"

"Ouch," she said. "You know what I mean."

He nodded. "Something will break our way in the next day or so."

She didn't say anything. She knew Marks. He wasn't always mister optimistic. She wasn't sure he believed what he had said.

•   •   •

Anders was ready to take a big bite out of a beef sandwich when Tammy Glaser slipped into the booth across from him. On a Tuesday, Lifers was pretty quiet. Tammy saw a couple of regulars at the bar. She hoped she wouldn't end up like them, drinking alone at a townie bar.

"You want something to eat?" Anders said.

"I ate earlier at home. I know you guys had a rough day."

"It's been a long week already."

"For a rookie, you get a murder and a kidnapping in two days."

He smiled. "Not really a rookie. We had a murder in Sterling. A wife shot her husband when he walked through the front door. He was holding flowers for her.

She felt bad about that, but not the ten times or so when he beat her up."

"Heart- warming story."

Anders took another bite of his beef and followed it with a drink of his beer. The waitress brought over a gin and tonic for Tammy. "You know this guy, Ricky Burnett?"

"Know of him," she said. "He's a little older, silver spoon kid, kind of a wimp."

"He acted like he knew Marks, but Steve said he only knew a little about him."

"He wasn't in Marks' group. That much I know. Marks, TH Brown, and a few others were the cool kids of that class. Guys like Ricky Burnett hung out at the country club and fretted over their putting stroke."

"Both him and his wife acted bizarre when questioned, kind of out of it. It was very weird."

"I can't imagine having my kid taken from my house," Tammy said. "Learn much at your homeless dinner?" She took a sip of her drink. It was light on gin.

"Not too much. Herbert appears to have had a little bit of a reputation as a thief. Not much more there. Our only lead is the allusive Big Tony. Carries a knife and a bad temper. Just got to find him."

She held up a piece of paper. "Anthony Michael Peters. Age forty-four. Last known residence was with his brother on his soybean farm near Platteville. Served time twice for breaking and entering. Served again for sexual abuse of a young lady. One more time for possession of an illegal substance. Couldn't find more than that. Seems like a small time, career loser."

"And his brother, the farmer?"

"Robert John Peters. Age forty-seven. Occupation, soybean farmer. Twenty-seven- eighteen County Road W. Platteville, Wisconsin. About an hour away."

Anders smiled. "That's great news. How can I repay you?"

She took another drink and smiled. "I'm sure we can work something out."

CHAPTER 4

April 2009

Mike Burke was sitting at his desk in the second precinct trying really hard not to smoke another cigarette. He had promised and told his wife that he had cut it down to a pack a day. He had only been off about fifty percent. He stuck the cigarette back in the box and put the pack in his pocket. He looked up as Eli Roach approached him.

"I saw the report from the coroner, Mike. What do you think?" Eli sat down on the chair next to Mike's desk.

"Not sure. The guy on lower Wacker was killed with a different knife than the guy behind Allegretti's. Could be that the killer just uses whatever knife he has on him at the time."

"That's what I was thinking. Definitely think it's the same guy?"

Mike shrugged. He wanted that smoke. "Two guys stabbed in the throat, both homeless guys, seems a possibility."

"Somebody who doesn't like homeless guys?"

"Or another homeless guy."

"So what do we do? You talk to other homeless guys or women in the area and nobody knows or saw anything."

"Can't blame them for not wanting to get involved. I'm pretty sure their lives are fucked up enough."

"I hear you on that, but in this case they could be next if it is some random guy walking around looking for their next victim. You know, like a serial killer."

Mike's stomach hurt. It was only two so far, five months apart. Were they connected? Was there someone really out there trying to kill off homeless men? He reached into his pocket for the cigarette pack.

. . .

The excitement that Anders had when Marks pulled up to get him waned when he saw the look on Marks' face. He knew something had changed as soon as he got in the car. "What happened to Henry Burnett?" he asked.

"It's not Henry. They found another body, a homeless guy, washed up under the bridge near Route 20."

"Jesus," Anders said. He put off telling Marks about the news about Big Tony.

Route 20 crosses from Illinois into Iowa on a sizeable expansion bridge that crosses the Mississippi. The bridge was located about a mile and half from the Aces Casino. Marks and Anders had no trouble spotting the flashing cop lights as they pulled up to the base of the bridge.

The dead man was lying in about six inches of water as waves loosely splashed around him. He was face up and his eyes were wide open. His face was bloated and was almost white. You didn't have to be a detective to tell that the cause of death was the rather large hole just below the victim's Adams apple.

"Killed the same way as Herbert," John Mack, the county coroner said. "Looks like somebody just stabbed him right in the throat and he bled out."

"He wasn't killed here, was he John?" Marks said.

"Don't think so. It looks like he has been in the water a couple of days. I think he was killed somewhere else and went into the river. I think he drifted over here with the current."

Marks noted that the current was running from the south. "You think he's been in the water a couple of days?"

"Kind of hard to tell, but from the decomposition I can see, I'd say a couple of days."

"Maybe from Sunday night?"

"Could be. Maybe Monday night. Until I can get him out of the river and run some tests, I can't give you a firm response."

"Get him out of the river," Marks said.

As they watched the members of the coroner's department hoist the body out of the water, Anders felt it was time to tell Marks about Big Tony's brother. "You think this guy was killed the same day as Herbert?"

"I'm thinking that. I think he might have been killed up the river a bit and drifted down here. We have to look for signs of where he came from, south of here."

"Tammy got us a lead on the brother of Big Tony. He owns a soybean farm near Platteville. She also found a bunch of stuff on Tony's past. He's been in and out of prison a number of times."

"That's good, Anders, and not surprising. First, we have to dispatch a team to look for any idea where this guy came from. Now we have to go interview the Burnetts. After that, we can look at Tony's brother."

"Busy, busy," Anders said. "Think Tony is our guy?"

"Now, you're pushing it, but he is the only one right now who has a bad temper and carries a knife."

•　•　•

Richard and Susan Burnett's house was located on the opposite side of the golf course from Ricky's home. It provided an excellent view of the tenth green and the pond that lay in front of it. Today was going to be sunny, but cold. The early sun light shined on the glass- like surface of the water.

"Would either of you like a muffin or coffee or tea?" Susan asked.

They had arrived almost an hour late after dealing with the body at the bridge. Both of them were hungry and wanted coffee, but Marks declined. "Thanks for the offer, but we're terribly busy and need to keep moving forward."

Susan looked upset that the two cops declined what she offered; Richard spoke up. "Have you learned anything about what happened to Henry?"

It had been nearly twenty-four hours since Henry had been taken. There had been no calls with any ransom demand. The cop who was staying with Ricky and Lisa said there had only been calls from friends or family, no demands from anyone. "We have learned very little at this point," Marks said. "I thought we would have received a call for ransom."

"Do you think we need to call in anyone else?" Richard asked. "Maybe the FBI?"

"At this point, I'm not sure whoever took Henry has crossed state lines. It's not a Federal issue until that happens."

"So you don't really know anything?" Susan said loudly.

Marks felt his face flush. "Like I said, Mrs. Burnett, we know very little at this time."

She leaned forward in her chair. Her hair was swept back in a strict cut; her face looked like work had been done on it. "Are you sure the Milton Police Department has the capability to investigate Henry being taken?"

"We do," Marks said. He thought it came out a little timidly. "We have also notified the state police and the Illinois Bureau of Investigation. Other local departments have been put on notice."

"Have you looked hard at Lisa?" Susan blurted. Her anger showed in her face.

"Susan, please," Richard said.

"Stop, Richard. Let Detective Marks answer me."

Marks took a breath in and exhaled; Anders felt his heartbeat hasten. "Why do you think your daughter-in-law would have something to do with the kidnapping of her own child?" Marks asked.

"It's the way she behaves, she's always running here and there, leaving that woman to watch Henry."

"Mrs. Lopez?" Marks asked.

"Yes, Mrs. Lopez," Susan said. "Every opportunity she gets she runs out."

"Just because Lisa goes out a lot doesn't mean that she would be involved in the Henry's kidnapping," Marks said. "Is there a rift between Lisa and you?"

Susan sat back in her chair. "I wouldn't call it a rift," she said.

"Susan has never cared for Lisa. She has never thought that Lisa was the right person for Ricky," Richard said.

Susan leaned forward again. "She married Ricky for his money."

"Is there a pre-nuptial agreement?" Anders asked. He was hoping to defuse to situation a bit.

"Of course," Susan said.

"Let's forget this for a moment," Marks said loudly. "Let's get back to Lisa's morning routine. Who would know anything about that?"

"Obviously, Ricky and Marguerite," Richard said. "They would know her exact movements on Tuesday and Thursday."

"We all know about that," Susan said loudly. "What about her little night excursions where she goes out shopping and down to Jack Wheeler's? These happen regularly. Who does she see and talk to during these little outings? Maybe there is someone out there who she told about what she does on those mornings. That's what I have been talking about. You need to talk to her, especially since you don't seem to have anything else to go on. Does that seem so stupid?" She was so upset; spit was flying from her mouth.

Marks leaned back in his chair. He really needed some coffee. "That doesn't seem very stupid to me at all. We'll look into that."

A smirk covered Susan's face. "Please do," she said.

"She seems pretty convinced that Lisa is behind Henry's kidnapping," Anders said. They were back in the car.

"She doesn't like her. That's for sure, but it's not the Tuesday/Thursday stuff that has me concerned. It's this other running around that Lisa does."

"The where does she go and who does she see stuff that Susan mentioned?"

"That's what we've got to look at," Marks said. His stomach growled loudly. Coffee and food were needed soon.

"What now?"

"We stop by and ask Lisa a few questions. After that, we need to split up. You get Tony's brother, and I'll get back to the body under the bridge."

Anders swallowed hard. "I'll be alright talking to Tony's brother?"

Marks smiled. "Find out what he knows about his brother and where he might be. Not much more than that."

"I've got it," Anders said.

"You do."

• • •

Lisa greeted them at the door. She was dressed in jeans and a sweater, hair done and makeup applied. "Ricky had to go into the Milton store for a bit," she said.

The Milton officer, Donny Briggs, rolled his eyes at that comment. He was sitting in the room where they had all met the time before. "We wanted to meet with you for a moment, Mrs. Burnett," Marks said.

She seemed a bit surprised but led them back to her husband's den. There was no offer of coffee or muffins.

"I take it there has been no contact from anyone about Henry?" Marks asked.

She shook her head. "Not at all. Hardly anyone calls the land line and our cell phones have just been friends checking in. We are getting quite worried."

Marks thought of Ricky, running off to check on his stores. "That's understandable. We'd like to ask you a few questions."

"Me?" she said.

"Yes. We understand that sometimes you go out at night. We hear that you go shopping sometimes and other times you go to some clubs. Can you elaborate on this?"

"Well, it's not all the time," she said.

"But you do go out quite often?"

"Sometimes. Where is this going?"

"Again, Mrs. Burnett, we are trying to figure out who might have known about your regular weekday patterns. Maybe, during your nighttime outings, you may have told someone that you shower while Henry is sleeping. This would give someone the opportunity to get in your house and take Henry."

She nodded but looked confused. Marks thought she looked like she was thinking of possibilities. "I don't think that I have ever told anyone my routine."

Marks nodded this time. "Where is it that you go on these outings?"

She shifted nervously in here chair. "Mostly the mall over in Dubuque. I can get some shopping in until around nine."

"Any other spots?"

"Sometimes I go to the bar at Jack Wheeler's. I meet some girlfriends there."

Jack Wheeler's was a popular steak house with a great bar, viewing the Mississippi. "How often do you go to Wheeler's?" Anders asked.

She stared at the young cop for a moment. It wouldn't do her any good to lie. "I usually go there on Thursday nights for a couple of drinks."

"Every Thursday?" Marks said.

"Not every Thursday," she answered too quickly, "but often."

Marks was making notes; Anders was staring back at her. "I'm very sure that I never told anyone at Wheeler's anything about my routine."

"What do you think?" Anders asked. They were driving back to headquarters to get a car for Anders.

"We are going to have to visit Wheeler's and The River Club to see who she spoke to." They had asked Lisa to compile a list of people she spoke to at the health club and steak house bar.

"What about Ricky? Would you be running off to work if your kid was kidnapped?"

"A little odd, I guess. He does run a pretty big business, so he's got to make sure that things are running smoothly. Then again, everyone deals with stress in their own way. Maybe waiting for a call, and not knowing anything, is driving him a little crazy. Maybe getting over to the store for a bit takes his mind off of things."

"I think I'd be paralyzed if my son were kidnapped. I don't think I'd be able to do anything."

Marks thought about it for a bit. How would he react? Probably more like Anders than Ricky, but who's to say?

•   •   •

Marks received a call from Stanley Cooper, another Milton detective, soon after he had dropped Anders off.

The patrolmen assigned to searching the river had found something about a mile and a half from where the second homeless man's body had been found. Marks notified Anders and then headed in that direction.

Stanley Cooper had been a longtime patrolman under Teddy Brown and had only been promoted to detective in the last five years. Marks thought Stanley was a good detective, especially with the domestic crap that Marks hated. He knew that Stanley always played it straight and never got caught up in any of Chief Brown's illicit games. He was also sure that this was Stanley's first exposure to a murder case. He liked Stanley. Stanley carried a big Colt .45. He always said if he had to shoot someone he wanted them to stay down.

The area that they had taped off was near a small outcropping of rocks right near the edge of the river. There was a small cave with an opening just big enough for a man. Stanley Cooper was standing just outside the cave, smoking a thin cigar. He was a tall man, skinny and always wore a suit with cowboy boots.

"This is the spot, Steve," Stanley said as Marks walked down the path that led to the river. Stanley wore a big smile.

"The spot?" Marks asked.

"Our guy was killed here, no doubt about it."

The small cave was hidden from view by a large number of bushes and small trees. The cave was located on a bluff about twenty feet from the surface of the river that rumbled below. Marks noted the small opening in the cave. He also saw the remnants of a small fire that had burned itself out. In the ashes was a small soup pot; an empty soup can was lying on its side by the dead ashes.

"I peeked inside the little cave, flashed a light in there," Stanley said. "There's some clothes and a bedroll, not much more."

"What makes you think this guy was killed here?"

"Look here." He walked about fifteen feet from the cave, close to the edge of the bluff. The surface here was mostly rock, with some straggly plants trying to come up for spring.

It was a bright morning. The ground was easy to see and Marks could make out what Stanley was pointing at. There were several clear splotches of blood near the edge of the bluff.

"I'm thinking the killer came up on this guy when he was cooking his dinner. He turned to face him and he was stabbed in the throat, took a couple of steps backward, fell down, bled all over and either fell or was pushed into the water," Stanley said.

Marks could now see that clearly. He looked back at the fire. "The guy was out here cooking his soup?"

"He was. The pot was empty so I'm thinking an animal ate it when it cooled. There are no signs that the man got to eat it."

"So he's cooking, the killer sneaks up on him, stabs him and somehow the man ends up in the river," Marks said.

"That's it exactly," Stanley said. He exhaled smoke from the cigar. "It's pretty damn isolated up here, Steve.

Whoever killed that man had to know he lived up here. They had to do some pretty damn good reconnaissance before they killed him."

Marks looked around. That's what he thought, too. "Let's bag whatever is in the cave, the pot and the soup can. We need blood samples to match up with the body even though we know where it came from. Maybe from his belongings we can find out who this was."

"Kind of a shitty way to die," Stanley said.

"If you ask me, it was kind of a shitty way to live, Stanley, up in some fucking cave."

Stanley nodded and flicked a big ash off of his cigar.

•   •   •

When the detectives finally left, Lisa did her best to call as many of her friends that she went to yoga class and to Jack Wheeler's with. After getting through all of the comments about how awful everyone felt about Henry's kidnapping, Lisa explained that the cops might come around and ask questions about her. With the friends she saw at Jack Wheeler's this was a little easier. She didn't go to Wheeler's all the time; she didn't always see the same women there. She wasn't sure any of the women that she had drinks with could pinpoint a day that she was there or not. She was also pretty sure that not all of them knew that she had built a relationship with Jack Wheeler, Jr. In the past couple of months there would be no credit card receipts from the bar. Her drinks had been on the house for a while. There were also the nights that she went right to young Jack's condo, skipping the bar completely.

With her friends from the yoga classes, it was different. Most knew that she hadn't been in class for a while. Some knew that she was seeing Kyle James. All didn't care one way or another. What she asked these women, if the cops did come around, was that they couldn't remember the last time she'd been in class or not. It was a simple request. She didn't want Ricky to find out about Kyle. Her friends were good about the request. A couple told her to call off the little game with Kyle, stating he was nothing but a moron with a great body. She didn't comment further.

When Lisa stepped out of the back den she almost walked right into Ricky. He had just come into the house from the garage.

"Everything okay, Lisa?" he asked.

The question surprised her. "Okay? What could be okay? Henry is still missing."

"I know that," he said. "I meant there is nothing new?"

"Nothing. Our son is missing and we have a full-time cop living in our living room."

"Try and relax. Something will happen soon. Marks thinks that the kidnappers will demand ransom very shortly."

"What makes you think that your friend, Detective Marks, knows what he is talking about? This is a small town with a small-town police department. I also don't care for his smart aleck companion. Are these the right people to help Henry?"

Ricky thought on this for a minute. "Marks is a smart guy. I think he's got an idea about how to go about this investigation. I also think he knows when he is in over his head. If he feels he can't get anything done he will call in someone else."

Lisa suddenly began to cry; Ricky took her in his arms. "Who would take Henry? Why would someone do this to us?"

Ricky held her chin in his hand and wiped away a tear. "People know we have money. We are a target, no doubt. That's all I can reason. They are after money."

"It doesn't help the situation that your mother is pointing her fingers at me."

"I'm sorry about my mother. I don't know what else to say."

"She has never liked me."

"I don't think she has ever felt that any woman would be right for me. She was never particularly nice to anyone I dated."

"And you can't think of anyone that might be behind this?" she said.

"Look, I have a lot of people I see on a daily basis at the stores. You have friends from the club, the yoga classes and when you meet the girls at Jack Wheeler's. There's a lot of people who know who we are and what we have, but I can't point at any one person that would be behind this. How about you?"

She didn't want to say it out loud, but she had a thought. For some reason it had nagged at her. "Even though she has been very accommodating and faithful, I have this feeling that Marguerite may know something. I know for a fact that her and her family are always in need of cash. I know she loves Henry, but the need for money takes over. That, and I also think that her husband is not the best citizen out there."

"Should we point Marks towards them?"

"Not just yet. I don't want to jump ahead. I was just thinking."

"That makes me uneasy. I think we should fire Marguerite."

"Not yet, Ricky. We don't need her now, but when Henry is returned we'll make that decision."

That comment caused Lisa to shed a few more tears. Ricky pulled her close to him. "He will be returned, won't he?" Lisa said.

Ricky hugged her tightly. "He'll be returned."

• • •

Robert Peters' farm wasn't located in Platteville but was only about a mile outside of the town's boundaries. It wasn't hard for Anders to find the place. There was a big sign that said "Peters Soybeans" just off of the county road. Anders followed the long gravel road back to the house that sat on top of a small hill; there were barren fields on either side of him. The sun was shining brightly.

The house was well maintained, painted a light blue. Anders wondered how long it had been sitting here. He had called ahead to say he was coming. Robert Peters told him to come on out. He rang the doorbell. It was answered by a short, plump woman with gnarly brown hair. "Come on in," she said. "Robert is waiting for you in the living room."

He followed the woman to the back of the house. The living room faced more empty fields. Anders could see a variety of farm equipment parked near an old shed. The man that stood to greet him was huge, well over six feet, barrel chested, big gut and a full beard. He could have easily played football at any level, just based on size. He extended a big hand to Anders. "Bob Peters," he said.

Anders took a seat in a nice chair and was offered coffee from Mrs. Peters. He settled on water. When she returned with it, she took a seat on the sofa by her husband.

"So what did Tony do now?" Robert asked.

Anders cleared his throat and sipped at the water. "We are not sure that he did anything. We are just trying to find him to ask some questions with regards to an investigation."

"About that homeless guy killed near the casino in Milton?" Robert had leaned forward; his look was intense.

"Unfortunately, his name has come up a couple of times. We've heard that he has a bad temper and that he carries a knife."

Peters laughed. "A temper? He's got more than a temper. He's crazy. Gets the feeling that anybody who looks at him wants to fight him. Growing up he got in more fights that I can count. He started most of them. Most people just walked away. Tony is a big boy like me."

Anders nodded. "Some people say that Tony may have been provoked by the dead man's dog or perhaps he accused the dead guy of stealing from him."

Peters laughed. "Or the dead guy was just there and maybe, and I emphasize maybe, he looked at Tony the wrong way."

"You're serious about people looking at him and setting him off?"

"Yes, sir. Tony suffers from extreme paranoia."

Anders made some notes. "Is he on any medication?"

"He was and he's supposed to be, but who knows? Who knows when he last went to a doctor? As they say, he's been off the grid for a while."

"Can I ask why?"

"Why? He can't be in a relationship. He can't hold a job. He can't show up for Thanksgiving without causing arguments and ruining the day. He is against the government, the establishment, social norms, and people in general. He is not a pleasant person and I think he is capable of just about anything."

Anders listened intently and tried to write down as much as he could. Big Tony was looking like somebody they should find and in a hurry. "Any idea where he is?"

"None. Zero."

"Do you remember the last time that you saw him?"

"Sure. We joke about it. It was the day that my brother Tony died."

Anders swallowed hard. "Can you explain that?"

"This was in the spring, four years ago. He knew I'd need help so he came here looking for work. I took him in. He stayed here. It was terrible. He tried to countermand every order I gave to the crew. We almost got in two fights. There were other problems."

"He came after me," Mrs. Peters said.

"I'm sorry," Anders said.

"He tried to convince me that I had married the wrong Peters brother. He tried to make it clear that he was much better for me than Bob," she said.

"Did he physically assault you?"

Her face turned a bright red. "He came up from behind me. I didn't hear him and he grabbed my breasts."

"That was the end of it," Robert Peters said. "I told him he had to go after what he tried with Val. I fired him and told him to get out."

"This didn't lead to a fight?" Anders asked.

Peters smiled. "Before I took over my dad's farm, I spent six years in the Special Forces. This may have pissed Tony off, too. He always thought he was the baddest one in the family, but I proved him wrong on a number of occasions.

Anders believed him. "One last thing. Do you have even the smallest idea where he might be?"

"Not for sure, but one thought came to me. He has a buddy, Doug Chalmers, another anti-everything nut.

Doug has a hunting shack near Savannah. Doug does have a job. He runs a bait and tackle place right outside of the town, Chalmers Bait and Tackle. I know Tony shacked up there a couple of times, but it's just a guess."

Anders finished his notes. "You've been a big help."

"I didn't tell you that much, Detective," Peters said, "but I hope you get the point. You've got to find my baby brother. I think he might be behind this."

· · ·

Marks and Anders had both barely gotten back into headquarters when they were called into a meeting with Lou Katz. It was past lunchtime and neither one had eaten. Marks thought for one of the first times in his Milton career that he was a little tense. He wondered if the small department was over its head; he wondered if they knew what they were doing.

Lou Katz was sitting behind his desk with his feet up on the top of it. He looked more relaxed than Marks thought he should. "You guys look like you've been through the wringer," he said.

"There's a little bit going on, Lou, and maybe we're a bit short staffed," Marks said.

Lou nodded. "I get that, but right now these are local issues. The murders for sure, but the kidnapping might be more than that."

"We don't know that Henry has been taken across any state lines. There is no demand for any ransom to date. In other words, we don't know shit."

"Well, as you can imagine, Wilson Garrett, is having a cow. The Burnetts are long time Milton people and big supporters of Wilson."

Wilson Garrett was the mayor of Milton. During the Fatty Fuller case, Marks had discovered that Wilson had an unsavory past. He never made it public knowledge. "This can't get political, Lou. It doesn't work that way. Like I said, Henry Burnett was taken from his home. We know very little and are trying to piece together clues. No one knows anything. Ricky and Lisa Burnett seem like they are off in space somewhere. Ricky seems more interested in his stores and Lisa, nice looking lady, seems like she's thinking about anything, but Henry."

"I met her at a fundraiser one time. I think she thought that the people were there to see her."

"We're working it, Lou. I'm thinking that something will break with a ransom demand shortly."

Lou wasn't sure he agreed with Marks but did think they were covering the case as well as they could. "What about these homeless guys?"

Marks laughed. "One is named Herbert; the other Victim Two. This is a strange community of people. Nobody saw or heard anything with Herbert's murder. Victim Two was killed on a bluff near the south end of town, kind of remote. Nothing there yet. John Mack hasn't completed an autopsy yet and may not do one. The victim was stabbed with the same kind of knife, a long-serrated type. There was significant bleeding at the site. John said the cause of death was loss of blood or hypothermia, or both. The knife wound would have killed him."

"Jesus," Lou said. "No ID on the guy?"

"Stanley is going through whatever belongings the guy had. I'm hoping for something later."

"No leads at all?"

Marks looked to Anders. "Tell him what we've got."

Anders cleared his throat. "There's a homeless guy out there, goes by the name of Big Tony. He is a big guy and carries a large hunting knife. This guy is known to have a bad temper and he's got a record indicating a violent past. I met his brother today out by Platteville. He described his brother as anti-social and anti-society. He says Tony never saw an opportunity to pass up a fight. He came right out and said that Tony could be behind these murders."

"But why murder Herbert?" Lou said loudly. He took his feet off of his desk and sat up quickly.

"Herbert has been known to steal some things and his little dog might have peed where Tony was trying to sleep once," Marks said.

"Yeah, the animal hospital called about the dog. They wanted to know if the department or Detective Marks was picking up the tab for the mutt," Lou said.

"I told them I'd pay."

"Well, at least that's solved. What about Tony?"

"Missing, "Anders said, "but he's a big man. Shouldn't be too hard to find. I've got a lead on a friend of his near Savannah that owns a bait and tackle shop and a hunting cabin. He's next on the list."

"I don't suppose there's much I can do for you guys?" Lou asked.

"Hire more detectives," Marks said. "Right now it's me, Anders and Stanley. We're a little thin."

"Just between us girls, what do you think?"

Marks shrugged. "I think we are going to get a ransom demand for Henry and something will turn up on these homeless murders to point us to the killer."

"I hope you're right. Right now, there's not much of a panic amongst the natives, but we've got to get something positive done and soon."

Neither Marks nor Anders responded.

"One more thing," Lou said. "Teddy Brown died last night. He had a massive stroke."

Teddy Brown had been waiting for a trial since being indicted for murder the past fall. He had been awaiting his day in court in a nearby nursing home. "You don't say," Marks said.

"All true. I would imagine this means that the two Brown boys will be in town soon. The last time they were here our lily-white record of low crime went out the window."

Marks laughed. "TH Brown popped the lid off of decades of crime and corruption."

"That's a fact," Lou said. "I just don't want any more dead bodies than we have right now."

Marks yawned at the same time his stomach growled.

"Get something to eat," Lou said. "And get me some results so I can shut up Wilson Garrett."

• • •

"I heard a little about Teddy Brown and some of the corruption that went on here in Milton," Anders said. They were in the car on their way to Savannah.

Marks laughed. "Oh he was corrupt and he had three lieutenants that would follow his every order. They ran the town for ages."

"Those are the three cops who were killed up near Dubuque in that drug raid?"

"They weren't really cops at the time they were killed and the drug raid theory is a little thin."

Anders let that comment go. "What about the Brown brothers? Are they bad apples?"

"Not at all. Richie is a homicide cop in Kansas City; TH is a recovering kleptomaniac who became a repo man in California. Based on the way they were raised and how Teddy treated them, I would say that they both turned out pretty well. The Fatty Fuller murder doesn't get solved without them and Teddy Brown would never have been indicted."

"I take it Teddy Brown was not the ideal father?"

Marks thought of his own father. Not very ideal, either. "He was an abusive, overbearing animal."

"Don't beat around the bush."

Chalmers Bait and Tackle was located in the center of the small town of Savannah, Illinois. Savannah is located ten miles to the south of Milton. The sign in the window of the small shop read OPEN. When they entered the store they were greeted by an obese woman reading a PEOPLE magazine. She stared at the two cops when they entered the store.

Marks flashed his badge. "We're looking for Greg Chalmers."

"For what?" the woman asked.

"For questioning."

"He's been clean for several years so don't be hassling him about any bullshit drug charges."

"Who are you?"

She smiled. "I'm Liz Chalmers, his wife."

"Well, Liz Chalmers, we are not here about any drug charges. We want to talk to Greg about a friend of his and we are a little short on time. Where is he?"

"He's out back, doing some work on the kayaks we rent out. He's not in any trouble, is he?"

"Right now, no, but that could change."

"Shit," she said. "Go through that back door. Kayak storage is right behind this building."

The storage shed was an aluminum building, rusted, that had seen better days. The door was open so they walked in. Greg Chalmers was sitting at a bench, polishing a two-man kayak that was braced on two sawhorses. Unlike his wife, Chalmers was very thin, wore his long hair in a ponytail and had once suffered from bad acne. He looked up when Marks and Anders came into the building.

"I ain't sold anything in a long while," Chalmers said.

"We don't care about that," Marks said. "We are looking for a pal of yours, Tony Peters."

Chalmers gave them the con, quizzical look. "Tony Peters?"

"You probably know him as Big Tony and like we told Liz, we don't have a lot of time to fuck around."

This seemed to bring clarity. "I haven't seen Tony in quite some time, a long time."

"Define long time."

"Years, maybe two."

"And no idea where he is today?"

"Nope. He'd come by here once in a while looking to borrow some cash or for a place to crash, but after a while I told him I couldn't help him any longer. He got a little mad, but he understood. He left and I haven't seen him since."

"But he knows where your hunting shack is?"

"Oh, yeah he knows. Why?"

"Can you tell us where your shack is? We think he could be staying there."

The shack was located west of Route 84, just off Post Oak Road. Post Oak Road wasn't much of a road, mostly frozen tire ruts with some spots of crushed rock and mulch. At the end of the road they found the gathering of seven or eight hunting or fishing shacks. Chalmers had said his would be easy to find. Liz had the shack painted a dark green.

The shack look unoccupied. They walked up the walkway and stopped on the small porch. It was too cold for fishing and it wasn't hunting season. There were no leaves to make noises in the trees from the wind. The woods were silent.

"Do we knock?" Anders asked. He giggled.

"Draw your gun," Marks said, pulling his own Glock. Leading the way, he turned the handle on the door and pushed it open; Anders followed with his drawn Ruger.

There were no lights on in the shack, but it was dimly lit. The entire place was about three hundred square feet. There was a kitchen area to the left. A bed, chair and fireplace were on the right. In the center of the room was a round wooden table with two chairs. In one of these chairs sat an enormous man. Anders saw the resemblance right away to Bob Peters, but he thought Big Tony looked bigger. Tony was at the table eating canned sardines and crackers. He smiled at the two cops.

"You Big Tony?" Marks asked. He knew the answer.

Tony stood up and grabbed a large hunting knife that had been sitting on the table. He ran his finger along the dull edge. "You two cop boys come to play?"

Marks leveled the Glock at Tony's chest. "Might be smart if you put that knife back on the table. We're just here to talk to you."

"No. Fuck that. I'm not going back to any more hospitals or jail. You guys want to talk you're going to have to drag me out of here and I ain't going easy if you know what I mean."

Anders took a step forward to the right of Marks. His gun was also pointed at the big man.

"You boys just going to shoot me like a dog? That would be murder, wouldn't it? I mean, you're going to murder me for trespassing up here? I might be a piece of shit, but they will still put you in a cage for a long time."

Marks thought for a second. "Think about where you're at. You are in the woods, us, and you. Nobody else is out here. You are, as you say, a piece of shit. You have a criminal past. You are known to be violent. You came at us with that big hunting knife. My young partner and I had no choice, but to shoot you. Make sense? By the way, we are not here about you trespassing."

"I ain't done nothing wrong."

"Let's talk about that."

"I'll give you two minutes," Tony said.

"Watch him," Marks said. He moved to his left into the kitchen area. There was a stove, a fridge, and a small sink. In the sink there was a long bladed, serrated knife. It was the only thing in the sink. "When did you get here?" he asked.

"Couple of nights ago."

"You anywhere near the casino Sunday night?"

"You talking about that dirty, old Herbert. Him and that fucking dog. That dog peed next to me one time. If Herbert hadn't pulled the leash, I would have cut that dog's throat. Pretty sure Herbert stole some stuff from me. He was a thief. He deserved to die."

Anders whistled. "You have anything to do with him dying, Tony?" Marks asked.

Tony smiled. "I may have willed him dead."

"How about a guy that lives in a cave up on a bluff?"

"Ronnie? He's a crazy bastard, too. Sees all kinds of visions. Not a very big guy, but scary. Can't be trusted. I tried with him, but it was too much."

"So what did you do to Ronnie?

"Took him out of my circle?"

"Your circle?"

"Like DeNiro in that Fokkers movie. My circle of trust. I couldn't have him there anymore."

Marks had heard enough. He raised his gun again. "Tony, you are going to have to come with us into Milton. We are going to question you some more. We really want this to happen peacefully."

Tony raised the hunting knife and kissed the blade. "I'm not a joker, cop boy. You can try, but I ain't leaving here without a fight. One of you, both of you, are going to get hurt."

Marks took several steps towards Tony; Tony got into a fighters' stance.

"Drop the knife now," Marks said. "I'm going to cuff you. If you don't drop it, I am going to shoot you in the fucking head. From this range, your head will look like a busted melon."

Tony shrugged. "Your rules, I guess."

"Your brother was asking about you," Anders said suddenly.

Tony turned towards Anders. "Bobby was asking about me?"

"Bobby and Val. Told me how much they missed you. Wanted you to get back on the farm to help them out with the planting. Told me how much they missed you, how they needed you. They were really worried about you."

Tony lowered his knife. "They want me back?"

"They want you back. They want to make everything okay again."

Tony looked from one cop to the other. He slowly nodded his head several times. "I'll go with you if I can go back to Bobby and Val. I'll talk with you if I can see Bobby first. I'll tell you what I know."

"Drop the knife, Tony, and let us take you to Milton without a fight," Anders said.

"If I can talk with Bobby first."

"We'll make sure you get to talk with Bobby first," Anders said.

There was silence between the three of them. The next sound made was the large, hunting knife being dropped on the floor.

• • •

It was late in the day when they got Big Tony processed and into a cell in the basement of the headquarters building. The long, serrated kitchen knife had been sent over to the lab to be tested to see if it was the weapon that was used in the two murders. Bob Peters had been contacted and agreed to come in to see his brother the next morning. Lou Katz had been ecstatic about the arrest, but Marks told him not to get too excited. There was still a lot of work to be done before the case was closed.

"That was quite a brilliant idea you had, telling Tony that his brother and sister-in-law wanted him back on the farm," Marks said to Anders in the break room. Both were drinking coffee; Anders was eating a pack of Saltines.

"It just popped into my head. I didn't think he was going to drop that knife and it was looking like we were going to have to shoot him. Would you have shot him?"

"Did you see that knife?"

"It was kind of like that was all that I could see."

"I hear you. Tomorrow is Thursday."

"And that means?"

"You're going to the yoga class at The River Club that Lisa normally goes to. Maybe some of the ladies there can shed some light on who has Henry."

Anders threw the cracker wrapper into the trash. "You're going to watch over the talk between Bob Peters and Big Tony?"

"That's the plan."

"Think he did it?"

"I think he's crazy and he didn't hide his feelings about Herbert. I'm just not sure."

Anders nodded. "And nothing new from the Burnett house?"

"Nothing. Two days and nothing."

"Do you think someone just took Henry to keep him?"

"Maybe so. Lou is thinking of calling in the FBI."

"Would they take over the case?"

"They will work with us is what I heard, but also heard they can be big bullies. They think we're all yokels. I'm not against them being involved, but I am going to see what I can find until they tell me to stop."

"Okay," Anders said. "What about Jack Wheeler's."

"Lisa liked to go there on Thursday nights. Again, tomorrow is Thursday. We should be there after the dinner hour."

"Can we stop somewhere along the way tomorrow to get something to eat?"

Marks laughed. "Saltines aren't enough for you?"

Anders winced and rubbed his jaw.

"I say something to hurt you?" Marks asked.

"It's this bad tooth, been aching for a couple of days."

"I told you to get that checked."

• • • •

Anders and Tammy were sitting in Lifers. It was close to nine o'clock. Anders had eaten two cheeseburgers and drank three beers. He was both stuffed and tired. His jaw throbbed a bit. Tammy was on her third gin and tonic. An old Credence song was playing on the jukebox.

"I love this song," Anders said. "I can never remember the name of it."

"It's 'Fortunate Son.' The title is in the song," she said.

"A little before my time."

She leaned over and kissed him on the cheek. "A lot was before your time."

"I'm not that much younger than you."

"In dog years it would be a lot."

"Maybe, but it's all good."

"Detective Marks was singing your praises today. I heard him after you guys got back after arresting that gorilla you brought in. He was saying how you talked the guy down from an almost certain physical encounter."

"I don't know how physical it would have gotten. Big Tony had a knife, a big one. Marks had a Glock and I had a Ruger. Might not have been a fair fight."

"Take the praise, Anders. Marks doesn't dole it out that often."

"You like him?"

"What's not to like. He's tall, handsome, dresses well and he can be funny."

"Not married, though?"

"No. He lives with his artist girlfriend, Tori Rooks, in a condo at The Point."

"That's the nice high-rise overlooking the river."

"She does well from what I hear and she's very good looking."

He grabbed her hand. "Like you're good looking."

"I need to lose a few pounds and I have too many freckles," she said. "Anyway, you have a suspect for the homeless killings, but nothing on the Burnett kidnapping?"

"Nothing. No calls for ransom and no great leads. Lou might call in the FBI because Richard Burnett and the mayor were breathing down his neck."

"The mayor? What a joke, but Richard Burnett can make a little noise. What do you think?"

Anders looked into the bottom of his beer glass, debated one more and put the glass back on the bar. "Marks was thinking it was a case where ransom would be demanded and quickly. It's been two days. I think it's leaning towards someone taking Henry to keep him."

"Or sell him."

"What?"

"Don't act naïve. The black market for babies is real. The black market for white babies is lucrative."

"You're kidding."

"It's out there, Anders. Trust me."

"In Milton, Illinois?"

"In wherever you have a buyer with a lot of cash."

Anders waved to the bartender for another round of drinks. "I really think it's someone who was very aware of Lisa's daily routine, a friend or maybe someone at one of Ricky's stores."

"My guess would be the nanny. It's always the fucking nanny."

"Marguerite Lopez? Don't think so. The woman is afraid of her own shadow. She couldn't stop trembling when we talked with her."

"I bet it's someone connected to her. I'm going to look into that."

"You do that. I'm going to Lisa's yoga class in the morning to address the attendees to see if anyone knows anything. Tomorrow night, it's off to Jack Wheelers to chat with Lisa's bar buddies."

"So you're pretty much going to be hanging out all day with privileged, good-looking women?"

"Something like that."

"Somebody must know something."

The round of drinks came. Anders took a sip of his beer. "Somebody knows something. We just haven't found them yet."

• • •

Steve Marks was slumped on the couch, a half-eaten meal in front of him. The TV was on and there was a basketball game in progress, but he had no idea who was winning or even playing. His neck and shoulder muscles ached. He was trying to get his brain to slow down, but the overwhelming thoughts from both cases weren't going to allow that to happen.

Tori came in from the kitchen where she had cleaned up most of the dinner mess. She was worried about Marks; she was worried about both of them. "You didn't finish your dinner."

He smiled. "I thought I was hungry, but I guess I wasn't."

She noticed that the glass of beer was empty. "Do you want something more to drink?"

He shook his head. "I'm good. Just trying to figure some things out."

"You said you picked up a suspect in the murder case."

"More like a prospect, but the guy was so weird, so detached, I don't know. Could be something, but I have my doubts."

"And nothing on the kidnapping?"

"Nothing, but political problems and pressure. Lou may be forced to call in the FBI by the mayor."

"Does that make you guys look bad?"

"I don't think so. Somebody took Henry. Somebody or more than one person knows where Henry is. Somebody will get lucky and find out who did."

"You thought there might be a ransom demand."

"Thought so, but two days later, I don't know. I don't know much. It's been an exhausting and frustrating two days."

Tori thought carefully about her next words. "This might not be the best time to bring this up, but I was thinking of going to Chicago for a bit."

"Chicago?" Marks said dumbly.

She sat down on the couch. "I know. Sounds a little strange, doesn't it, but when you started talking about going up there I looked into some possibilities. I think there could be some opportunities that I want to explore. Betty thinks it could be good for me."

"How long, Tor?"

She grabbed his hand. "No real time frame. I just want to go up there and see how it goes. I haven't put any time frame on it."

Marks felt his neck and shoulders tighten even more. "You're disappointed I didn't take the Chicago job?"

"No. Not disappointed. I just thought you were going to do it."

He pulled his hand away. "Kind of hard to leave Lou with two murders and a kidnapping. I thought you'd understand that."

"I do, but this is something I have to do for me."

"And what does this do for us?"

She wondered the same thing. "Right now, nothing. I check out what is going on in Chicago and you work your two cases. Once that's done we can figure out our next move."

"I turned down the Chicago offer. I doubt they'll reopen it when these two cases are solved."

She knew that. She also knew she didn't have any truthful answer to his question about where this change left them. "Let's see what happens," she said.

Marks said nothing; he knew there wasn't much more he could say without escalating things into a fight. He got up from the couch and went into the bedroom, closing the door behind him.

CHAPTER 5

Chicago, August 2009

The third victim was found underneath the El tracks at Fullerton. Within two blocks of the crime scene were a number of restaurants and bars. The entire area had been packed earlier in the night; the Cubs had hosted a night game against the Phillies. The area was also heavily populated and was considered upper middle class; DePaul University was within walking distance. The temperature had hit a hundred at two o'clock; it was ninety-two now at three-fifteen in the morning.

Eli Roach was standing by the dead body, smoke drifting upwards from his cigarette. "Same way, Mike. Somebody just stabbed this poor bastard in the throat."

Mike Burke had a hangover. He didn't think he'd get called in and decided tonight was a good night to hit the scotch. Four drinks later and only a couple of hours of sleep resulted in a nice headache. "Who found the body?"

"A couple of students wandering down the alley. They saw him leaning against the beam for the EL tracks. One of them thought he looked funny."

Mike noticed that there was plenty of lighting near the scene. "We don't know what time this guy was killed, but up until about two o'clock this area was jumping.

Coogan's and O'Leary's are less than half a block away. Cubs are in town. There had to be a bunch of people crammed around here."

"No doubt. And nobody saw or heard a damn thing?"

"Well, nobody called in any sighting of the actual crime."

"Pretty bold to walk up to this guy with all of these people around and stab him in the throat."

Mike looked around. "Some of these bar people park under the tracks, by the apartment buildings."

"Somebody could have walked by minutes before or after the murder took place. Whoever did this had balls, not caring about how many people were about."

Lots of people, thought Burke. Most of them drunk or on the way. Nobody had called in saying they saw anything suspicious. "Unless somebody reports something tomorrow, it would be useless to ask around the bars in the area. Asking the apartment dwellers just as useless. I'm thinking nobody saw anyone back here doing anything wrong."

Eli flicked his cigarette away. "What do we do?"

Mike Burke laughed. "Let the ME bag this guy and see if we can ID him. Then I guess we can put out a bulletin asking for information about anyone knowing anything about a killer going around and stabbing bums in the throat."

"What a fucking mess," Eli said.

"We'll put some guys out to canvas the area, see if anyone saw or heard anything, but that's all we can do."

Eli grunted and walked away.

The medical examiner's report came back days later. The dead man, not yet identified, was killed with a long bladed, serrated knife, the same as the second victim. The first dead man had been killed with a shorter knife, not serrated. Only the first man had been identified; the only known object missing was his cell phone, never found.

Mike Burke read the report at his desk. It was back over a hundred outside. The precinct's air was trying hard to cool the office, but not doing very well. Mike was hungry, wanted a smoke and a drink. It was only eleven-thirty in the morning. He had three murders, only one known victim, no clues and only one real idea about the cases. He had a serial killer working his area. A serial killer who walked up to homeless men and stabbed them in the throat.

•   •   •

The news that Tori might go up to Chicago on her own did nothing for Marks' mood. That coupled with two cases with no clues in sight made for a bad night of sleep. There was nagging tension at the base of his neck as he waited for the interview with the Peters brothers, scheduled for nine. He rubbed at his neck and thought of taking some ibuprofen but got more coffee instead. Marks wasn't sure about Big Tony. The man was unstable, but was he a killer? He was also reeling from the lack of a ransom demand for little Henry Burnett. Had someone really kidnapped the boy to keep him?

That seemed too bold. Eventually, someone would figure out where Henry was, right?

There was a knock on his door and Marks looked up to see the tall figure of Stanley Cooper. He waved him in. Stanley looked as tired as Marks felt.

"I've got some stuff back from John Mack at the coroner's office and the evidence techs," Stanley said.

"Stuff?" Marks asked.

"I guess some of it is stuff, some might be real evidence. The boys over there were up all night trying to piece some of this together."

"Give me the evidence first."

"The guy in the river had been in the water a couple of days. From what I can find, he goes by the name of Ronnie. No known last name. John said he was pretty convinced he died the same night as Herbert. Cause of death the same. One deep thrust of a long, serrated knife into the throat. The guy would have bled to death, but the icy cold of the river didn't help."

"The blood on the rocks overlooking the bluff?"

"Clear match for victim two."

"How about the knife we found in the shack where Big Tony was hiding?"

"Hard to tell for certain, but John thinks both Herbert and the river guy were killed with a longer blade. He's trying to run more tests, but that is going to take some time."

Marks nodded. "Can John tell how far apart in time the killings took place?"

"Again, hard to tell. An hour, maybe more. The victim in the river had his rigor slowed by the water temperature. John was pretty certain about the time Herbert died."

Marks leaned back in his chair. "So what do you think, Stanley?"

"I know you might think you have a suspect in Big Tony, but what I'm finding hard to swallow is how Tony kills Herbert up by the casino and then gets all the way over to kill the river guy up on that bluff or vice versa. It's close to a couple of miles away and it was freezing cold that night. He had no car and I don't believe anyone would pick up a hitchhiker. There's no reports of stolen cars. How'd he manage to get all of this done?"

"So Tony's a waste of time?"

"Unless you have two killers offing homeless guys in the same manner."

"Jesus."

"That's not all. The river guy, Ronnie, had one of those cloth string bags that he kept in the cave. We found a couple of notebooks in in. The guy was a bit of a poet."

"He wrote poems?"

"Poems, rhymes and just one sentence notes summing up his life."

"And?"

Stanley checked his notes, sliding on his reading glasses first. "In several of his latest entries there is mention of a black shadow that he has seen along the river and near his cave on the bluff. There's at least three entries detailing this. In the last entry he makes the analogy that this black shadow is a portent of coming death. He then writes a small prayer, 'God, don't let the black shadow come for me.' That's the last thing in the notebook."

"Any dates on the entries?"

"All of them. The last one was dated three days before he went into the river."

"The Black Shadow. What the fuck is that?"

Stanley took his glasses off. "That's for us detectives to figure out, but John Mack reminded me. These guys that were killed have not been properly nourished and are more than likely not mentally all there. These sightings of this Black Shadow could be completely delusional."

Marks looked at his watch. Ten minutes to nine. Time to deal with Big Tony. "Get over to evidence and get those papers for further analysis. Let me deal with Big Tony now."

"Don't get too wound up with that guy, Steve. I don't think he's the guy."

Marks nodded. He didn't think so, either.

•   •   •

Marks wasn't a small guy, but with the two Peters brothers in one room he felt tiny. The brothers were huge. Marks had told Bob Peters the lie that Anders had told Big Tony about him wanting Tony to come back to work on the farm. Bob wasn't pleased about that but promised to work through it. Marks let Bob take the lead while talking to his brother.

"There's a couple of things the police would like to learn from you," Bob said.

"They said you wanted me to come back and work on the farm."

"I said I would take you back on the farm if you got some help and some treatment."

Tony's face reddened and he moved about in his chair. His hands were manacled to the table. "I'm not going back into any cages."

"Tony, listen," Bob said. "We can get you some treatment and get you some medication without you having to go into a cage. There's a shelter right there in Platteville. You can stay there until you get better and then we can try and get you back on the farm. I'm trying to help you, brother, but I need your help, too."

Tony thought for a moment. He was making a series of odd faces as he considered this. "I think I can do that."

Bob smiled. "Do you think you can help the police? They are trying hard to track a killer."

"I know about Herbert and Ronnie," Tony said.

"Do you know anything about who might have killed those two men?" Marks asked.

Tony frowned. "Herbert's mangy dog peed by me and I think Herbert stole something from me."

"Do you know anything about how Herbert died?"

"Yeah. Somebody stabbed him."

"Do you know who?" Marks persisted.

Tony hung his head. "No. I don't know who killed Herbert."

Marks expected this answer. "What about Ronnie?"

"I knew Ronnie a little bit. Kind of a scary dude. Lived up on that bluff in that cave. Only went into town looking for handouts. He never bothered anyone."

"But somebody went up there and stabbed him and pushed him into the river."

"Ronnie was afraid of the shadow," Tony said.

"You mean like his own shadow?" Bob said.

"What shadow?" Marks said.

"Ronnie said there was a dark shadow that he'd seen near his bluff and along the river. I saw it once in back of the casino, near where they say Herbert was killed. Ronnie was real afraid of it."

"That's silly," Bob said.

"Hold on," Marks said. "When you say shadow do you mean a person?"

Tony shrugged. "I think, yeah, a person, but I don't know for sure. I never saw a face or anything. It was moving away from me when I saw it. Quickly. Looked all black like it was wearing some sort of cape. To be honest. It spooked me. I stayed put. The shadow disappeared behind some of the smaller storage buildings back there."

"How many times did Ronnie see it?"

"More than once," Tony said. "He thought the shadow was stalking him."

Great, Marks thought. Now they had a clue and it turned out to be something known as The Shadow. The tension in his neck and shoulders tightened.

· · ·

Anders was walking through the parking lot of The River Club after meeting with the women who attended the yoga class that Lisa Burnett usually went to. The instructor introduced him to the class as it was ending and Anders took his time detailing what he could about Henry's kidnapping. He said they were looking for any information at all about who was Henry's abductor. He also mentioned Lisa and her habits and would anyone of them have any idea who might be aware of her habits on Tuesdays and Thursdays that might have led to the kidnapping. Not surprisingly, there was no response from the women. There was a bit of head shaking, but that was it. Dumbly, Anders thanked them for their time and left the room. He was almost to his car when he heard his name being called.

Anders turned and saw a small woman approaching him. She was a blonde and was wearing an open ski coat over her top and leggings. Anders could see that she was very pretty. "Can I help you?" he asked.

"Maybe I can help you," she said. "I just don't want to get anyone in any trouble."

"What's your name?"

"Karen. Karen Dubois."

"Why do you think you'd get anyone in any trouble?"

She looked over her shoulder to see if anyone was behind them. "Well, if I tell you something and it turns out to be nothing, you know what I mean."

"Karen, look, we are searching for a missing two-year-old. Anything you can tell us may help us. We'll make sure that no one gets into any trouble unless they really did something wrong."

She thought about this for a moment and looked over her shoulder again. "I'm not really very sure about this, but there's something going on with Lisa Burnett."

"What do you mean there is something going on with her?"

"There's been a few rumors, and Lisa has missed several classes in the past few weeks, but I just thought it was a coincidence the way she was acting and then the kidnapping."

"Come on over here," Anders said. He led her behind a work van where she would be out of view from anyone else in the lot. "What rumors and how has she been acting?"

Karen shivered and took a moment to zip her jacket. "Like I said, she's missed a bunch of classes recently and she was always like clockwork attending them."

"I got that part. What about the rumors?"

"A lot of the girls say she's been missing classes and seeing this guy named Kyle James."

Anders wrote down the name. "Who is Kyle James?"

"He went to high school here, played football. Nice looking guy, but a bit of a dimwit. He's an auto mechanic."

"These are just rumors about this Kyle fellow?"

She shrugged. "Lisa told a couple of the girls that she was having some fun with him. I overheard her."

"Okay, I see. What makes you think something like this is important?"

"Can't you see it?" she snapped. "You're the detective. Lisa starts missing these classes. Her son gets kidnapped. Lisa is married to Ricky Burnett who has a lot of money. Kyle James doesn't have much money and probably knows every move Lisa makes. Doesn't that make sense?"

Anders smiled. "It makes a lot of sense. I just wanted to hear exactly what you were thinking. What you described is a very probable scenario."

"You're not going to get me into any trouble, are you?"

Anders shook his head. "You are not the one who's going to be in trouble if this is true. If it's not true, your name will never come up."

• • •

They all got together in Lou Katz' office when Anders returned. Lou seemed more tense than Marks had ever seen him. He knew there was pressure from the mayor and from the Burnett family on the kidnapping. The two murders of the homeless men weren't helping the situation.

"So where are we?" Lou asked.

"Big Tony, as nutty as he is, is not a suspect in the murders," Marks said.

"Who is?" Lou said.

Marks laughed. "Only The Shadow knows."

"I'm not really in a joking mood, Steve, so if you have something please tell me."

"The second guy, goes by Ronnie, mentioned in his notebook something about a shadow lurking around the bluffs and along the river. He made notes that he feared the shadow was stalking him. He thought the shadow was going to kill him."

"Okay, so now we have some homeless guy talking about a shadow stalking him. This is our most reliable source?"

"I thought it was goofy, too, Lou, but then Big Tony claimed he'd heard about and saw the shadow himself. He couldn't identify whether it was a man or a woman, but claimed he saw it behind the casino. Looked like it was wearing a cape. He didn't pursue it or anything, but he did see it."

"So there could be a nut running around wearing a cape and killing these homeless guys?"

"Could be. I've got Stanley and his crew hitting the streets to talk with other homeless people to see who has seen this shadow."

Lou shook his head. He thought he was getting a headache. "Please tell me something a little more solid on Henry Burnett."

Anders cleared his throat. "It turns out Lisa Burnett has been missing some of her Tuesday and Thursday yoga classes. One of the ladies who goes to these classes told me that rumor has it that Lisa is seeing an auto mechanic named Kyle James."

Lou's face lit up. "The Kyle James, our former classmate?"

Marks shrugged. "Only Kyle James I know in town."

Anders continued. "Kyle goes to the same gym. My source told me Lisa has skipped classes and goes to Kyle's instead."

"Let's talk with Kyle," Lou said.

"On our way as soon as we're done here," Marks said.

"And nothing else? No ransom calls?"

"Nothing else, Lou. It's starting to worry me."

"What do you mean?"

"I thought Henry had been taken as a tool to get ransom. Now I'm starting to think he might have been taken by someone to keep him."

"Or trade him," Anders said.

Lou and Marks stared at Anders. "There's apparently a market for white babies. The babies are stolen and then moved out of the country or at least far enough away so that no one asks too many questions."

"Oh, Jesus," Lou said. "Let's hit on Kyle James, first. And let me know what Stanley finds out about the shadow."

Marks and Anders got up from their chairs. "One more thing, Steve," Lou said. "TH Brown stopped by when you were talking with Big Tony. He's staying out on 20. He said Richie would be coming in later for the funeral. Richie was going to stay by Rachel's."

Marks nodded. "I'll give TH a call."

"Remember, Steve. The last time those two were in town a bunch of people ended up dead. I can't have that right now."

"Lou, the Brown boys are here to bury Teddy. I don't think anyone is going to end up dead."

"I've just got a bad feeling about them being in town."

Marks wondered how much of that feeling had to do with TH once dating Lou's wife, Mary. "I'll talk with TH."

• • •

After going by his apartment and seeing that he wasn't home, Marks and Anders went by Mercury Auto Repair to track down Kyle James. They were told that Kyle was in the back area of the garage installing new brakes on an old pick-up. The garage was on Central and was good size. Marks knew there were multiple exits on the back of the building, but he didn't think that Kyle would try and run. At least he was thinking that as they approached the truck Kyle was working on.

Kyle took his eyes off the brake pads he was installing and saw the two detectives walking towards him. He thought immediately of the call from Lisa Burnett. Something tightened in his stomach.

"Hey, Kyle," Marks said.

Kyle removed his protective eyewear. In the back of the shop it was very hot. Kyle wore only a tee shirt which he filled out impressively. "Steve Marks," he said. "Hear

131

something suspicious about this truck. It belongs to Jim McGrady. He's got more money than anyone and he's driving around in a twelve-year-old truck."

"We're not here about the truck, Kyle."

More tightening in his stomach. "What's this about, Steve?"

"We hear that you know Lisa Burnett."

Kyle cocked his head to one side like he was considering the remark. "Nice looking girl. Works out at the same club as me. Takes yoga. Somehow that dweeb Ricky Burnett ended up with her. Cash helps I guess."

"It can," Marks said. "We heard that you know her a little bit better than just seeing her at the River Club."

"Jesus, I knew this was going to end badly."

"You heard that her little boy, Henry, was kidnapped?"

Kyle's eyes shifted nervously between Marks and Anders. "You don't think I had anything to do with that?"

"Did you?"

"Not a fucking thing," he said, raising his voice. "You're going to get me in enough trouble just coming in here and talking to me. Tying me to that kidnapping will cost me my job."

"Relax, Kyle. Just tell us what you know about Lisa Burnett."

Kyle laughed. "What's there to tell you? The woman is hot. We met at the club and one night we had a drink. She came on to me like crazy; it was way too easy. Last couple of months she skips yoga and stops by my place. We have sex and then she goes home. That's it."

Kyle always came off as a little stupid. Marks wasn't getting that impression now. His answers were clear and concise. "So you are pretty aware of her Tuesday and Thursday morning routines?"

"When she texts me and says she's coming by, sure. Somedays I don't get a text. When she does, she comes by, we have sex and she leaves. That's what I know."

Marks nodded. "She tell you anything about what she does when she gets home?"

Kyle shook his head. "I have no idea. In my room we talk and laugh, but it's not about anything important. She will once in a while make fun of Ricky, but not too bad. I always had the feeling that the guy was a pansy. I got the feeling Lisa wanted to be with a different type, if you know what I mean?" Now he smiled.

"Like a stud?" Anders said. It was the first time he'd spoken.

"Man, you look like you're twelve."

"I won't look that way if I have to book you," Anders said.

The smile left Kyle's face. "I didn't mean anything," he said, "but, yeah, she wanted a bigger guy with a better body. She told me so."

"Do you know anyone who might want to get at the Burnetts? Anybody that might want to do them harm?" Marks asked.

"Look, Ricky Burnett was a spoiled little, rich kid. Driving a BMW in junior year. Come on. A lot of people were jealous. I'm sure some hated him, just for being wealthy, but if you're asking if I have any idea who might have taken their little boy, the answer is no. I was fooling around with Ricky's wife, but it had nothing to do with hurting the Burnetts. Have you seen her?"

Marks was one of those who didn't like Ricky in high school because of the wealth he paraded. He'd also seen Lisa Burnett. "Watch yourself with her, Kyle," he said.

Kyle put his safety glasses back on. "I've got to finish these brakes and them I'm sure the boss is going to want to know why the cops came to see me."

• • •

"Seems pretty simple what his game was with Lisa," Anders said on the drive back.

"Yeah, but you never know. Could be he was bullshitting us but doing a good job. We'll keep in touch with him."

"I've got Jack Wheeler's covered tonight. Wonder what we'll find out about Lisa there."

Marks laughed. "She does seem like a character."

"Where to, now."

"Drop me by the McDonald's on 20. I've got to see what TH Brown is up to. TH makes Lou nervous. When I get back we'll see if Stanley found anything about the shadow Big Tony and Ronnie mentioned."

• • •

TH Brown was seated in a booth near the back of the McDonalds. It was well past the lunch hour and the place was mostly empty. He waved at Marks when he walked through the door. Marks smiled as he approached the table.

"I didn't think I'd see you so soon," Marks said. It had been less than six months since the Fatty Fuller case ended.

"Can't control when people die, big fellow," TH said. He was finishing the last of his French fries. "You've got a better tan than me."

"Ten days in Florida will do that for you," Marks said. "Sorry about your dad."

"Don't be. It's no great loss for anyone. You know what kind of person he was. Milton and the world will be a better place."

"I heard Richie is due in later?"

"Later today, I think."

"Lou wanted to make sure you guys behaved. Can't have any dead bodies in or around Milton."

"I'm just here to bury Teddy and then I'm going back to LA. Anyway, he can blame old Teddy for the dead bodies."

Marks laughed. "I'm just messing with you. You guys have a wake scheduled?"

"No wake. We are here to plant the son of a bitch and get back to our lives. We wouldn't be here if Rachel didn't need some help straightening out some stuff."

"Is it a mess?"

"I'm not a lawyer, but there's no will or trust. Everything was in his name so I guess it will go to probate. I don't really care. I don't want anything."

"Not even some cash?"

"Rachel can have my share," TH said. "That's enough about my father. Talking about him gives me heartburn. What's new in Milton?"

"Remember Ricky Burnett?"

"BMW Burnett? Sure. Little rich kid who I hear cheated at golf. What did he do?"

"Somebody kidnapped his little boy. No clues, no ransom demands?"

"You don't say? That's got to be tough on them."

"You would think so, but Ricky seems more interested in what's happening at his stores and his wife, a real beauty named Lisa, is screwing Kyle James."

"The Kyle James, the fullback?"

"That's him. He's a mechanic now and a workout nut. He says it's purely physical. Says he knows nothing about the kidnapping."

"I always thought he was a little dense."

"He didn't seem that dumb when we talked with him."

"Tori doing okay?"

Marks was still smarting from the talk the other night. "She might go up to Chicago to work on a couple of projects. Other than that, things are fine."

TH noticed a hesitation in the answer. He switched topics. "A kidnapping is a pretty big case."

"Well, that's not all. Somebody went out Sunday night and stabbed two homeless guys in the throat, killing them. One behind Aces; the other on a bluff about two miles south on the river."

"Jesus, this is not the Milton I recall."

"A little out of character for our little town."

"This Burnett kidnapping, you really have no idea?"

"Really zero. Lisa comes home, goes in the shower and the kid disappears. No real idea."

TH rubbed his unshaven chin. "There's an LAPD cop I do some stuff for. He specializes in kidnappings and cases of moving migrants in from Mexico and Central America. I can ask him about it."

Marks leaned back against the hard bench. "What help could he be here, TH?"

"This guy Scanlon, he told me about this sudden development, the kidnapping of young white babies, moving them through Toronto and then onto Europe. He says it's gotten very big and aggressive lately."

"You mean it's in the Midwest?"

"Yeah. I thought he was talking about a west coast problem, but then he told me this group operates primarily in the Midwest. Illinois, Wisconsin, Michigan, Minnesota, and Iowa are hotspots. Kids are taken and nobody ever hears another word. Spooky, huh?"

Marks was stunned. He thought about what Anders had said. "Yeah. Real spooky."

"I'll talk to Scanlon and see what more he can tell me," TH said. "I'm off to see Joseph in a bit." Joseph Running Bear was another old classmate. He ran a hunting preserve near Sterling. He had been heavily involved in the Fatty Fuller mess.

"That's' good," Marks said, but his mind was spinning. "Say hi to Joseph."

137

. . .

Stanley Cooper was standing in Marks' office twiddling an unlit cigar in his fingers. Anders was seated in the chair facing Marks, drinking a cup of coffee. Marks was making notes on a pad of paper. "Nothing, Stanley?" he said finally.

"I wouldn't say nothing. We had one guy, goes by the name of Tommy, tell us that he's heard of this Shadow hanging out near the casino. He never saw it, but he heard people talking about it."

"I'm not sure that helps," Marks said.

"This Big Tony said he actually saw it?" Stanley asked.

"That's what he said. It all sounds pretty ludicrous, but right now that's what we've got."

"I can put the guys back on the street tomorrow to see if anyone else saw this Shadow," Stanley said. "I don't know. Seems like a bit of a time waster."

"Let me think a minute," Marks said. "We've talked to a bunch of these homeless people and nobody knows much."

"How about Kyle James and the Burnett lady?" Stanley asked.

"He admitted an affair with her but denied having anything to do with the kidnapping."

"I'm not surprised. Are you? Kyle is a good guy, a tad slow, but he's just an average Milton boy. I don't think he'd ever be involved in something that complicated."

Marks wrote something down on his pad again. "TH Brown is in town for the old man's funeral. He said a cop up in LA told him of some kidnappings in the Midwest. Children are taken and then shipped up to Toronto where they are sold off to Europeans. White kids seem to be the targets."

Stanley laughed. "That sounds like something out of a movie."

Anders cleared his throat. "That's what Tammy was talking about, this syndicate. She says there's a black market for white kids. She's seen some internet stuff on it, but mostly in the dark web."

"The whole ransom thing is bothering me," Marks said. "I thought for sure there would be a demand. Days later and we have nothing. Somebody took Henry Burnett to keep him."

"Or sell him," Anders said.

"Shit," Marks said. "Before the day ends, go and talk with Tammy. Have her do some more research on this group that's moving kids through Toronto. Also have Tammy look into Kyle James. I couldn't find anything, but she's the best at that."

"How do you want me to play it tonight at Jack Wheelers?" Anders said.

Marks smiled. "Just be your charming self with the ladies and see what more you can find out about Lisa. Maybe it's nothing, but you never know."

"I can put a couple of patrol cars along the river roads the next couple of nights," Stanley said. 'Maybe they can get lucky and see something."

"Better yet," Marks said, "tell them to put on search clothes and walk the banks and accessible areas. Driving around and sitting in their cars, they won't see anything and will most likely be seen. Maybe strolling through those areas will produce something."

"Never thought I'd be chasing a damn shadow," Stanley said.

"Especially one that kills by stabbing people in the throat," Marks answered.

• • • •

It was just past eight when Kyle James stepped out of his pickup and walked toward his apartment. The lot was dark and it was cold. He was walking with his head down. He looked up suddenly when he heard a noise in front of him. There was a short, wide-bodied man in front of him. The man had a crew cut, but that was all Kyle could make out.

"Hello, Kyle," the man said.

Kyle's heart rate quickened. "Do I know you?"

"Don't think so." The man took a step forward.

"What do you want?"

The man was now only about five feet away. His eyes were dark and seemed to have shadows under them. His nose was twisted to the left. His ears were funny shaped. "You seem like a good guy, Kyle, but maybe you should stop being a fuckup while you still can."

Kyle thought of Lisa Burnett and then of Steve Marks. Now this little, squat guy. "What did I do?"

With that the man took a quick step forward and swung a thick crowbar at Kyle's left knee. There was a crunching sound and Kyle felt extreme pain. He fell to the ground and grabbed for the knee. The man hovered over him for a moment and Kyle felt for sure a more damaging blow was coming.

"Don't be so fucking stupid and don't do it again," the man said and he quickly disappeared between some parked cars.

Kyle stayed put on the cold pavement for a minute. He wasn't sure he could get up. His knee was throbbing. He reached for his phone. Who could he call? The cops? His mother? An ambulance? He started to cry.

•　•　•

Jack Wheeler's was crowded for a Thursday night. Anders got there around eight-thirty; there were still people eating their dinner and the bar area was packed. There was a special going on for half- priced martinis if you ordered a vodka the bar was pushing. Wheelers was known for its overpriced steaks and drinks so any special was considered a deal. The bar also had great views of the Mississippi and the Iowa bluffs across the river.

Before Anders left headquarters for the day he had called down to Tammy Glaser. He told her it might be a late night and he had an early start in the morning.

"You're not blowing me off, are you?" she asked.

Anders hesitated. "No. Of course not. Why would I do that?"

"I'm just busting your chops," she said. "Tonight's the night you meet with all of the high society gals?"

"Just checking on Lisa Burnett's visits to Jack Wheeler's."

"Watch those women, Anders. A few might want to get their claws in you and then I'd have to kill them."

"That could be problematic, but I'll behave."

"I'll know."

He laughed. "Anything come up on Rodrigo Lopez?"

"Nothing. I can't find a damn thing. I'm wondering if that's his legal name."

"We may have to ask. Can I ask you one more favor?"

"Sure."

"I need to you to a check on Kyle James."

"The Kyle James, the lunkhead car mechanic?"

"That's him. Apparently he's been working on Lisa Burnett's engine as well."

"Pretty good for him. Nice looking guy, but dumb as a rock would be a great compliment for him."

"See what you can find if anything. Obviously, he said he knows and did nothing, but he's spent some time with Lisa. Also, can you find out more about that black market for white babies you mentioned to me? We heard a little more about it today."

Anders ran back to his small apartment and changed into casual slacks and a sport coat. He wanted to look relaxed, not like a cop seeking information. He wandered up to the bar and took a lone empty seat near the end of it. He ordered a beer from the bartender, a nice-looking woman wearing black slacks, a white shirt, and a red bow tie.

She smiled at Anders. "Do I need to ask you for your ID?" she said.

"Probably should," he said. He flipped open the case holding the temporary Milton PD Detective shield. "They're hiring us right out of high school. My name is Anders Hedberg."

She reached a hand across the bar and shook Anders. "Martha Cleary."

"Martha? Kind of an old-fashioned name."

"What's wrong with being old fashioned?"

"Not a thing," he said. "Just don't meet many Marthas who aren't eighty."

"Good point. What can I do for you tonight, Detective?"

"We need to be a little discreet, but I'm looking for the friends of Lisa Burnett."

"You mean the TNBC?"

"What's that?"

"Thursday Night Bitches Club. "

"Nice name. I suppose there's a reason for it."

"That's what they are. It's a shame about the kidnapping, but there's something about that family that is totally dysfunctional and Lisa might be the most dysfunctional one."

"Why do you say that?"

"Well, she's married to a rich guy, has everything she needs, has a beautiful baby boy and her two biggest pleasures in life are banging Kyle James and Jack Wheeler, Junior."

"Wow! Word seems to travel fast on the Kyle James thing."

"Not really. I've known about it for a while. Nothing stays a secret in a town like Milton."

"And Jack Wheeler, Junior?"

"That's relatively new, maybe a month. Lisa stopped coming by here on Thursdays. Now she goes, or did go, to Jack's condo."

"You seem pretty sure about the timing on all this."

"I am sure. About a month ago Jack stopped banging old Martha here and started up with Lisa Burnett."

Anders wandered over to the table where the TNBC was having their weekly meeting. There were seven women, somewhere between thirty and mid-thirties, all dressed up, sitting at a large table by the windows. They had an excellent view of the river, but none seemed to care about the view. They were chatting and laughing and barely noticed when Anders walked up to the table. There was an empty chair and he sat down. The women immediately stopped talking.

"Good evening, ladies," he said, scanning the table for reactions.

"Is it Boy Scout night?" one of the ladies asked. She was a redhead, wearing a top that exposed impressive cleavage.

"I couldn't get in the Boy Scouts because I ate a Brownie," Anders said. When nobody laughed at the old joke, he took out his badge and opened it on the table.

"Oh! You're the new cop working with Stevie Marks," another woman said, a small blonde with white, perfectly capped teeth.

"I am."

"Stevie's a good man and cute," the blonde said.

"Except that he's smitten with the cold bitch artist he lives with," the redhead responded.

"I don't know Tori," Anders said. "I would like to ask a few questions."

There was no comment from any of the women. A few reached for their drinks and took a sip. "If you don't mind?" Anders asked.

"You're with the police," the redhead said. "We can't stop you from asking."

"I was hoping to get some answers, too."

The redhead crossed her arms over her chest. "We'll have to see."

Anders smiled. "All we're trying to do is find Henry. We want to try and find anyone that might be aware of Lisa Burnett's patterns especially on Tuesday and Thursdays when she goes out. We know she's been missing her yoga classes and we've just learned that she has stopped coming by here on Thursday nights. Anything you can tell me would be helpful."

"Is Henry going to be okay?" the little blonde asked.

"We hope so. We hope someone comes up with a demand for ransom. Right now, like I said, we're just looking for anyone who knows anything."

"Well, Kyle James would sure know a lot about Lisa's habits on yoga mornings," the redhead said.

"Angie!" a pudgy woman said. She was seated close to Anders.

"Oh, come on, Grace," the redhead continued. "Half the town knows Lisa is seeing Kyle James."

There was no response to that. "What about Jack Wheeler, Junior?" Anders asked.

"Another good looking one," Angie, the redhead said. "The problem with Junior is that he will screw anything that moves. I'm not sure why Lisa went after him. I'm not sure why Lisa does a lot of what she does."

That comment caused Anders to think for a moment. The women at the table all seemed to be staring at him, waiting for him to speak. "So why does Lisa do what she does?" he asked. "She's married to a successful man, has a little boy, a big house on a golf course and probably gets whatever she wants."

"You mean why does she run around?" Janet asked.

"That's exactly what I mean. Some of her behavior could have led someone to take Henry. Not for sure, of course, but you never know."

The women again looked down at their cocktails; they seemed to have hit a collective mute button. "Look," Anders said. "Forget all of that bullshit about squealing on Lisa or telling her dark secrets. Somewhere out there is a little boy, two and half years old, wondering where mommy and daddy are. He's probably not understanding anything and he's scared. I'm really just trying to bring him home. You holding back what you know or think is not helping me find Henry."

The table was quiet and then the little blonde cleared her throat. "It's no secret," she said. "We've all talked about it. Lisa was okay when she was just married to Ricky. She could do whatever she wanted. When his father retired, he became obsessed with running the stores. That took a lot of the time he spent with Lisa away. Then Henry came along. That diminished her free time even more. In the last year she has become a little out of control. She has been acting like a single woman, not like the mother of a two-year-old. These affairs with Kyle and Jack make us sick, but if you mention it to Lisa, she'll cut you off. She's struggling, Detective. She's struggling with who she is and who she wants to be. It's not a healthy situation."

All of the women were looking at Anders as he scanned the table. Most were slowly nodding their heads at him. "How many of you have children?" he asked.

All of the women raised their hands. Anders thought he knew how they would feel if their kid had been taken from them. He wasn't getting that feeling from Lisa Burnett.

"Learn anything from the ladies," Martha the bartender said as Anders stopped to thank her.

"Maybe a little," he said.

"Those seven, you know, they get all dressed up, come in for a few drinks and then they go home. I know a little about all of them. I was a little harsh about them. They're really not bad people."

"But Lisa Burnett?"

Martha laughed. "She's a different breed. That one has got a screw loose."

CHAPTER 6

Chicago, Fall 2009

The guy's name was Woody. He was small, just over five feet and skinny. He had long, stringy hair and a dirty beard. His clothes were worn and torn. He smelled like the back of an alley. Half of his teeth were missing.

Mike Burke had asked the patrol units in the area to ask any of the homeless people that they came across if they had seen someone suspicious around in the past few months. Most of the people the cops talked to had nothing to say. Some said that there were always suspicious looking people around. Woody said something specific. He was waiting in a second-floor interrogation room for Burke and Eli Roach to talk to him. He had been given a Coke and a bag of chips. He ate the chips like it was a Thanksgiving meal.

"You think we can trust what this guy says?" Eli asked.

"Maybe not everything, but our list of leads is at zero, so maybe we can get a nugget or two."

"He ate those chips like hadn't had anything in days."

Burke looked in on Woody. There were chip crumbles in his beard. "Man, what a fucking life."

They entered the room. Woody was sitting at the head of the table. Mike and Eli took seats on each side of him. Woody's eyes looked frantically from one detective to the other; both cops noticed the smell.

"Relax, Woody," Mike said. "We just want to ask you some questions based on the comments you made to Officer Higgins last night."

"He was a nice cop," Woody said.

Mike smiled. "Aren't they all nice?"

Woody shook his head. "No, sir. Some of them will just fuck with you for no reason. Some of them are mean."

"I'm sorry about that. We are just here today to follow up with you. You are not in any trouble or anything."

"That's what the cop said. I will help if I can."

"Officer Higgins said that you told him that you saw something kind of strange about a week ago. Can you tell us what you saw?"

Woody's nose ran a bit. He used the sleeve of his shirt to wipe it. He coughed once. "There were a few of us sitting under the El tracks near Wilson. It was a warm night and humid. That's why what I saw was so strange."

Mike sat back in his chair. "What was it?"

"There was a person down there, too. They walked under the tracks, looking at us. There were five or six of us just talking, keeping each other company."

"What did this person look like?" Eli asked.

"That's the thing. It was hot, like I said. Real hot. This person, who was just kind of creeping along, had on this long coat and kind of a cowboy hat."

"A cowboy hat?" Eli said.

"Maybe not that. Just wide brimmed," Woody answered.

"Can you describe the coat?" Mike asked.

"Like I said, long and black. All black, the coat and hat."

"Tall or short person?"

"I think tall. At least I thought they were tall."

"Male or female?" Mike said.

Woody shook his head. "That's what I told the cop. I didn't see the face. I just saw this person walking near us, looking over at us, but never getting close enough to make out the face. The person circled us a couple of times and then kind of just vanished. For a minute, I thought I was seeing things, but Jimmy saw it, too."

"Jimmy who?" Eli said.

Woody shrugged. "Man, I don't know anyone's last name. But Jimmy said he saw it. He said it looked like a shadow, like that old comic book character. This person is all in black and then you blink your eyes and it's gone. Like a damn shadow."

"That's it?" Mike said.

"That's all. I been down there a long time and that was one of the spookiest things I'd ever seen and nothing really happened."

Mike smiled. "You did good, Woody. At least we have something to go on."

"This is about them homeless people being murdered, isn't it?" Woody asked. His eyes were wide open.

"It is," Mike said.

"Please find that bastard before he gets more of us."

"We're trying. Can we get a patrol car to give you a lift?"

Woody nodded. "Can I get some more chips?"

Mike Burke went into his wallet and took out a twenty. "Get yourself something good to eat."

When Woody was gone the two detectives had a smoke in the interrogation room. The smoke helped diminish the Woody smell.

"Nothing much," Eli said.

"Oh, I don't know," Burke said. "A tall person in a long black coat and a wide brimmed hat on a hot night is not nothing. Could be a man. Could be a woman."

"Only The Shadow knows for sure," Eli said and he laughed.

"Ain't that the fucking truth?"

• • •

Kyle James was lying in a bed on the second floor of County Memorial Hospital. His left leg was heavily bandaged and was elevated. The doctors had told Marks and Anders that X-rays had revealed that the kneecap had been badly damaged. They weren't sure whether Kyle needed a replacement or just some surgery. They needed the extensive swelling to go down. Until then, they wouldn't know what path to take. They had given Kyle some pain killers, but he was still alert. Now was as good a time to interview him as any.

Kyle looked pensive when they walked into his room. He was watching a morning talk show but was spending more time looking out the window. His look saddened when he saw who his new visitors were.

"How are you doing, Kyle?" Marks asked.

Kyle smirked. "That is a real dumb question, Steve," he said. "First you guys show up at work and question me about some kidnapping and then this goon kneecaps me in my apartment parking lot. How am I doing, you ask?"

"Okay," Marks said. "A dumb question. Why don't you tell us what happened?"

"Like I said, I get out of my truck and had just started towards my place when this guy steps out of the shadows, tells me to stop being a fuckup and pops me in the knee. I knew the knee was gone as soon as he hit me."

"That was all he said?"

"That was it, short and sweet and then he hit me."

"Can you describe him?"

"Short guy, fire hydrant like, with a real short haircut. I couldn't make out the face, but it was kind of round. The eyes seemed dark."

"So what you do think?" Anders asked.

"What do I think?" he yelled. "You guys are the cops and you're asking me? It's pretty obvious that Lisa Burnett thinks I had something to do with her boy being kidnapped and she sent this little warning to me. She must think I know something and she wants me to start talking."

"You really believe that?" Marks asked.

"What else, Steve. I'm a nice guy, the nice town mechanic. I don't piss people off. I'm really nice to everyone. Who else would want to do this to me?"

"How about Ricky Burnett?" Anders said.

"Ricky? You've got to be kidding me. Ricky is a little pansy. He's so worried about screwing up the business his daddy started that he's become obsessed with it. He's so obsessed that he forgot what a beautiful wife he has. He doesn't even think about her."

Marks and Anders were outside of the hospital. Marks lit a cigarette. "So who put the hitman up to this, Lisa, or Ricky?"

"I'm going to go with Ricky, but even that bothers me. Both of them have cops all around them every minute of the day right now. Would you be ordering up someone to kneecap somebody?"

Marks exhaled. He was smoking way too much. It wasn't helping his headache or tense neck muscles. "This is too bizarre. I can't see Kyle being involved in a kidnapping and I really can't see Ricky being the vengeful type. Way too bizarre."

"More bizarre then the Shadow theory on the homeless guys?"

Marks had to laugh. "Maybe not that bizarre. Tell me about Jack Wheeler's."

"I met a nice group of women, some talked, and some didn't. One told me that Lisa lost her identity when

Henry was born; she's trying to find it but seems to be getting on the wild side of things."

"Such as?"

"We know all about Kyle James. I learned last night that she's been seeing quite a bit of Jack Wheeler, Junior."

"Good looking guy with some cash," Marks said.

"Apparently, Lisa has missed some of the Thursday night gatherings and has gone straight to young Jack's condo."

"Geez. What are we going to hear next? This woman is some trouble. We just don't know how much or what kind."

• • •

They left the hospital and were on their way back to headquarters when the call came in about the ransom. They reversed their course and headed in the direction of the Burnett home.

"Think it's real?" Anders asked.

"Better than nothing, but let's see." Marks wasn't sure, but they had next to nothing. "All this stuff on Lisa and now a ransom call. This is a bit too much."

The whole Burnett family was at the house when they got there. The look of tension on their faces was obvious. Marks had to wonder if any of them knew anything about the kidnapping; they looked so worn out.

Donny Briggs, who was the cop who was with the family, got up and approached Marks as he came into the house. "The call came in about twenty-five minutes ago. Ricky Burnett took it."

Ricky was seated by the window that faced the fairway. He stood up. "The caller said that the directions would come in within the next hour. He said I should gather the whole family and be prepared to write down everything. He also said no cops had better be involved."

"That's a line from a book or a movie, Ricky," Marks said. "It was a man that called?"

"Yes. For sure."

"No attempt to hide the voice?"

"Not really. Normal voice, nothing unique."

"What do we do?" Ricky's father asked.

"When the call comes, we'll put it on speaker. We'll record Ricky and the caller's interaction. I don't want anyone to get too excited. This could be a hoax."

"Why would you say that?" Lisa Burnett spoke up. She was dressed in slacks and a tight sweater. Her figure was on full display.

Marks regretted the comment right away. "What I mean is let's hear what the caller says before we determine what we should do."

"You don't seem very confident," Ricky's mother said.

Marks took a deep breath. "I'm afraid I can't be until I know what we have."

There was an awkward silence for the next ten minutes. The call came to the landline. It was put on speaker. Anders started the video on his phone. Marks told Ricky to answer the phone.

"I'm only going to say this once, so don't fuck it up," the caller said. It was a man. There was nothing too unusual about the voice. Marks thought he might be younger. "You got that?"

"Yes," Ricky said.

"In Galena, across from Grant's home, there is a candy store. In front of this candy store there is a concrete planter. Right now, the tree in it is dead. Tomorrow at eleven o'clock, Mrs. Burnett, the young one, will place a briefcase holding one hundred thousand dollars in the planter. She will drop it off and she will walk to the north up Main.

"Once she is a couple of blocks up the street the briefcase will be picked up. Once this courier is back safe and sound with the money, we will tell you where you can find Henry. Again, and I'm only going to tell you this once, we get any idea that the cops are involved or that the courier was followed and this deal is off. You won't see Henry for a long time."

Ricky swallowed hard. "You won't hurt Henry?"

There was a short laugh. "I can't make you any promises, dude, but let's keep it simple. You've got the money, find a briefcase and put it in there and then have your pretty wife put it in the planter. Simple shit. We get the money and you get Henry back. Clear?"

"Yes, it's clear. Is Henry okay?"

Another laugh. "What do you think we are? Of course he's okay. Who would hurt a little two-year-old boy? Do as we say and everything will work out right."

"How soon after we deliver the money can we get Henry?"

They all heard the click on the other end of the line. The phone was dead. The Burnett family in unison turned to Marks. "Can you get the money together?" he asked.

"Of course we can, "Ricky's father said. "Should we trust this call?"

"Right now, we have to. Don't pay any attention to that threat about no cops being involved. We will closely monitor the situation."

"You can't do that," Lisa burst out. "They said they'll hide Henry for a long time if the cops are involved."

"Okay," Marks said. "If the call is real and we give them the money, they should tell us where to find Henry. If it's a hoax, you will lose one hundred thousand dollars. I will promise you that we won't compromise the situation. They'll never see us. My idea is to get Henry and the money back."

Ricky's father stepped forward. "I hope you know what you are doing, Detective Marks. I think you should call in the FBI."

"This is a local situation. Technically it is out of their jurisdiction. I have complete confidence that we can handle this."

"I hope you are right," the father said. "Something like this that goes badly could cost someone a career."

"You didn't say anything when Ricky's dad threatened you," Anders said. They were back in the car, leaving the Burnett's to get the money together for the drop.

"Just emotions speaking, Anders. What was I going to do, tell him to go fuck himself?"

"I might have."

"You are young and stupid."

"Where to now?"

"Galena. I know the police chief there. I'm going to tell him what's going on and ask him not to interfere with what we are doing. Then we'll scope out the area and make a plan."

"They can't see us."

"They won't. They can't. If they think we are on to them the whole thing will be blown and Mr. Burnett will have it right. The shit will hit the fan."

• • •

TH Brown was sitting in the back booth at the Start of the Day Café eating a late breakfast when his cell phone buzzed. He picked up the phone without answering and noticed the LA number. He didn't recognize the number; it was just past nine in California. He pushed the receive button. "Hello," he said.

"TH, this is Johnny Scanlon."

"Hey Johnny. I didn't recognize the number."

"I saw your message and I'm calling from home. I thought if you were calling from up there it was probably important."

"I'm just probing on something. There's been a kidnapping here in my hometown and I was thinking about that group in the Midwest that moves white babies into Toronto and then Europe. You mentioned it to me once and I was wondering what kind of legs it had."

"It's got a lot of legs. Like I told you there is major cash in moving these children to Europe. Anybody can get on a plane with a baby and nobody pays attention."

"What kind of cash is major?"

"Maybe two-fifty to five hundred K. It's not a small market item. White babies up for adoption are in big demand."

"And people are okay with stolen ones?"

"Yeah. Pretty sick, huh?"

"No kidding. How much hard info is available on this group or is a lot of this hearsay?"

"Not that much. The Feds arrested a guy that told a whole story about this baby moving syndicate. He was trying to cut a deal for a totally unrelated incident. Unfortunately, he was very light on details such as names and places, but he did a pretty good job of explaining the disappearance of a two-year-old from Eden Prairie, Minnesota. He explained how the kidnapping went down but couldn't tell anyone anything about how the kid was transported up to Canada and then out of the continent. The Feds poked around but couldn't prove anything."

"But there's been this activity in the Midwest?"

"TH, kids disappear all the time, but most of them aren't related to celebrities, politicians or rich people. These are children of ordinary folks. They disappear and nobody hears about them because the media doesn't think the stories are front page worthy. Sad but true."

"That is incredibly sad."

"Hey, you know, I was looking at a map of the Midwest, pretty detailed, and I found your little Milton there on the Mississippi. Across the river is Dubuque, Iowa, right?"

"That's right."

"This guy the Feds caught, he told them that all of the stolen babies were funneled through Dubuque and then into Minnesota and then onto Canada. Thought that was interesting."

TH looked at his empty coffee cup. He felt a little burn in his stomach. "Yeah. That is something," he said.

• • •

Anders found Tammy at her cubicle on the lower level of the building. There was a meeting set up with Lou Katz in an hour to discuss Henry's ransom demand. Marks was rounding up unmarked cars for the surveillance of the pickup.

"Hello, stranger," Tammy said. She smiled as she could see how tired Anders looked.

"There's been a ransom demand for Henry."

"Really?"

"Yeah. We're meeting with Lou in an hour to go over all the details."

"You don't sound very encouraged."

Anders took the seat next to Tammy's desk. He noticed how pretty she looked. He liked her. "It's just a gut feeling, but somehow I've got this bad feeling about Lisa Burnett."

"Wait a minute," she said. "You think Lisa is involved in the kidnapping of her own little boy?"

"Sounds weird, huh? I don't know. The woman is detached. She's also running all over town and having multiple affairs. Something is definitely going on with her."

"The one affair I know about is with Kyle James. I did a little research. Kyle got busted for breaking and entering a few years back. Him, and a couple of buddies, looted a few houses. Minor stuff, but he did ninety days.'

"Little odd twist, there. Somebody knee-capped him in the parking lot of his apartment building last night. He's in the hospital recovering."

"So who hired who to do that?"

"Great question. Did Lisa hire somebody because she thought Kyle was involved in the kidnapping?"

"Or did Ricky hire someone because Kyle was banging his wife?"

"That's for us detectives to figure out."

She laughed. "You said that Lisa was having affairs, plural. Do you know who else she's supposedly seeing?"

"Jack Wheeler, Junior, son of the steakhouse owner."

"I know who Jack Wheeler, Junior is. Quite the playboy. His father is supposedly beside himself because young Jack won't commit himself to anything except screwing half the ladies who come into the restaurant."

"That's what I heard. I guess he got his mitts on Lisa."

"Another fun fact. Jack, Junior has had his allowance cut by daddy. Young Jack is pissed off. He is also a bigtime cocaine guy. This cut in funding has slowed his usage. He's not happy with daddy."

Anders rubbed his sore jaw; the tooth ached. "He might also be looking for ways to get some quick cash."

"He would know an awful lot about Lisa's coming and goings."

"I've mentioned it to Marks. We're going to talk to Jack. Anything new on Marguerite Lopez's husband?"

"Not a thing. I can't find anything on the guy. He might be illegal. I looked under Rodrigo Lopez and found a driver's license, but that's it."

"Could he get a license using some other form of fake ID?"

"Happens all the time. I'll keep plugging, but right now he is a bit of a mystery."

Anders stood up. "I'd better get back upstairs."

"How does tonight look?"

"I've got to be here bright and early tomorrow and alert. Probably not too good."

She smiled and blew him a kiss. "I look forward to double the attention tomorrow night."

"I'll be ready," he said.

• • •

The meeting was in the small conference room on the first floor. Marks had always liked this room because during boring meetings it had a great view of the parking area and the comings and goings of the station. Today wouldn't be boring. There was too much going on and it wasn't mundane. The tension in his neck and shoulders never seemed to go away. Now this ransom demand. Was it real or a ploy to get quick cash out of the Burnetts? Only time would tell.

When Marks entered the conference room, Lou Katz was seated at the head of the table with Anders on one side of him and Stanley Cooper on the other. Jeff Blakely the nighttime watch commander was seated next to Stanley. Marks took the seat by Anders.

"Let's start with the murders. Anything new on either Herbert or Ronnie?" Lou asked.

They all looked at Marks. "All we have on them is first names. They're both in the morgue awaiting any further identification, but I don't think that is coming. I suppose in the near future we are just going to be looking at burial."

Lou grimaced and nodded. "I suppose our only new lead is the one involving the Shadow. Is this a joke or is it real?"

"Real," Marks said. "Big Tony claims to have seen it. The guy Ronnie had a number of writings in a notebook, poems, and little anecdotes. He mentioned the Shadow a few times. In one poem he mentioned that he was sure that the Shadow was out to get him. Jeff and Stanley had guys out last night rousting the homeless to see what they could find."

Blakely cleared his throat. "We had the guys all dress in plainclothes, no uniforms, and walk the areas where we know the homeless hang out. We interviewed, or I should say talked to seventeen people. Five of these people know of at least a sighting or hearing about the Shadow. One of them heard Ronnie talk about the Shadow and his fear that it would kill him. One other person, George Emerson, said he saw the Shadow."

"Actually saw it?" Lou asked.

"That's what he said. He saw it along the river walkway behind the casino, a couple of weeks ago. Tall guy, long black coat, and some type of wide brimmed hat. The Shadow was walking away from him and he didn't want to get any closer. He said he watched him for a few minutes until he disappeared behind the casino building. Then he said he turned and went in the opposite direction."

"What do you think, Stevie?" Lou said.

"We've had multiple sightings. Even though Big Tony is a little on the nutty side, I got the impression he was clear when he told us about him. I think that's who we are looking for."

"So what do we do?"

"I'd say flood the heavily known areas of homeless people with plainclothes guys, especially at night. Between Route 20 and up to two miles north and south along the river. Maybe we'll get lucky and get a hit."

Lou nodded. "I want your best guys on that, Jeff. We're talking four total miles along the river. Maybe use six guys. So far the killer hasn't come away from the river so let's concentrate on that area. Agreed?"

The other four nodded their heads. "Now let's get to this ransom demand."

"Excuse me, Lou," Anders said.

"You have something to say, Anders?"

"Before we talk about the ransom demand, I think we should spend a little time talking about Lisa Burnett."

Lou leaned back and crossed his arms over his chest. "What about Lisa?"

"For lack of a better word," Marks said, "she's become unhinged."

"Let Anders get his say in," Lou said.

"Steve is right," Anders said. "Lately, she has been running around a lot and is in the midst of two separate affairs, one with Kyle James and the other with Jack Wheeler, Junior."

"Kyle James?" Lou asked. "I saw his name come across the morning briefings as an assault victim."

"Yeah. Somebody whacked him in the knee last night in his parking lot. He's at the hospital now and the knee is in really bad shape," Marks said.

"So Kyle was having an affair with Lisa and he ends up getting kneecapped?"

"That's it," Lou," Anders said, "And don't forget Jack Wheeler."

"Stop for a minute. Why are we looking at Lisa? Do we think she might have something to do with the kidnapping or her own son?"

"It's complicated, Lou," Marks said. "Her friends tell us that she is trying to regain some lost identity that she had before Henry was born. Trying to regain her freedom. Part of this is sleeping with half of the men in Milton; the other part might be getting rid of Henry."

Lou laughed. "Come on fellas. That's preposterous."

"I'm not sure," Marks answered. "There is supposedly a black market for white babies in the Midwest. A group moves the kidnapped kids up into Canada and then to Europe."

"Who is your source on this? Didn't Tammy mention this?

Marks hesitated a moment. "Yes and TH Brown knew something about it."

"TH? I guess he'd know something about stealing things. I didn't know he was an expert on black market kidnappings."

"Hold on, Lew. Tammy Glaser told me about this kidnapping ring," Anders interjected. "She also found some things about James and Wheeler, Junior."

"What things?" Lou was getting more agitated.

"Kyle has an old arrest record for breaking and entering, a conviction. Wheeler is a heavy coke user and has been cut off from Daddy for his allowance. Both may have a reason and a past for wanting to get some extra income, a large amount of income."

"But now Lisa thinks Kyle is involved and has his knee broken?"

"Maybe," Marks said. "Maybe she just sent him a reminder about talking too much to the police. It's a bit of a stretch, but she's running a little wild and these two guys fit the bill for helping her out."

"I have to admit this all sounds a little fictional," Lou said. "I trust Tammy. I don't trust TH. I'm not saying the whole thing is bullshit, but we need something more on it. Keep an eye on Kyle and also Wheeler. I know Kyle. He's a simpleton and I don't think he'd get involved in anything like this. As far as Wheeler, junior, he's just a punk that mooches off his dad. I really don't see either of them involved."

"Okay," Marks said. "It came up and we're looking at it. Other than this ransom call, we have nothing else. There is a lot of money involved if they are trying to move Henry though this syndicate. There's also Lisa Burnett. You have seen her?"

Lou smiled for the first time. "I have and people have done some dumb things to gain the attention of a woman." The others laughed at his comment. "Probably everyone in this room. Now what about the ransom call and our response."

"Just so you know, I cleared everything with Denny Lucas," Marks said. Lucas was the Chief of Police in Galena.

"We don't ever have a problem with Denny," Lou said.

"Anyway, there is a concrete planter directly across the street from Grant's home. Lisa Burnett is to place the briefcase with the cash in it at eleven o'clock. Denny has agreed that no cruisers will be on Main Street from ten-forty-five until eleven-fifteen. That will give us time to survey the area and watch for the drop and pickup."

Lou leaned back in his chair. "How do you intend to pull that off?"

"There's an east-west street pointing right at the planter with a no parking zone. I will be there in an unmarked car watching. Anders will be down the street facing south; Stanley will up the street facing north. When the pickup takes place we'll be able to trace what's going on and hopefully be able to follow undetected."

Lou let out a deep breath. "And then what?"

Marks shrugged. "Then we see what happens. Once the pickup is completed, there is supposed to be instructions about how we can get Henry back. If we can keep track of these guys, we can get Henry back and catch them."

"I suppose it doesn't go that smoothly if you guys are seen following the pickup car?" Lou said.

"The plan is to not be seen," Marks said.

Lou looked around at the small group of men. There weren't any further comments. It was a plan. How safe

169

and secure it was wouldn't be known for a while, but it was something. "Okay, let's move on it."

• • •

TH Brown was at the bar in Lifers when Marks walked into the place. TH was drinking a Bud Light. Marks immediately ordered a Jack Daniels on the rocks.

"Tough day, Steve?" TH asked.

"One of the toughest I've had as a Milton cop. Homeless guys getting murdered and little boys getting kidnapped is not good for the system."

TH waited for the bartender to put Marks' drink in front of him before he spoke. The bar was quiet; the juke box was playing some country songs. "I talked to my LA contact. He confirmed that there is a group in the Midwest that kidnaps white babies, gets them up to Toronto and then onto European buyers. Very sophisticated and very high end. He also told me one of the central funneling points for these kids is right across the river in Dubuque."

Marks sipped his whiskey and felt the warmth go through his body; he had hoped the drink would take the edge off of his tension. "Not the case here. This syndicate that you talk about doesn't look for ransom since they're being paid by the eventual buyers. We have a ransom demand for little Henry. We're not sure about it, but it's what we have right now."

TH smiled broadly. "Well, that's good news. I guess the people I'm talking about aren't involved."

"I don't think so, but it is wild that your source says that Dubuque is one central cities involved."

"Dubuque only served me as a place that Mary and I could sneak to in our younger days." Mary was now Mary Katz, Lou's wife.

"That was really a long time ago."

"Yeah, like fifteen, sixteen years. Clay Johnson still running things in Dubuque?"

Clay Johnson, like Marks, had been a Milton cop, rising to Detective. When he figured there was little room for advancement there he moved up to Dubuque. He had been the Chief of Police for two years. "He's the man in charge."

"You were never a big fan of Clay's."

"That's an understatement. We didn't like each other"

"I remember that going back to high school. There was a pretty good fist fight if I recall."

Marks laughed. "We each got our licks in."

"I could talk with Clay. We used to get along. I can see if he knows much about this baby snatching ring."

Marks stared over his glass at TH for a moment. "Not yet. Let me see how this ransom demand works out."

TH nodded. "No clues on your murders?"

"Who said that? Our biggest clue is someone known as The Shadow, dresses all in black, and is terrorizing our homeless community."

"Sounds promising."

Marks knocked back the drink. "It's all we have. More than a few sightings of this person."

"You in a rush?"

"Just a big day tomorrow, but I'll be in touch. When is the funeral?"

"Day after tomorrow. Family only. Tori doing okay?"

Marks hadn't thought much about what Tori said about going up to Chicago. He had too much to focus on to worry about that right now. "Yeah, she's fine."

TH had noticed the hesitation in his old friend's answer. "Don't fuck that one up, Stevie. That's a once in a lifetime opportunity."

Marks stood and patted TH on the back. "Don't worry. I know that," he said, but he wasn't sure anymore. "Give my regards to your family."

CHAPTER 7

Chicago, Day after Thanksgiving, 2009

The dinner for the homeless had taken place in the basement of Our Lady of Lourdes Catholic Church. It had run from five o'clock until seven. The victim had been found only a block and a half away. She was lying on her back, covered in some old blankets, in a deserted garage behind a house on Ashland Avenue. The garage had been condemned by the city and was due to come down. The body had been found by two kids who had snuck into the garage to smoke a joint around eleven in the morning. One of the kids, Jimmy Phelps, had volunteered and worked the homeless dinner the night before. He recognized the victim because of the bright red coat the woman wore. The woman had mostly orange hair except for where her black roots showed through. Her hair and coat color were visible because of the slats that were missing in the roof of the garage that let the sunshine through.

"Nice Turkey Day?" Eli Roach asked. He was chewing on an unlit cigar.

"Sure," Mike Burke said. "I ate too much turkey, drank a half a bottle of scotch, and fell asleep on the front room couch. I woke up about four and the gout in my foot was yelling at me. I was supposed to clean up the back yard today until I got called in. Now Carol is mad at me."

"Because somebody got murdered?"

"Something like that, but I think it was the scotch."

"Sorry about that, but here we are again."

"These two kids found the body?"

"Yeah. They stepped in here to smoke some weed and almost fell over the body."

Mike stepped past Eli and looked at the body. "A woman this time," he said.

"Yep. There's a nice hole in the throat. Looks like the killer followed the same M.O."

"And one of the boys said that this lady was at a homeless dinner last night?"

"He was working it at Lourdes. He recognized the red coat and the orange hair."

Mike thought for a minute. "That's a five-minute walk from here. This woman ate her dinner and wandered over here to hunker down for the night. I bet the killer stalked her and killed her once she was in this garage. God, it's fucking cold."

Eli shifted the cigar in his mouth. "The dinner ended around seven. By the time this woman walked down the alley to get to the garage, it was dark and most of the neighborhood was like you, half in the bag. If anyone saw anything they didn't report it."

"Who would be able to see The Shadow anyway?"

"True," Eli Said. "And what time did the woman in the red coat get here and what time did the killer make his visit?"

"All things for the great homicide detectives to figure out."

"Think we're going to catch this guy?"

Mike's bad foot started throbbing. "Who goes around stabbing homeless people in the throat and why?"

"Only The Shadow knows for sure."

"That wasn't funny the first time," Mike said and he went outside to talk with the two boys who had found the body.

• • •

It was a few minutes before eleven and they were all set for the drop. Marks was parked directly across the street with a clear view of the planter. The weather was warming up a bit. The sky was clear and the sun was shining brightly. Anders and Stanley Cooper had made contact and were in place. Now all that was needed was for Lisa Burnett to make her drop and for the kidnappers to grab the briefcase. Then they would see where things went from there.

The foot traffic for the stores in Galena was picking up. On such a nice day, Marks knew there might be a chance of some interference from people not involved. He hoped it was minimal.

The clock on his dashboard hit eleven. There was no sight of Lisa. Anders checked in and Marks told him to relax. At eleven-o- one, there was still no sign of her and Marks heartbeat quickened. At eleven-o-two he saw her walking across the street holding a battered, brown briefcase. She wore a tan raincoat, but with her blonde hair and good looks she still stood out. Marks watched as she calmly placed the briefcase in the planter, looked to her left and right and then walked down the street.

"Get ready, boys," Marks said into his mouthpiece.

It seemed like minutes went by, but it was less than two. Marks watched several cars drive past the drop zone as well as a number of pedestrians on the sidewalk. None stopped to look at the briefcase. Marks took a deep breath; he noticed he was perspiring. His neck muscles tightened.

It was almost ten after when Marks saw a bicyclist approach from his right. The man, dressed in an all-black racing outfit, slowed in front of the planter, took the bike up onto the sidewalk, grabbed the briefcase and quickly got back down onto Main Street. He began to quickly peddle south in the direction of Anders. Marks was able to watch as he turned on Queens Street and headed for River Road. Marks knew Queens dead ended so the biker was going to have to go right or left.

"The guy is on a bike, all dressed in black. He's headed west towards River. He's got to out either north or south. Get over to River, now."

Ander shifted into drive and quickly made the two-block drive over to River Road. He pulled into a spot near the corner and waited. "No sign yet," he said.

"None here either," Stanley Cooper said.

"Wait," Marks said.

It was then that Anders saw the cyclist. He could have been any other biking enthusiast except for the briefcase he carried in his right hand. He was doing all the steering with his left hand. He cautiously pulled past where Anders was sitting; the traffic on River was moderate. It was not hard for Anders to slip in four cars behind the bike.

"I've got him," Anders said.

No sooner had Anders started following the bike, the cyclist got into the left lane to go east on Route 20. Anders was still five cars behind him. The biker was spending so much time steering and holding the briefcase, it didn't look like he cared who followed him.

"Heading east on 20," Anders said. "I'm five cars back. I don't think he has a clue I'm here."

"Don't get seen," Marks said.

"He's having enough trouble steering and holding that briefcase; I don't think he knows that I'm here."

About a mile after making the turn on 20, the biker made a right turn on Maple Crest Road. Two other cars followed so Anders felt no threat when he turned. The area was still country like, but there were several houses, spread apart, lining the west side of the street. A farmer's field was on the left. A quarter of a mile up the street the biker pulled into the driveway of a small, light blue, frame house. Anders pulled past him and continued to drive up the road. He looked into his rearview mirror and saw the man get off the bike and go up the stairs in front of the house. He walked right in the door with briefcase in hand. Anders turned around and parked on the opposite side of the road on the crest of a small rise. He had a perfect view of the house.

"He pulled into a blue house on Maple Crest Road. Parked the bike and walked right into the house. Didn't knock or anything," he said. "I'm parked about two hundred yards away on the east side of the street."

"Any vehicles near the house? Any signs of other people?" Marks asked.

"Negative on both. Place looks like a little serene country house. What do you want me to do?"

"Nothing. Sit tight. Instructions for getting Henry should come soon if they were telling the truth. Don't let anybody come or go out of that house without letting me know. Stanley, get over to Maple Crest. Park on the west side of the street, down from the house. We can't let anybody get out of that house."

"Got that," Stanley said.

Marks took a deep breath. His cell phone buzzed. It was Lou Katz. "We've got the pickup covered. It was a guy on a bike. Grabbed the case and drove to a house on Maple Crest. Anders has him covered. Stanley is on his way for backup."

"That's great, Steve. Keep me posted on that," Lou said. He sounded weird.

"Everything okay there, Lou?"

"I need you to get over to Uncle Billy's as long as things are under control there." Uncle Billy's was poker room.

"I don't suppose I have to ask why?"

"You don't. The Shadow strikes again."

The body had been discovered by two workers who were coming in for the early shift. Billy's was open from noon until four in the morning. The two dealers were coming into the back entrance when they noticed an old shoe lying in front of some garbage cans. A closer look showed the dead body slumped behind the cans.

John Mack, the coroner was standing about twenty feet from the cans, puffing on a cigarette. The temperature was getting warmer by the hour, the area near the garbage was starting to smell. Marks remembered the scene behind Aces with Herbert's murder. There was a close resemblance.

"Sorry it took so long to get here, John," Marks said. "I had to make the drive from Galena."

"No worries, Steve. I wasn't that busy and our latest client wasn't going anywhere."

"What have you got?"

"You can take a look, but it's pretty similar. An older guy, I'd say late fifties. Deep puncture wound at the base of the throat. Bled out. I'm thinking he's been there from midnight until now. Just guessing, of course."

Marks walked over to the garbage cans, saw the lone shoe, and looked behind the receptacles. Same as before was an accurate description for what he was looking at. The dead man was short, under five foot six, skinny and with a dirty beard. He was wearing an old torn sports coat and filthy gray slacks. The shirt he wore under the coat was saturated with blood. The bottom of the long beard looked like it had been dipped in red ink. In contrast, the man's eyes were closed and his face looked peaceful, an image that suggested sleep not violent death. Marks turned back to John Mack.

"Of course, nobody saw a damn thing?"

"Other than these two dealers who were walking in the back door for their shift, no. The patrol cops who made the first stop asked around, but nobody heard or saw anything."

Marks lit his own cigarette. "Other than Aces, this is the busiest spot in town and nobody sees someone walk up to another person and plunge a knife into their throat?"

Mack knew that Marks was talking out loud, not really to him. "The killer seems to be completely aware of where he is while selecting targets."

"In back of Billy's? This is a thousand times more out in the open than the spots along the river for the first two victims."

"The killer is becoming bolder."

"Or crazier."

"Okay to bag him?"

Marks flicked away the half-smoked cigarette. "Can't do too much with him lying here and nobody knows anything."

Marks called Lou on his way into headquarters. With the new murder, he didn't know whether to go there or back to Galena.

"Guy was killed in the same fashion?" Lou asked.

"Identical. That and nobody saw or heard anything."

"Well, here's some news. The occupants of the house that the kidnappers are in are Audrey and Phillip Ranier, like the mountain. They are renters and have been in the house three years. She is a poet. He delivers dairy for Wellstone Dairies. The Burnetts are on his route."

"Wow. He would have a pretty good idea about their daily habits."

"Thought so, too. What do you suggest?"

Marks thought for a moment. "We don't know if they have Henry in that house or if they have him at all. Could be a bluff. Let's sit on it for a bit. Anders and Stanley have the place covered. I'd hate to blow the whole thing and rush the house if Henry isn't there. If the Raniers have accomplices who have the boy that could really mess things up."

"You know, the mayor is going to shit over this new murder, especially since it took place in the heart of town."

"I know. I know. I'm not sure what else we can do."

"Get me a suspect, Steve."

"Sure, Lou."

Coming along Route 20, Marks saw the animal hospital on his left. He quickly slowed and turned into the place; there was a parking spot right in front. When he entered the hospital, Susie, the young girl who had helped him with Buster was behind the reception desk. She smiled.

"Hello, Detective Marks. Did you come to get Buster?"

"No. Not at all, but can I see him?"

Susie frowned. "Doc was hoping you'd come get him soon. He's out to lunch now so I can take you back to see Buster."

Susie led Marks back into the area where the animals were kept. Buster was the lone occupant. He jumped up when Susie approached his cage and got really excited when he saw Marks. His tail was wagging rapidly.

"He likes you, Detective," she said.

Marks noticed that Buster looked a lot cleaner and healthier. A bath and decent food had revived him. "I like him, too. I just can't take him. Not yet, anyway."

"Doc was hoping you'd come get him."

"Yeah. I heard that. Let me pay you for what I owe you and just keep taking care of him until I can find a good spot for him."

As they were leaving the cage area, Marks looked back at Buster. The dog wore a forlorn look and his tail no longer wagged. This did not help Marks' already bad disposition.

•   •   •

Marks checked in with Anders and Stanley Cooper on his way back to the Burnett's house. He told them there had been a new homeless murder but could offer little more information. He didn't have anything to tell them. He asked about the Raniers and the house on Maple Crest.

"No change," Anders said. "I haven't seen any movement since the bike rider went into the house with the briefcase. The bike is still parked in the driveway."

"Nothing from my end either," Stanley added."

"Well, we ID'd the guy. His name is Phillip Ranier. He delivers dairy to the Burnetts. No known criminal record, but he might have a pretty good idea of their daily habits."

"They are the ones that took the cash," Anders said. "I say we just sit on them for a bit."

"That's what I thought," Marks said. "Any sign of any vehicle on the premises."

"I can't see any," Stanley said.

"There is a separate garage in the back. If there's a vehicle, it's probably in there."

"Okay, keep up the watch. I'm going to see the Burnetts."

All four of the Burnetts were present when Marks got back to the house. All of them were seated around a coffee table, drinking coffee, and staring at a landline phone in the middle of the table. Donny Briggs was seated in the corner of the room. He shrugged at Marks when he came into the room.

"You haven't heard from anyone?" Marks asked.

"Nothing," Ricky's father said. "We're you able to track the person who picked up the briefcase?"

"Yes. He is someone that you have come in contact with. His name is Phillip Ranier. He delivers your dairy products from Wellstone."

"Phil?" Ricky Burnett said.

"You talk to him much, Ricky?" Marks asked.

"Not that much. Hello and goodbye if I see him on my way out in the morning. That's about it. Nothing more substantial."

"How about you, Lisa?"

She turned to face Marks. The beauty was still there, but so was a new sadness on her face. "I have never spoken a word to the dairy delivery man."

Marks nodded. It would have helped if he had knowledge that someone had spoken to Phillip Ranier, telling him parts of their daily routine.

"But Marguerite has. She speaks to him almost all the time when he delivers something. I see them chatting on the porch," Lisa said.

"Marguerite Lopez?" Marks absently said aloud.

"That would be the only Marguerite that we know, Detective," Lisa said.

• • •

The Lopez family lived in a small house, just outside of the Milton city limits. The house frame, one story that looked to be well kept. The house had no garage and there was only one small sedan in the driveway that

Marks knew belonged to Marguerite. He parked behind it and walked up the walkway to the house. He rang the doorbell.

It didn't take long for the door to be opened. Marguerite Lopez stood there in in old jeans and a dark sweatshirt. "Detective Marks," she said. "I didn't expect you. I just got back from Milton. I work in the offices."

Marks nodded. "Can I have a minute of your time?"

She hesitated. "Yes, of course. Rodrigo is out with the children right now. Please come in."

The house looked clean and was decorated with older furniture. Marguerite led Marks into the living room. "Would you like something to drink?" she asked.

Marks remained standing. "No. I just have a couple of quick questions for you."

"More questions about Henry?"

"Yes. Well, his case at least. Do you know Phillip Ranier?"

She seemed to think for a second. "I don't know that name."

"Maybe you don't know his last name, but I'm talking about Phil who delivers the dairy to the Burnett residence."

She smiled. "Oh, Phil. Yes, I know Phil."

"I understand that you talk with him when he made deliveries."

"Yes. When I see him come up the stairs I would come out and talk with him. He's very nice. Why do you ask?"

"Is it possible that you might have told him about Lisa Burnett's daily routine? Is it possible that you might have told him what she does after she comes home from the health club on Tuesday morning?"

Her bright look faded. "I don't know. I don't remember exactly."

"Marguerite, this is very important. Think about what you might have told him. Did you tell him anything about the time that Lisa Burnett comes home and when you leave the house?"

She hung her head. "We talked a lot about our jobs. He would tell me about his route, the nice people, and the mean people. He said the few times he had met Mrs. Burnett, she had barely spoken to him. I told him she was nice."

"But how about anything with regards to you putting Henry down for his nap and Lisa going into the shower?"

She lifted her head. Tears were forming at the corners of her eyes. "He asked me what time I get done working for the Burnetts. I think I told him when she gets back from her health club, I put Henry down and she goes into the shower and gets ready for the day. I told him that is when I leave the house."

There was a sudden feeling of relief in Marks' neck and shoulders. He nodded slowly.

"Am I in any trouble, Detective Marks?" A large tear ran down her face.

"No, I don't think so. Sometime, tomorrow, I will need you to come into the station and make a formal statement."

"Did Phil take Henry?"

Marks hesitated. "We don't know yet, but he may be involved."

"Oh my god! Because of me?"

"Don't think that way. Because we say things, that doesn't mean that we are responsible for bad things people do."

"But you can get Henry back?"

Marks thought for a moment. Where exactly was Henry? Could they get him back? "We'll get him back," he said."

•　　•　　•

Marks checked with the Burnett residence. There had been no contact from anyone regarding Henry or his release. He checked with Anders and Stanley. The Raniers were still in their house on Maple Crest. There was so sign of any movement. He called Lou and gave him the new update on the talks between Marguerite Lopez and Phillip Ranier.

"Gotta be them," Lou said.

"They took the money, but do they have Henry."

"Do you want to hit the house?"

"Not yet. I don't want to jeopardize anything. If someone else is holding Henry that could really screw things up, but Anders and Stanley are going to need relief soon."

"I thought it could be you and Jeff Blakely for a bit, to give the guys a break."

As much as Marks didn't care for Blakely, he saw little damage the watch commander could do watching a house. "I'm thinking an hour and a half."

"That would work, but I need you to come by here right now. We picked up a homeless guy who identified the dead guy by Billy's and also says he saw The Shadow."

"Are you kidding?"

"Nope. Guy's name is Lenny. Waiting for you downstairs."

On the way back to headquarters, Marks put in a call to Tori. It went straight to her voicemail, but Marks didn't' leave a message. They hadn't talked much since Tori said she might go to Chicago. Marks really didn't have any idea what he would say to her anyway.

• • • •

"What's your full name?" Marks asked the man sitting across from him.

"Lenny. Lenny Myers." Lenny was only about five-nine, slight in build with a ruddy complexion and deep-set eyes that looked vacant, like they were missing eyeballs. He was wearing torn jeans, a dirty white shirt, and an old Army jacket with a 101st Airborne patch on the left sleeve. Somebody had given him a Diet Coke.

"You knew the man that was killed behind Billy's?"

"I knew him. That was Charlie. We used to talk a little."

Marks made a note. "What was he doing behind Billy's?"

Lenny shrugged. "Probably looking for something to eat. There's nothing else back there except garbage cans."

"When did you last see Charlie?"

Lenny took a sip of the drink. "I remembered that I was talking with Charlie when I heard the church bells chime midnight. I remember thinking another day was starting and how fucking cold it was."

Marks smiled. "What's with the Army jacket?"

"I did my time, Detective, but this was my older brother's. He was with the 101st in Nam. Went in with sixty-eight other guys. Came out with twenty-six."

Marks nodded. "No family?"

"No family that gives a shit. No family that listens."

"I'm sorry to hear that. How long have you been on the streets?"

"Like forever, man. I tried to get along, tried to fit in, but nothing ever worked. You know what I mean?"

Marks didn't. "I heard that you might have seen someone lurking around Billy's."

Lenny's eyes widened; the eyeballs became visible. "I saw it, The Shadow they say. When I left Charlie down by Billy's, I was walking down the alley when this person came towards me. Tall, dressed in black, long cape, black hat. Scared the crap out of me."

"Did The Shadow look at you?"

"No. he kept his head down and I walked past him. I don't even think he saw me on the other side of the alley."

"Sure it was a man?"

"I don't know. I never saw the face."

"He was heading towards Billy's?"

"Right back to where I left Charlie."

"That was all you saw?"

"You bet. I got the hell outta there."

"I don't blame you."

"You gonna get this son of a bitch, Detective?"

Like getting Henry back, Marks wasn't sure. "We'll get him."

• • •

Marks and Jeff Blakely rode to Maple Crest Road in separate cars. Marks was going to relieve Anders; Blakely was there for Stanley. Marks watched as Blakely pulled in behind Stanley's car. He proceeded down the street, past the blue house, the bike still in the driveway and up the road toward Anders. He did a U-turn and pulled up behind Anders. He looked down the road at the house. If you didn't know that the people inside had taken the ransom, you would think nothing of the place. It was about as nondescript as you could get.

Just as he had that thought he saw two people emerge from the rear of the house, a man, and a woman. They were dressed in jeans and heavy coats. Each was pulling a piece of luggage on wheels. The man carried a briefcase. "Jesus," Marks said into his microphone. "They are going to run for it." He watched as the man, oblivious to the cops watching him, keyed in numbers to open the garage door in the back of the house. The door started to slide up slowly.

"What are we doing here, Steve?" Stanley asked.

"I'm sure they are coming in your direction towards 20. When they turn out of their drive, I want you and Jeff to pull your cars across the road, blocking them. Anders and I will pull up behind them and do the same thing."

The two people were in the garage, but out of sight. Marks imagined them placing the luggage into the rear of the vehicle. He noticed that his heartbeat had quickened. The palms of his hands were perspiring. Then he remembered he hadn't seen them carrying anything that would suggest that they had Henry. He took a deep breath.

"They are moving," Stanley said.

Marks looked again and saw a blue van, older, moving slowly out of the garage and onto the driveway. It was blocked by the side of the house and then eased past the bike. It got to the street and began to turn left as Marks suggested.

"Let them come out a bit, Stanley. Get ready to go Anders," he said.

The van slowly turned left onto Maple and headed in the direction of Stanley and Blakely. Marks noticed that Anders had started slowly down the street. He put his own car in drive and followed. Up ahead, he could see the van's taillights light up. He could see Stanley's car park across the road. Anders was about fifty yards in front of him. He saw him turn the car to the left, blocking the van in. He quickly pulled in behind him.

"Draw your weapon and hold tight. If either one of them makes a quick move to get out of the car be ready," Marks said.

Marks was the first one out of the cars. He moved slowly up the street with his Glock drawn. When he got within thirty feet of the van, the driver's door opened. Phillip Ranier slowly stepped out of the van, holding the old briefcase that held the cash. He turned slowly and faced Marks.

"Be a good idea, Phillip, if you put the briefcase down and your hands up," Marks said. The gun he held in his hand was levelled at Phillip's chest.

Phillip Ranier said nothing and placed the briefcase on the ground. He raised his hands above his head. The look on his face said total compliance. Marks noticed that Stanley had gotten out of his car and was approaching Phillip from the opposite side; Anders had walked up behind Marks.

"Now tell your wife to come out of the van on her side. Tell her to come out and put her hands above her head."

Phillip turned his head and said something through the open van door. It didn't take long for his wife to come out of the van on the other side and put her hands in the air. Marks approached Phillip and got a good look at him. Older guy, mid-forties, a little beer gut and a wimpy mustache. The wife was plainly attractive with long blonde hair and a slightly turned up nose.

"Stanley, you get to cuff Phillip and Anders please take care of the Mrs. Please be sure to give both their Miranda rights.

•　•　•

"It was a stupid idea," Phillip Ranier said. He was talking with Marks and Anders in the first-floor interrogation room. He was completely calm. "I knew from the news that there hadn't been much progress in solving the kidnapping. I knew there was potential for nabbing a ransom request."

"You didn't think we'd be watching?" Marks asked.

Phillip smiled. "I thought the cops would stay away, not wanting to hurt the chance of getting Henry back and I also thought going up there on a bike would raise fewer questions."

"Part of your message to the Burnetts said that once the ransom was received they would get instructions on how to get Henry back."

Phillip laughed a bit. "We would never take a little boy form his mother and father. Our whole goal was to get the cash and go. We had nothing to do with the kidnapping."

"And you have no idea where Henry is?"

"I do not, I'm afraid. He's a cute little guy. I've seen him a few times; I hope you get him back safely."

Marks stomach dropped a bit. "What the hell were you going to do with the money?"

"Man, we were just going to go someplace else, maybe out west. We just wanted a chance to start over. The cash would have helped us do that. Our lives here were just stuck in the mud. We just wanted to get a fresh start. Like I said, it was a stupid idea."

• • •

It had been a long day with the new murder and the fake ransom move. Marks was tired; everyone was. The two cases, running side by side, were wearing on the department. The mayor was upset about the murders and the kidnapping, constantly calling Lou Katz. Richard Burnett had called Lou earlier in the day and asked if the FBI should be called in. Lou hadn't given him any kind of answer. Lou wanted to call Marks and tell him to get something fast, but he didn't. He knew that Marks already knew this.

Somehow they ended up at Lifers. Somebody suggested they needed a break and no one argued. Marks, Anders, Tammy Glaser, Stanley and his girlfriend, Margie were all standing or sitting around the juke box in the rear of the bar. They'd all had too many drinks and had taken to playing old songs from the sixties. There was some dancing and laughing, but everyone knew the day had been a failure. Several times during the night, Marks checked his phone, looking for something from Tori, but there was nothing. During a break in the songs, Tammy excused herself for a bathroom break and Anders wandered over to where marks was sitting.

"Long day, huh?" Anders said.

Marks looked at the young cop. His eyes were glassy, but alert. "Very perceptive, Anders."

"So what do you think?"

"I think we have another dead homeless guy and we're still missing a little two-year-old boy. Other than that, I don't think much."

Anders nodded slowly. "But we do have a witness that saw The Shadow sometime before the new murder?"

"We do. Another homeless guy says he saw him walking down the alley towards Billy's. A lot of people claim to have seen him, but it's never one of our guys."

Anders gave Marks a tap on the shoulder. "We'll get something soon."

"I think we'd better or the mayor will have our badges."

"What about Jack Wheeler, junior?"

"I was thinking about him. We should take a drive over tomorrow and pay him a visit."

There were some greetings from the front of the bar as some new patrons arrived. Marks turned to see TH Brown and Joseph Running Bear enter the place. They took a booth up near the front windows.

"I've got to see these two guys for a minute," Marks said and he got up and moved away from Anders.

Marks got to the booth before the waitress arrived. He slipped into the seat next to TH. There was no room next to the big frame of Joseph.

"I wondered if you could go up to Dubuque and ask our old friend if he has any idea about this Midwest kidnapping ring." Marks asked.

"You don't say hello first anymore?" TH said.

"No time for small·talk. We have no fucking clue, no pun intended, where little Henry is. The FBI is about to be called in, we're catching heat from Wilson Garrett and I'm getting worried we might not ever find the boy."

"If you remember, the last time we were in Dubuque, some bad shit happened," TH said.

"I didn't ask you to kill anyone."

"Sure. I'll go. We'll go up tomorrow after the funeral. Joseph will go, too. He's got nothing to do until hunting season. I might even ask Richie to go, but he might be into the vodka."

"I just need anything that might help us. I know it's a long shot, but we've got nothing."

TH could see the fear I Marks' eyes. "We'll go, Steve. We'll see what we can learn."

• • •

It was past eleven o'clock when Marks got back to the condo. There were no lights on which was unusual, but he hadn't spoken to Tori so she had no idea where he was or had been. He turned on the lights in the kitchen and put his keys, wallet and phone in the little dish Tori had bought. He noticed her phone wasn't in there. He looked around a bit and noticed the envelope on the table. He opened it and removed the single piece of paper, a note:

Steve, I know you are busy and I didn't want to stress you out any more than necessary. I went to Chicago with Helen. I will be gone a few days. I will give you a call.

Love, Tor

Marks read the note again and nodded. Yes, he was busy and stressed, but if there was one person he thought would support him it was Tori, and now she was gone.

CHAPTER 8

December 23rd, 2009

It was under a decorated pine tree, just outside of the Lincoln Park Zoo, that they found the last body. It was a man again, dressed in a heavy overcoat and beat up black boots. The man was not wearing a hat, but there was a crumpled watch cap sitting several feet from the body. There was one difference in this case. The man was found lying on his stomach in a large pool of his own blood.

"Quite the contrast," Eli Roach said. "This fancy Christmas tree and a dead guy lying underneath it."

Mike Burke flicked his cigarette away. "Fuck Christmas," he said. His stomach hurt and he was already cold. "Right out in the open this time. This killer doesn't give a shit about where he kills them."

"This one less than a month after the last one. He's getting a little more active."

"Just what we need," Burke said.

The young Laskey kid from the coroner's office came up. The body on the ground had been turned over. The gaping hole was present in the throat. The twinkling Christmas lights danced across his face. "It's not much different from the rest," he said, "but take a look at this. Come closer."

Laskey moved up next to the body and shone a flashlight on the victim's left hand. "Check out the hand, under the nails. Theres's quite a bit of blood there and I'm thinking some skin fragments. If I had to make a guess, I'm going to say that this guy went out with a bit of a fight. Looks to me like he grabbed a good piece of the killer and we now have some blood and skin samples."

Burke whistled. "Maybe I was a little harsh on Christmas. You think that's for real?"

Laskey turned off the flashlight. "Unless he had a fight with someone else tonight."

"How long to run the tests on the samples?"

"We put a rush on them, a couple of weeks. Based on what we are chasing, maybe we get a break, and it gets prioritized."

"Put a rush on it Laskey. This killer is now doing somebody every month. We have thirty days, maybe less."

"I'll do what I can, Detective. I just can't be responsible for the other agency's response."

Eli Roach stepped forward before Burke could. "Laskey, just speed it up. We'll worry about any shit that we cause."

Laskey nodded, turned, and headed back to his van.

"Dickhead," Eli said.

"Most appointees are."

"What's that?" Burke said, pointing at an object on the ground.

Eli walked over and looked at it. "Looks like a heal off of a woman's shoe."

Burke shrugged. "Put it in an evidence bag."

•   •   •   •

They heard back from testing center within ten days. The reports were conclusive. "The blood and the skin fragments came from a woman," Laskey said.

"You're sure?" Burke asked. They were in a second-floor interrogation room.

"One hundred percent. The bad news is that nothing in the DNA reports indicate who this woman is."

"Or if this woman is the one who is the killer," Eli said.

"Exactly," Laskey said. "The samples came from someone who has no police record anywhere. It could be from the killer or it could be from someone who the dead guy got into a fight with earlier the night he was killed."

"I'm thinking that," Eli said. "I can't see a woman doing this."

"No," Burke said slowly. "I'm thinking that our killer is a woman and that those samples belong to her. I'm thinking the broken heal is also from our gal."

•   •   •   •

That night as they sat in the living room of their small Rogers Park home, Burke thought that he was entering a depressive state. The DNA said that the killer was a woman; others in his unit didn't think that. Why, he didn't know? Women committed awful crimes. The internet was full of stories of them. Start with Lizzie Borden and her forty whacks. Why would it be impossible for a woman to be roaming around Chicago and killing homeless people?

"Are you okay, Mike?" his wife Carol asked. She was reading a book; Mike had ESPN on with no sound.

"I'm good," he said. "Just thinking."

"Correction, drinking and thinking."

She was right. Burke was into his fourth scotch. His back ached, he was putting on weight and sleeping like shit. Carol went to yoga, Pilates and did the Stairmaster four times a week. She looked ten, fifteen years younger than him. "You're right. This damn homeless case is driving me nuts."

Carol took off her reading glasses and looked at her husband. This was as bad as she'd ever seen him. "What's got you down so much today?"

"We recovered some DNA samples from the latest victim, the guy killed in Lincoln Park. The samples indicate that the killer might be a woman. No one seems to believe that a woman could be the killer. Even Eli doubts it."

"Eli always agrees with you."

"Not this time. He refuses to believe it could be a woman. He says that women don't go around stabbing random guys in the throat. He was trying to make a joke, but he said it wasn't in their DNA."

"I mean, I think women can do some awfully gruesome things, but aren't most of them in response to something else, a reaction rather than some thought out plan?"

"I don't know about that. I doubt if there are statistics about how much planning women do before killing someone."

"But there's not that many female serial killers."

"That's true, but there are some."

"Extremely rare."

Burke took a sip. The scotch was tasting sour. Maybe he'd had enough. "Yeah, that's what I learned, but that doesn't mean I couldn't catch one."

She smiled. "You're going to be fifty-five in October. There's plenty of time after that to head south and find a spot to stay for the winter. Of course, we'd be back here for Thanksgiving and Christmas, but we'd have a lot of time to look for a winter home."

Burke felt an odd warmth coming over him. "Thirty years is a long time to be a cop anywhere. In Chicago, it feels like sixty."

"Honey, you have done so much for that department and so much for this family. I talked to the kids and they are good with it. We'll only be a plane ride away and we can get a small place for the summer. I think that would be the best thing for both of us."

Burke took another sip. It wasn't that bad. There was a lot of time between now and October. Time to catch one more killer. "That is absolutely the best plan ever."

Carol laughed out loud. Mike laughed; too, but still thought he was looking at a woman as his prime suspect.

Marks stopped by to see his mother before he went into headquarters. As he walked the halls of the home, the antiseptic smell overwhelming, he felt tense. How would his mother be? He wasn't sure he could handle a repeat of the last visit where she seemed spaced out and didn't even know who he was.

Janet Marks was lying in her bed with her head propped up by two pillows. She was wearing her glasses and had the TV on. She turned towards the door as Marks entered the room. "Oh, hello, Steven. I was wondering when you'd stop by and see your old mom."

This one little comment made Marks relax. He smiled. "I'm sorry, mom. I've been a little busy this past week."

"Catching all the bad guys that Milton has to offer?"

"There are few," he said. "How are you feeling?"

She smiled. "I'm sure you know this, Steven, but I am dying. I know this and I am okay with it. I know that the next life will be better than this one has been, but I am not complaining. I have had a great life and you are a good reason for it."

Marks felt his emotions rising. He got closer to his mother's bed and took her bony hand. "You're not going anywhere for a while."

"Maybe not until Good Morning America is over," she said, "but soon. I don't ask, but I can see it in the nurse's and doctor's eyes. I don't know how long, but my body tells me not to plan any long trips. My mind tells me I'm going to go on a much longer journey and that it will be good."

He squeezed her hand. "Is there anything that you need, mom?"

"No. You have given me much more than a mother could ask from a son."

Marks didn't want her to see him cry. "I've got to be going now, but I'll try and come by tomorrow."

"I'm fine," she said. "Be sure to say hi to Louis and TH Brown."

He smiled and leaned down to kiss her cold cheek. "I will, mom."

He got out into the hall, didn't notice the pungent smell, walked all the way out to his car and got in before he started crying. It took several minutes before he could stop.

• • •

It was just past nine when Marks and Anders got to the condominium building that Jack Wheeler, Jr. lived in. They knew he was home because his red Corvette was parked in a spot directly underneath his second-floor unit. What they didn't know was what kind of shape they'd find young Jack in. He was a known partier and cocaine user. Marks knew that sometimes these types didn't begin their day until well past noon. "Let's hope he's mobile and functional," he said.

Anders wasn't sure he was either of those two after the late night of drinking, but the coffee and aspirin had helped. His toothache was throbbing.

They rang Jack's doorbell and waited a few minutes before ringing it again. They heard someone inside shouting at them and then heard the door lock and latch being undone. Jack opened the door and peered at them through slightly closed eyes. "What the fuck is it?" he said. He was dressed in boxer shorts and a Vikings tee shirt.

Marks raised his badge up to where Jack had a clear view of it. "We'd like to talk with you for a few minutes, Jack."

Jack squinted as he looked at the shield. "I didn't do anything wrong."

"Possession of cocaine is not a legal activity, but we are not here to talk about that. We want to ask you a few questions about Lisa Burnett."

Jack's mind went right to Lisa's kidnapped little boy. "Oh, fuck," he said, but he backed up and let the two detectives into the unit.

Surprisingly to Marks, the condo was in immaculate shape. The furniture was all leather and wood, good stuff. Everything was all neat and tidy. For some reason,

Marks thought the place would resemble other places where druggies lived.

"I wasn't expecting company so forgive me for being short on hospitality," Jack said.

"We're good," Marks said. He looked at Jack. He put him in his late twenties, good looking with a full head of dark hair. His face looked like he was missing sleep, his nose was red and cracked underneath it. "Tough night, last night, Jack?"

"I thought you guys wanted to talk about Lisa."

"You're right. What can you tell us?"

Jack laughed. "What can I tell you? She's hot. I met her at the restaurant. She came onto me and we hit it off. We're friends."

"Friends?" Anders said. He got the feeling that Jack and he could never be friends.

Jack squinted again. "You really a cop?"

"Guilty," Anders said. "What kind of friends?"

Another short laugh. "We're fuck buddies. Friends with benefits, nothing more than that."

"When was the last time you saw her?" Marks asked.

Jack hesitated, thinking. "Would have been last Thursday. That's the night she usually goes to Wheeler's, but she just started coming over here."

"You know her son has been kidnapped?"

"I know that. You're not here about that, are you?"

"Know anything about it?"

"Not a fucking thing. Like I said, Lisa comes by here, she hangs out an hour or two and then she is gone."

"You know much about her daily routine?"

"You mean like what she does all day? No idea. I see her on Thursdays. We don't talk about whether she got her laundry done."

"She ever talk about her husband to you?"

"Yeah, sometimes. I get the impression she thinks the guy has lost interest in her. Says he's always working, doesn't have time for her. She said she thought he might have gone over to the other team."

"What?" Marks said.

"You mean, she thought he might be gay?" Anders responded.

"You got it," Jack said.

Marks shook his head. "What about little Henry? Hear much about him?"

Jack thought for a moment. "I knew she had a son. I think she mentioned his name a few times, but there's nothing that stands out."

"Do you know she attends yoga classes on Tuesday and Thursday mornings?"

"Not really, but I figured she worked out a bunch with a body like that."

Marks didn't think they were getting anywhere. Jack was just a little playboy having some fun. He might be a coke user, but not hooked up in a crime. "We heard your daddy cut your allowance?"

"Not true. Total rumor. My dad and I fight all the time. You know the bullshit about getting my act together. Dad's probably right, but he didn't cut my salary, or allowance, as you say. Mom would kill him."

Marks laughed. "Moms can be like that."

"Most of what I know about Lisa's husband is what she told me. It's a little thin because there's not much. What I will say about the guy is that I have seen him a couple of times at Wheelers. Each time he was with a hood named Micky Farrell."

"A hood?" Marks asked.

"That's me talking. My dad used Micky a few times for some collection issues on the catering side. I don't think they were pleasant negotiations."

On the way back in, Anders turned to Marks. "What do you think of this Micky Farrell guy?"

"I was thinking about that. I don't really know. We should ask Ricky."

"Micky and Ricky has a nice ring to it."

"Would you hire someone, a hood, to bust the kneecap of the guy who was banging your wife?"

'I don't have a wife, but if she looked like Lisa Burnett, I might."

"I don't have a wife either, but I have a live-in girlfriend. I don't think I'd feel particularly good if she were sharing the sheets with someone."

"But you and I are rational."

"Ricky doesn't seem that interested in Lisa these days, but you don't know. Plus, he knows Kyle James. That his wife is banging the nice guy, town mechanic might piss him off."

"Guess we'd better ask."

"You think you can ask Tammy to take a look at Micky Farrell?"

Anders smiled. "I guess I can ask."

"Maybe if you treat her extra nice, she'll find something that helps us."

"I'd say something derogatory, but it might only get me in trouble."

"Probably, don't say it."

• • •

The funeral wasn't much. Not counting family, there were maybe fifteen people at church for the mass. By the time they got to the cemetery that number was down to six or seven. Teddy Brown had died with few friends; most of his loyal allies had been gunned down in Iowa the past October. TH figured that those that came out to pay respects didn't really know him.

"Maybe we should have just fried him," TH had said earlier.

"TH, please," Rachel said.

"He's God's problem now," Richie said. He didn't look good. TH suspected his older brother hadn't given up the booze as promised.

"I'm not sure he's going to be interviewed by God," TH said.

"The Devil can have him," Rachel said.

When things were done at the cemetery, Rachel headed home to her kids. Richie said he was going up to Wisconsin for a couple of days. TH had a date to meet Joseph Running Bear at Lifers. The big Indian was sitting at the bar drinking a beer and munching on some wings.

"Everything go okay?" Joseph asked.

"As well as can be expected. The world is a better place."

"He was still your father, TH."

Teddy Brown's people had harassed Joseph over the years. He was the last one he'd thought he'd hear anything positive about his father. TH avoided the remark. "Almost done with your little snack?"

Joseph ate the last little wing and drank the half of beer that was left. "If I get heartburn, it's your fault."

"I told Marks I'd get up to Dubuque and get back. They are trying to find Henry Burnett."

"We can go," Joseph said.

The traffic on the bridge over the river was backed up. Somebody had blown a tire in the left lane and couldn't get over to the right shoulder. The normal fifteen-minute drive to Dubuque took almost thirty. TH had called Clay Johnson and said they wanted to talk. Clay didn't suspect anything and said come on by.

The Dubuque Police Department was in a new six story building in the center of town. Clay Johnson's office was on the third floor with a nice view of the bluffs lining the Mississippi. Clay was a big man and had let his gut go to where it was hanging over his belt. He'd also grown his hair where it was covering his ears. He looked a little sloppy in his uniform.

"Sorry to hear about your dad, TH?" Clay said. He was behind his desk; TH and Joseph took the two chairs in front of him.

"Thanks," TH said. Clay had worked for his father but left when Lou Katz 's star had begun rising in the department.

"You still got your hunting lodge, Joe?"

Joseph laughed. "No lodge, Clay. Just land where the hunters can get their deer."

Clay nodded. "You mentioned Marks, TH. You said you were doing him a favor."

"I know how close you two are," TH said. "I was here and thought I'd come up and ask a few questions."

Clay leaned back and rested his hands on his prominent belly. "About what?"

TH sensed the tone. "You heard about Ricky Burnett's kid?"

"Who hasn't in these parts? We put out an APB. We're looking, but so far nothing."

"Marks is working full time on it. That and the homeless guys getting murdered."

"Heard about that, too. Keep that guy on that side of the river."

TH smiled. "I was talking with this detective I know in LA. He says there's a ring of kidnappers operating out of the Midwest that will kidnap kids and move them up north into Canada where they find passage to Europe. White kids, babies."

Clay's face didn't change. "Don't know anything about that one. Sounds a little like make believe."

"This cop, his name is Scanlon, he told me that Dubuque is considered one of the hubs for moving the kids."

Now Clay Johnson laughed, a belly jiggling laugh. "My Dubuque? We're the hub for moving white babies up to Canada?"

"No joke, Clay. From here to Minnesota and then Toronto."

Clay sat forward and pressed his arms on his desk. "That is the biggest bunch of bullshit that I have ever heard. Something like one of those bad cop flicks on Netflix."

TH shrugged. "Hey Clay, I'm not trying to ruffle your feathers. It's just something that Scanlon told me, and I told Marks I'd ask you what you know."

The look on Clay's face softened. "We run a tight ship here. Not tight like Teddy used to run, but we keep things clean and smooth. I'd know if there was even a rumor of something like that going on and there isn't."

"That's good, Clay. I'll let Marks know. We were just looking because, you know, we all went to school with Ricky Burnett, and this hits home a little bit."

"I hear you," Clay said. "I always thought Ricky was a little pussy, but nobody should have their baby taken from them. What's your interest, other than helping Marks a bit?"

"That's really it."

"Not thinking of trying to find the baby up here in Dubuque and stealing him back?"

TH smiled again. "Nothing like that, Clay."

"The last time anyone from Milton got involved in something shady up here, some people shot the hell out of them. You guys know about that?"

"We do. Doesn't surprise me that Ack and his buddies were killed in a shootout. I don't think they were actually the law-abiding types."

"Wasn't a shootout. More like an ambush. I don't need that shit anymore."

"Even if I knew that Henry Burnett was here, I wouldn't come up here and try and steal him back."

Clay laughed. "I was just fucking with you, TH. I knew you wouldn't pull anything stupid like that."

On the drive back, TH lit a cigarette and flicked an ash out of the window.

"If you knew where Ricky Burnett's son was, you would go and get him," Joseph Running Bear said.

TH looked at Joseph, the smoke dangling from his lips. "In a heartbeat."

"You let me know if you are going to do that. My history of providing backup in Dubuque is good."

• • •

Tammy caught up with Anders in the break room on the lower level. He was hoping to have another cup of coffee before they went to see Ricky Burnett. Tammy looked excited.

"I'm glad I caught you," she said.

There was no one around so he leaned in and kissed her on the cheek. "I'm glad you did, too."

"Business first," she said.

Anders took the cup out of the machine and took a sip. He winced. "That's not good, but you are right. Business first."

"First of all, what I could find on Micky Farrell. It's not too far off from what Jack Wheeler told you. The guy used to be some sort of amateur boxer, Golden Gloves, that sort of thing. He's small so he was just a bantam back then. He tried to go pro, but that fizzled fast. He got into enforcement."

Anders took another sip. Better this time. "Meaning what?"

"He runs a collection service out of Dubuque. There's not a whole lot us cops can prove, but it is alleged that's he's broken a few bones and noses over his career at the behest of his clients. He's been arrested a few times but has never served. He did probation for beating up a guy, but there was some proof that the guy came at him first with an umbrella."

"Probably not the best decision."

"No. The guy ended up with a broken jaw and a Grade 2 concussion. What this proves, Anders, is that this is probably the guy that went after Kyle James. It would seem to me that the logical choice for the hiring was Ricky Burnett since Kyle was boinking his wife."

"Well, Jack Wheeler placed them together in the restaurant. We are going to talk with Ricky."

"I found something else that I thought you would find interesting. Remember I couldn't find much on Rodrigo Lopez?"

"Marguerite's husband? Yeah."

"Well, I found something. When he came across the border, his name was Rodrigo Suarez. Somewhere the name got changed on the records and it stuck."

"Okay. Anything more than the name change?"

"Got busted for soliciting a hooker on Brewster Way, but the charge was dropped. Records say he came into the US when he was twelve years old. He has a sister, Maria, three years younger. She also lives in Milton. No record of any kind."

"That's interesting, but I'm not so sure on Rodrigo. That's too obvious for him to be involved in Henry's kidnapping. I like the stuff on Farrell. We'll see what Ricky has to say."

"What do you think?"

Anders finished the small cup of coffee. "I think the clock is ticking on the FBI being called in. We really have nothing. I'm also real uneasy with Ricky and Lisa. He seems like he's got his head up his ass with anything other than his stores; she seems like she's only interested in regaining some life she lost. She's making quite the name for herself seducing the younger men of Milton. I really can't figure them out."

"So, who took Henry?"

"Fuck if I know." Anders reached a hand up and rubbed his jaw. "Damn tooth is killing me."

"You'd better get that looked at."

"Yeah. In my free time."

• • • •

"We're going to have to call in the FBI," Lou said. He had his back to Marks and was looking out of his office window. "This fake ransom deal and any lack of good suspects makes it necessary."

Marks couldn't disagree. "I can't argue with you on that."

Lou turned back to him. "Wilson Garrett is getting all kinds of grief from Ricky's dad. He told Wilson we were unequipped to find Henry. We didn't have the manpower or the resources."

"Well, there's no doubt on both of those issues that the FBI has us beat."

"You seem okay with this."

"Everyone I know who is working these two cases is working as hard as they can. The cases are totally different, but remarkably similar. A kidnapping and a multiple murderer in little Milton. Who would have thunk it? In each case we have no suspects, no one heard or sees anything. That's not true. We do have sightings on the mysterious Shadow. In Henry's case, we don't have anything other than a mother who is sleeping around and a father who'd rather be in his stores than home helping his family get through this."

"More like "48 Hours" than a Disney story?" Lou said.

"Exactly. So, we keep on working Henry's case or we back off?"

"No. We keep working it. They'll ask for what we have and run their own game. It's still technically our case but try and stay out of their way and don't cause any trouble."

"Fuck it. I just hope they find Henry."

"Who took him, Steve?"

"I don't have any idea who took Henry, but somebody that we've contacted knows something."

Lou smiled. "And the Shadow murders?"

"He'll make a mistake if he keeps prowling Milton and preying on the homeless. Somebody will really see him, and we'll catch him."

"Not too many more murders, I hope. Makes our town's tourism brochure look like shit."

"I finally looked at that. It was a shitty brochure to begin with."

• • •

On the drive to see Ricky Burnett, Marks told Anders about the FBI being called into the case. Anders told Marks what Tammy had found out about Rodrigo Lopez and Micky Farrell.

"So, what does the FBI being involved do to us?" Anders asked.

"They will do their thing and we'll continue to do ours. Mostly they'll want us out of the way."

"What can they find that we couldn't?"

"That's a good one. I think Henry might be gone. I think he could be on his way to Canada and then Europe, but the thing is, somebody locally knows something and that's what we have to focus on."

"What about Rodrigo and his sister?"

"Well, the name thing is a little weird and the fact that he has a sister doesn't tell me much, so I don't know. Nothing there sparks my interest."

"What about Micky Farrell?"

"Let's see what Ricky has to say about that one."

They found the whole family sitting in the living room, looking at each other, and saying nothing. Marks thought the mood in the room was somewhere between frustration and disdain for each other, a toxic mix. Donny Briggs, the Milton cop, looked ready to take a nap as he sat in his corner of the room.

"The FBI is being called into the case," Ricky's father said. "Should have been done sooner than today."

"I really hope they can turn over something that we couldn't find," Marks said. His comment quieted the father. "We need to speak with Ricky privately."

All the family turned towards Ricky. "You want to speak with me?" Ricky asked.

"Privately," Marks said.

They retreated to Ricky's den and the door was closed. None of the men took a seat. "What is this about?" Ricky said.

"You know a guy named Micky Farrell?"

Ricky was thinking. "I can't say that I do."

"You sure, Ricky?" Marks said. "We have a witness that spotted you with Micky at Wheeler's."

Ricky's shoulders drooped. "Okay. I know Micky Farrell. What does this have to do with anything?"

"Well, then you must know something about Micky. His background is not that great."

"He has chased some bad collection items for me. My father used him as well."

"Just collections?"

"What else would there be?"

"Micky Farrell has a reputation for being an enforcer."

"I never used Micky to use force to collect some money."

"What about Kyle James?"

"Kyle James? What about Kyle James?"

"Come on, Ricky."

"Okay, Steve. I know. I know that Lisa was seeing Kyle on the side. Bad thoughts crossed my mind about Kyle James, but if you think that I hired Micky Farrell to bash in Kyle's knee you are barking up the wrong tree."

"So, you know of no one that would just arbitrarily attack Kyle James?"

"You tell me. The man is sleeping with a married woman. What else could he be doing? Are there other people in Milton that he has pissed off so badly that they wanted his knee broken? What does any of this have to do with finding Henry? We are wasting time here."

Marks nodded his head. "None of this has anything to do with Henry's case, but what happened with Kyle is still a crime. We are a small department. We still have to look at the other crimes in the town."

"I agree," Ricky said. "You have poor Kyle getting his knee smashed. You have someone killing homeless people along the river. That, plus Henry, is too much for the Milton PD to handle. That's why the FBI is being called in."

Ricky's face was red; his eyes were wide open. Marks could see his point. A small department with not enough manpower handling two major cases and stuck with handling the piddly ones. Maybe they weren't up to the challenge.

· · ·

There was a message on Marks' phone that TH Brown wanted to meet him at Lifers at four o'clock. There was nothing in the message about what the content of the meeting was about which led Marks to think it wasn't that important. Marks decided to bring Anders long anyway.

"Are you mentoring high school kids?" TH asked when he first saw Anders.

Anders shook his hand. "I hear you are a thief?"

"Easy boys," Marks said. "Anders is my partner, an associate detective; TH is a respected repo man from Southern California."

TH laughed. "Still looks like a sophomore."

They moved from the front of the bar to a booth near the back. The place was mostly empty. TH ordered a round of beers for the three of them.

"Funeral went okay, I take it?" Marks asked.

"Sure," TH said. "The big debate was whether we should have had him planted or fried."

Anders whistled. "You're talking about your father?"

"You didn't know him," TH said. "Believe all of the bad stuff. Be extremely cautious about the good stuff you hear."

The beers came and all three tapped their bottles together. "I guess you called this meeting to tell me you have solved Henry's kidnapping?" Marks asked.

"I saw your old friend, Clay Johnson, in Dubuque after the funeral."

Marks turned to Anders. "We weren't friends or close to it."

"Mortal enemies," TH said, "which is why I made a courtesy visit."

"And he knows nothing?"

"That is not true. He knows that he runs the tightest ship in law enforcement. He knows everything that goes on in the little hamlet of Dubuque. Also threw a tremendous amount of water on this story about the kidnapping ring funneling kids through his city. Says it's ridiculous."

"That's not much," Marks said.

"Sorry. He was very clear about the ring and clear that if Henry Burnett were in Dubuque, he would have heard about it."

"Guess he can see things we can't."

"He's just the same pompous ass he used to be," TH said. "Nothing new on your end?"

"The biggest news is that we think Ricky hired a guy named Micky Farrell to break Kyle James' kneecap because Kyle was sleeping with Lisa."

"No shit? Our Kyle? Good move for him on the wife. I hear she's a knockout. Not good news on the broken kneecap. Does it have anything to do with the kidnapping?"

"Probably not and we have no proof that Ricky was behind it, but Ricky was seen in Wheelers with this guy Farrell. Tammy Glaser says Micky Farrell is a thug who specializes in debt collection and may resort to less than legal methods to enact payment."

"I'm sorry I wasn't more help for you," TH said. "I wish there was more that I could do."

Marks picked up his beer and took a long swallow. He wished that, too. He wished for something good to happen.

· · ·

Ricky Burnett went into the kitchen to get more coffee for the four family members who were waiting for any word on Henry. He had refilled only two of the four cups when Lisa came into the kitchen behind him.

"Why did the police want to talk with you privately?" she asked. She was wearing a snug pair of jeans and a button-down white shirt. The two top buttons were undone.

Ricky felt his face flush and took a conscious effort to control his temper. "They asked about an old high school friend of mine."

"Is this person a suspect?"

"I don't think so. His name is Kyle James. He's a mechanic in town. Somebody paid him a visit the other night and broke his kneecap. He's in the hospital recuperating."

Lisa felt her stomach sink. She hadn't heard this. "Oh my God," she said. "Why would they question you?"

"Kyle bought a bunch of furniture and decided not to pay on it," he lied. "One of the collection people we use has a reputation for using violence to collect debts. They were wondering if we put this guy onto Kyle, which is absurd. We don't employ thugs to collect our debts."

Lisa was looking doe eyed at Ricky as he spoke. She was hearing him but thinking of Kyle. She realized that Ricky was done speaking. "Do you think we are going to get Henry back, Ricky? We have to get him back. I don't know what I'll do if we can't get him back."

Ricky thought this over for a minute. Lisa had constantly complained about Henry costing her too much of her free time and how she wished for the days of old. "We'll get him back," he said.

"How can you be so sure?" There were tears forming in her eyes.

Ricky finished pouring the last two cups of coffee. "My father thinks that the FBI will be a vast improvement over the Milton PD. He thinks they will be able to figure something out and quickly."

"But what do you think?"

"I think we'll get him back shortly."

Lisa took a step forward to hug her husband, but he had picked up the coffee tray blocking the move. "I think you should button at least one more button on your shirt. We all know you have big boobs, but I don't think my parents or Officer Briggs needs that clear a view of them."

•   •   •   •

The coroner, John Mack, was waiting for Marks when he returned to headquarters. He was sitting in his office reviewing notes in his file.

"Lose your way to your office, John?" Marks asked.

Mack looked up from his notes and smiled. "I might have found something on this guy who was killed behind Billy's."

"We're you able to identify him?"

Mack reached up and stroked his thick mustache. "No, nothing like that. Take a look at these photos."

Marks could see that Mack had spread three different, blown-up pictures on his desk. They were clearly pictures of a leg. Hair and veins were easy to see. What each picture showed that was unique was a stamp or an impression of a triangle. In each photo, the triangle, which was small stood out clearly, red in color.

"What is that, John?"

"I don't know. That's why I brought these down here for you to look at. I thought you or your guys might have an idea. The dead guy had these three triangles on three different spots on his left leg. They were imprinted with some force. We checked the pants the victim was wearing. There are no tear marks in them."

"You think the dead guy was whacked with something or poked?"

Mack shrugged. "That's my thought, but I have no idea what the object was and whether it could lead us to the killer. None of the first two dead guys had these marks, so I don't know. Just very weird."

"But the knife used was the same one?"

"No doubt about it. The instrument of death is the same one. Your killer in all three cases is the same person."

• • •

Her name was Gloria Forman. She had been a friend of Rachel Brown, a little older than TH. He remembered that Rachel had told him that Gloria had risen to the top accounting person in the Burnett Furniture chain. She worked out of the main store that was located just east of Brewster Way. TH had been able to reach her right before the store had closed and she agreed to meet him at Lifers for a drink. TH was a little worried because she had agreed to meet him so quickly.

Gloria Forman had been a bridesmaid in Rachel's first wedding. TH remembered an attractive girl with dark hair and a nice figure. She was now getting into her late thirties. The dark hair was streaked with strands of gray and she had put on a few pounds. "It's been a while, TH," she said. She had ordered some sort of colored martini before TH had arrived.

"I saw you at my sister's wake."

"That's true, but we didn't get much time to talk. It's been a rough six months for your family with Melissa and now your father."

"It's hasn't been the best."

"It seems Rachel is doing okay."

Rachel was struggling to raise her kids and worked at Walmart. TH let the comment go. "You're probably wondering why I asked you to come out for a drink."

She smiled, nice white teeth. "I was."

"I was talking with Steve Marks about the Burnett kidnapping, little Henry."

"That's a terrible thing. I don't know how Ricky manages to stay focused."

TH nodded. He wondered that, too, based on what Marks had told him. "It is an incredible ordeal. Anyway, I was trying to help Steve out by talking to some local people. I went and saw Clay Johnson up in Dubuque. There was supposed to be some kidnapping ring up there."

Gloria's smile dimmed when she realized the meeting had nothing to do with romance. "I remember Clay. Kind of a bully and thought all the girls loved him."

"That's Clay. I went up there because Steve and Clay weren't exactly pals."

She sipped her drink. "I don't know too much about Clay."

"It's not Clay I'm interested in. It's Ricky."

"Ricky Burnett? What would you want to know about Ricky?"

"Gloria, look, I'm not probing Ricky. We all know quite a bit about him. It's the people around him that I'm interested in. Somebody that Ricky was close to had a pretty good idea of what Ricky's wife did during the daytime. She follows the same schedule on Tuesday and Thursday mornings. Somebody knew she'd be in the shower at a certain time and came into the house and grabbed Henry."

She took another sip and brushed some hair out of her eyes. "I see Ricky every day. We interact all the time and I know nothing about what Lisa does. Ricky is all business when he comes into the stores. He's a totally different person since he's taken over for his father."

TH sipped his beer. "So, nobody that you can think of that is close to Ricky who might know something about their home life?"

Gloria started to chew on a nail on her right hand, stopped and looked around the bar. "There's a woman that started to work for us about a year ago. She works on the floor, so I don't have much to do with her."

"What's so special about this woman?"

"Well, you know, it's just rumors. I mean, we've got five stores but were still a small business. Everybody knows something about everyone."

"So, what about her?"

"She's a Latino, very pretty. I'd say closer to your age than mine. Exceptionally good shape. Like I said, she's been with us for maybe a year. Some of the people I talk with say that Ricky was talking and joking with her as soon as she started. There's other women that work for us, but nobody can remember Ricky stopping in the store to chat with them. Let's face it, he goes home to Lisa. He doesn't need to look far for a good-looking woman."

"So, there were rumors about the two of them?"

"Yeah. It almost seemed like neither of them cared. People would see them talking in the parking lot after we closed and then watched as they drove off on the same direction. A lot of their behavior was obvious. It was the closest I've ever seen Ricky with a regular employee."

"So, you think the two of them were doing more than talking?"

"Amongst the rumor crowd, that was the consensus. Now I don't have any idea whether Ricky told her anything about his home life and what Lisa did, but he's never joked, smiled and laughed with anyone like this before."

"What's this woman's name?"

"Suarez. Maria Saurez."

TH made a note on his I-phone. "Anything else?"

"When Henry was kidnapped, we were all stunned. When Ricky came into the store a few times, everyone stopped by to say something to him. Everyone except for Maria Saurez. She was nowhere in sight. This became a topic of the rumor crowd. Very weird, but Maria went on a two week vacation the day that Henry was abducted. None of us knows where she went, but someone thought she said Mexico."

• • •

Anders and Tammy Glaser were lying in the bed watching the end of one of the late-night talk shows. Anders had received a call that Marks wanted him in the office at nine o'clock to review some new evidence. Marks didn't tell him what the evidence was, but it pertained to the homeless men murders.

"You do a lot of research," Anders said. "Any idea what kind of evidence Marks could be talking about?"

Tammy yawned and turned on her side. "I have no idea, but he must think it's important if you guys are going to discuss it first thing."

"It would be nice to get a lead on anything. We have two major cases, a kidnapping and three murders, and no real idea pointing us where to go."

"Not like Columbo," she said, yawning again.

"Who?"

Tammy laughed. "Old cop show. The real thing is nothing like TV where with ten minutes to go in the show it becomes clear to the detective what is going on."

"No, it's nothing like that. At least with a civil disturbance you have a pretty good idea who hit who with the frying pan."

She stifled a third yawn. "Something will come up shortly."

Anders turned to look at her. "Almost forgot to tell you. I met your old friend TH Brown today."

"TH really wasn't a friend of mine. I knew his sisters Melissa and Rachel a little. TH was good friends with Marks. They played baseball together."

"He said he went up to Dubuque today to talk with the Chief of Police about that kidnapping ring that uses the city as a forwarding spot to get these children up to Minnesota and then Canada. Guy's name was Clay Johnson."

Tammy propped herself on one elbow. "Now, there is somebody that I know about."

"You know the guy?"

"If you were a girl older than thirteen and had a set of boobs, you heard from Clay Johnson. The joke was he picked being a cop over being a pimp. He hit on every girl in the damn town. He was a good cop but saw his chance in Iowa. That came true when word came down that Lou Katz was going to be the Assistant Chief. Did he know much about the ring?"

"TH said he knew nothing about it and doubted its existence. He said that if such an operation were going on in Dubuque, he would have heard something about it."

"That makes sense. Kind of ironic, though. He used to be sort of a fanboy of Ricky Burnett."

"Wait a minute. Clay Johnson admired Ricky Burnett?"

"Not really Ricky, but his money and cars. Clay would sometimes hang with Ricky because of the cars he drove and the cash he had. Some of the girls liked Ricky because of this, too. Clay didn't mind that either."

"So, they were friends?"

"They were from different sides of the tracks, but they hung out together for a while. Like I said, it might have been for the cars and money Ricky had."

"But Marks and Clay Johnson didn't get along?"

"Not close. They had a big fight in high school, a brawl. They never ironed out things even when they were on the force together. Everyone knew the story, so they were never assigned to work together."

Anders leaned over and kissed her on the cheek. "Interesting about Clay and Ricky, but hopefully tomorrow will bring a lead on one of these cases."

"Maybe," she said. "Forgot to ask. How's the tooth?"

"Not great. I've got to get in to see someone, but we've been so damn busy."

CHAPTER 9

They were all standing around a table in the first-floor conference room. Marks and Anders stood on one side of the table: Stanley Cooper and John Mack on the other. The photos of the leg with the red triangles on it were spread out on the table before them. All the men circled the table to look at each picture from a different angle.

"I sent the pictures up to the state crime lab to see if they could be any help in identifying what the marks are from," John Mack said. "I'm not sure if I will get a quick response."

"It looks like somebody took a hot poker and stuck this guy in the leg a few times," Stanley said.

"Anders?" Marks asked.

"Definitely looks like somebody stuck this guy with something," he said. "I can't even guess what it might have been."

They were all silently looking over the pictures and didn't notice that the door to the conference room had opened and a middle-aged, gray-haired man had entered the room. He walked up to the end of the table and peered at the photos.

"Who the hell are you?" Marks asked.

The man bent over and gave the pictures a good look. He straightened up. "These marks that you see on this leg came from the heel of a woman's shoe, a high-heel."

Marks shook his head. "I asked who you are and now I will ask what you are talking about?"

"My name is Mike Burke, Chicago PD, retired. Back in 2008 and 2009 we worked a case in Chicago where our killer murdered five homeless people, four men and one woman. The cause of death in each case was the plunging of a long knife into the throat of the victims. In the last case the victim was able to scratch the assailant, leaving skin fragments under his nails. From the DNA from the skin, we were able to determine that the killer was a woman. At the scene of the last victim we found a broken heel from a woman's shoe. The tip of the heel was shaped like a triangle."

"Wait a minute," Marks said. "You said that your cases came from 08 and 09?"

Mike Burke nodded and smiled. "I think my killer went on vacation, a long break, and has decided to resume his activities here in Milton. I think your killer is my killer."

Marks, Anders, and Mike Burke retreated to the break room on the lower level. Marks got them all a cup of coffee as they sat at a table near the windows. "How the heck did you hear about us?" Marks asked.

Burke smiled. "God bless the *USA Today*. They had an article the other day highlighting the homeless murders taking place in the small town of Milton, Illinois. I knew it was my killer as soon as I saw it. I decided to drive up right away."

"You're retired and still spend winters in Chicago?" Anders asked.

"I'm not stupid if that's what you think. It wasn't my idea. My children started to have their own children and my wife won't stay away for the whole winter. We went to Arizona for two weeks after New Year's Day. Other than that, I freeze my butt of in Chicago."

"Tell me about your cases," Marks said.

Burke sipped his coffee. "Five in all, four men and one woman. One behind a restaurant, one under Lower Wacker, one under the El Tracks, one in an abandoned garage and the last one under a Christmas tree near the Lincoln Park Zoo. All killed the same way, stabbed in the throat with a long knife. The clues we had were the skin under the nails and the heel."

"No suspects?" Marks said.

"Maybe two," Burke said.

"What does that mean?"

"The first victim, Richard Archer, was a younger guy. He became homeless on his own. He wanted to experience the minimalist society. He had a sister, Pauline. She demanded justice and would show up at the precinct berating the Captain for updates on her brother's murder. She was a little unhinged. Sometime after the fifth murder, a month or so, I thought I'd look her up because she had stopped coming around, but she had been killed in a car accident. We thought we had something with the skin fragments and the heel, but then the murders stopped, and the investigation went into the cold case file."

"Who did you think your killer might be?"

"We got the information that our killer was tall, wore a black raincoat and a full brimmed black hat. Nobody ever got a good look at the face."

"Jesus," Anders said. "That's fits the description of our killer. We've come up for a name for him, The Shadow."

Burke was sipping his coffee and nearly spit it out. "My God. That's what we called our killer and it might not be a him."

. . . .

TH tried to call Steve Marks, but the call went right into voicemail. He took it upon himself to look up Maria Suarez and found that she lived on Pleasant Avenue, about three blocks in from the river and not too far from the casino. TH waited until ten o'clock to head to the apartment complex. There were only two buildings, three stories, all brick. He parked between the two. In the building to his left, he found nothing that indicated that Maria lived there; in the second he found her name listed as the tenant for Apartment B212.

He rang the bell for the unit but was not surprised when there was no answer. He thought that someone would leave the building, giving him the opportunity to get up to the second floor. He had to wait about fifteen minutes before he saw a young man, bearded, get off the elevator. The man was in a hurry as he pushed open the exit door, oblivious to TH. The man smelled of pot as he left the building. TH walked calmly into the open elevator and pushed the button for floor two.

It was easy to find Apartment B212. TH tried the bell on the side of the door, but again there was no answer. He pounded loudly on the door, but no one came. He was about to give up when the door next to Maria's was opened and a woman came out. She was dressed in a wrinkled business suit and was carrying a stuffed briefcase and a fatter purse. She looked up at TH in surprise.

"Oh, you scared me," she said. Her dark hair showed a few grays, her face lines around the eyes and poorly applied makeup.

"Sorry," TH said. "I'm trying to locate Maria Suarez."

Now the woman eyed him suspiciously. "Are you a bill collector?"

TH smiled. "Do I look like one?" He was wearing jeans, a Bears sweatshirt, and a leather jacket.

"Not really," she said.

"I'm just an old friend. I was in town and thought I'd look her up. Her phone number seems to have changed so I thought I'd stop by."

"Your timing is not very good," the woman said. "Usually, she goes to work. She works at the Burnett Furniture store in downtown Milton."

"What do you mean usually."

"She's gone. I heard she was going to Mexico on a trip. It was last week. I saw her getting into the car to take her to the airport."

"Was it an Uber or a private limo?"

"That was what I thought was odd. It was a dark black Range Rover with heavily tinted windows. I saw a guy help her with her bags and then they both got in the car. I didn't see the guy very well."

"What was so odd?"

"The car had Iowa plates. Seemed odd because I thought she'd get a ride from someone from Illinois."

TH shrugged. "Maybe it was a friend from Iowa?"

"Maybe," she said, smiling broadly, "but the only guy I've seen around her was Ricky Burnett. I saw him here at least three times. Don't tell anyone I said so because that's not supposed to be happening."

TH rode the elevator back to the first floor and went out into the parking lot. He checked out some of the cars parked in front of the building. All the spots were marked with the unit numbers of the apartments. He found the spot allotted to apartment B212. There was an old Toyota Camry in the spot. TH looked in the window. All he could see were a travel coffee mug and a crucifix hanging from the rear-view mirror. On the front wind shield he saw a sticker for employee parking at Burnett Furniture.

He went back into the building a found the bell for the building manager. He didn't know if anyone would be around, but he hit the buzzer. There was no quick answer, so he hit it again. This time he was buzzed in. He walked back into the lobby area and found the directions for the manager's office. Before he got halfway there, a short, pudgy man came out of the office. He had a badly groomed, short beard and was chomping on an unlit cigar.

"What the rush?" the man said.

"No rush," TH said. "I'm just trying to locate one of your tenants. I'm worried about her."

The man folded his arms over his chest. "Who might "she" be?"

"Maria Suarez. She's in B212. I've tried calling her with no answer. I see her car is in her spot."

"She's gone. Went on a trip."

"You know this for a fact?"

"She stopped by last week to tell me she was off to Mexico for a bit."

"When last week?"

He thought for a moment. "Would have been Monday or Tuesday."

"Mind if you take me upstairs to look in her unit?"

"Why would I do that unless you are a cop?"

TH smiled. "I'm not a cop, but I am good friends with Lou Katz, the Police Chief and Steve Marks, a detective. I could call them to come over and they would. Or you can take this and just let me see her apartment. Less than five minutes." TH handed the man a hundred-dollar bill.

The manager looked at the bill and shoved it into his pocket. "Five minutes," he said.

They quickly rode the elevator up to two and the manager used his master key to open the apartment. They walked into the place and TH immediately noticed how neat everything looked. The place smelled like air freshener had recently been used. It was a small apartment, one bedroom, one bath with a living room and small kitchen area. TH just wanted to see one room. He walked into the bedroom with the manager trailing right behind him.

He went right to the closet and opened the double doors. The closet was empty except for one old bathrobe and a pair of Nike running shoes, both well worn. TH moved back and found the tall dresser in the corner of the room. He pulled open every drawer. Each was empty.

"What the fuck?" the manager said.

"That sums it up," TH said. "Miss Suarez may have gone to Mexico, but I don't think she is coming back. You don't go on vacation and take every stitch of clothing you own."

"What the fuck?" the manager repeated.

• • •

Ricky Burnett had tried to call Micky Farrell three times, but Farrell had not answered. The fourth time was the charm; Farrell answered on the first ring. "I was going to get back to you in a little bit, Ricky. I've been busy."

"We need to talk Micky. There's been some trouble."

"What kind of trouble?"

"Kyle James kind of trouble."

Micky laughed. "I thought I'd teach the punk a little bit of a lesson."

Ricky exhaled deeply. "I thought we talked about that. I thought I said to hold off on doing anything with Kyle."

"Yeah, we did. I really did it because it felt right. This one is free of charge. No cost to you, Ricky."

"Micky, the cops are asking me about it. I've got Henry missing and the cops are asking me what I know about someone bashing Kyle in the knee in his parking lot."

"That's easy. Tell them you know nothing."

"That's what I told them," Ricky said loudly. "Unfortunately, someone saw us together at Jack Wheeler's and told the cops. They found out about Lisa and Kyle and tied the attack to me. They think I hired you to take care of Kyle."

"Tell them they are full of shit. Tell them you don't know a fucking thing."

"I did. I'm not sure they believe me."

Again, Micky laughed. "That's their job, not to believe you. There's no evidence that you had anything to do with Kyle. We talked at Wheeler's about bill collections. That was it. Beyond that, tell them to fuck off."

"It might cause me some issues, Micky."

"Look, sorry about your kid."

"I wish you hadn't gone after Kyle."

"Oh well," Micky said and he yawned. "I've got to go, Ricky."

Ricky wanted to respond but said nothing. The line went dead.

• • •

Mike Burke agreed to bring in the files he had on the murdered Chicago victims. Marks retreated to his office and called Tori, but the call went directly to voicemail. He felt a short jab to the stomach. His phone buzzed and he thought it might be her calling back, but the ID indicated it was TH Brown.

"Morning, TH," Marks said.

"Listen to this, Steve," TH said. He was excited. "You remember Gloria Forman, went to school with Rachel?"

"Can't say I do."

"Forget that. Gloria works for Ricky's Milton store. I bought her a couple of drinks last night and she told me an interesting story. Ricky has a young lady working for him by the name of Maria Suarez, a very attractive Latino. It seems the two of them have hit it off. They have been seen leaving work in the same direction on several occasions."

Marks shifted in his chair. "Where's this going, TH?"

"Let me get there. I went by Maria's apartment this morning, just for a look see. I met her neighbor who tells me that Ricky has been a frequent visitor. I went to visit Maria, but there was no answer at her apartment. I got the superintendent to show me in. All of her clothes, every stitch, had been removed from her place."

"She's ducked out?"

"Both the neighbor and Gloria told me they thought she had gone to Mexico on a trip. The neighbor lady told me she saw Maria get into a Range Rover with Iowa plates. This was Monday or Tuesday; the day Henry was kidnapped."

"No shit?"

"This is no bullshit, Steve. The woman is gone and not on a vacation. Two distinct sources told me she was headed to Mexico. Maria had some strong connections to Ricky Burnett."

Marks felt his heart race accelerate. His palms were sweaty. "Let me get my guys together. Sit tight for a bit. I think we need to talk with Ricky. Sounds like his little girlfriend might be up to something."

Moments later, after finding Anders, they were gathered in Lou Katz' office. Lou listened to the story that TH had relayed to Marks. "So Ricky was banging this Maria and she has suddenly disappeared, maybe to Mexico and maybe on the day that Henry was kidnapped?" Lou said.

"That's what TH said. No proof of anything, but, I mean, way too much to overlook."

Lou scratched his chin. "You gotta talk to Ricky and I would say sooner than later."

"Yeah," Marks said. "First this thing with Kyle and now Maria Suarez."

"Wait a minute," Anders said. "What did you say her last name was?"

"Suarez," Marks said.

"Shit," Anders said. "That's the last name of Rodrigo Lopez' sister. Tammy just dug that up."

They all looked at each other for a minute, stunned. "We've really got to talk to Ricky and like now," Marks said.

"Let's not get too crazy here, Steve. Talk to him privately, not near his father. I don't want the dad calling the mayor about this," Lou said.

Right before they left, Marks phone buzzed again. He thought it might be Tori so he stopped for a moment. It wasn't Tori. It was the Animal Hospital. Probably looking for him to come and get Buster.

"Hello," he said.

"Detective Marks, it's Susie."

Marks exhaled deeply. "Yes, Susie. I'm a little busy."

"Oh, I'm sorry. Maybe I should call back later."

Marks instantly felt bad. "That's okay. How is Buster doing?"

"He's fine. He seems a lot happier than when you brought him in here. Doesn't smell anymore, either."

Marks smiled. "That's great, Susie, but I've got to run."

"Okay, okay. It's just that you told me to call you if someone came in and asked about Buster."

This caught Marks by surprises. "Repeat that."

"You said to call if someone came in and asked about Buster."

"I did. Did somebody come by?"

"Yeah, yesterday. I was on my lunch break, but Janie was here working the desk. She forgot to tell me until just now. She said some weird looking dude came in and wanted to know about Buster, you know, how he was doing."

"Is Janie working today?"

"Yeah, up until six. Is this important?"

"It might be. We've got a couple of other calls to make but tell Janie that we are going to come out and talk to her today."

"She's not in any trouble for forgetting to tell me, is she?"

Marks laughed. "No, not at all. Just tell her we're coming by." He hung up the phone as Anders appeared in his doorway.

"You're laughing," Anders said.

"Somebody came over to the Animal Hospital and asked how Buster was doing."

"Wow. Two leads in less than an hour."

"We'll head over there after talking to Ricky."

•　•　•

They quietly asked Ricky if they could speak to him in private. Ricky shrugged; the rest of the family said nothing as Ricky led them back to his den. He closed the door behind them. "What is this about?" Ricky asked.

"What this is about is Maria Suarez," Marks said.

Ricky swallowed hard; his face reddened. "What about Maria?"

Marks felt he was losing his patience. "What's going on with her, Ricky, and spare me the bullshit."

Ricky closed his eyes for a moment. "She's a woman that works for me. We became attracted to each other, but it's not what you think. It was just a fling. I told her that we had to end it. It was just one of those little fun things."

"And she is related to Rodrigo Lopez, who is the husband of Marguerite, who is your nanny?"

"She's is Rodrigo's sister, but so what? She's a nice girl. She has nothing to do with Henry."

"You're sure," Marks said loudly. "Where is she now?"

"When I broke it off, she said she wanted to go somewhere and be alone. She went to Mexico, I think, for a couple of weeks."

"And cleaned all of her clothes out of her apartment?"

"What?"

"Her apartment.. She has completely removed every piece of clothing and personal effects from her apartment. It doesn't look like two weeks. It looks more like forever."

Ricky hung his head and shook it slowly. "This has nothing to do with Henry."

"You didn't think it was important to tell us the Marguerite's sister-in-law works for you?" Anders said. "This is a woman who may have more than a casual knowledge of the daily habits of your family."

Ricky's head shot up. "Not from me," he said loudly.

"Relax, Ricky," Marks said. "No one is blaming you, but this Maria may have picked up information from

Marguerite, Rodrigo or you as time went by. We've got to find her."

Ricky nodded slowly. "She told me she was going to Mexico."

Reluctantly, Marks believed him. "We'll have to check with Marguerite and Rodrigo. Something is not right here."

Ricky placed his hand on Marks' arm. "Lisa and my parents don't need to hear about this, do they?"

Marks took Ricky's hand and lifted it off his arm. "Right now, there are more important things to worry about than what your family thinks about you dillying one of your employees."

"Might explain why he spent so much time in his stores," Anders said as they drove to the Lopez house.

"Or not at his stores, "Marks said. "What's good for Lisa is good for Ricky."

"Except maybe Ricky's fling may lead us to finding Henry," Anders said.

Marks was a little skeptical. "Maybe. We'll see."

• • •

Marguerite and Rodrigo were both home when the detectives arrived. They sent their children into their rooms while they talked to the police. Marguerite looked nervous; Rodrigo wore the look of someone who'd had trouble with the police before. Marks and Anders stood before them as they sat on a couch; Marguerite took Rodrigo's hand.

"Is Henry alright?" she asked.

"There is no word about Henry," Marks said.

"Why are you here?" Rodrigo said.

Marks looked at Rodrigo. He was a stout man, big gut and with a dark beard. Marks felt his dark eyes were trying to look through him. "We are looking for your sister, Maria."

Rodrigo's eyes widened. "Maria? Why are you looking for Maria?"

"She had suddenly become a person of interest in Henry's disappearance."

"Maria?" he said. "You are crazy if you believe that, detective."

"Why didn't you tell us that Maria worked for Ricky Burnett?" He addressed the question to Marguerite.

"Why? Is that important?" Rodrigo said loudly.

"It might be," Marks said. "It appears that she was carrying on a relationship with Ricky Burnett that was cozier than your normal employee/boss situation."

"That's ridiculous," Rodrigo said.

"Stop!" Marguerite suddenly said. "Stop all of this dodging the truth."

"Marguerite, don't," Rodrigo said.

"Don't what?" Marks said.

Marguerite rubbed away tears that had formed in the corner of her eyes; she took a deep breath. "Maria has been seeing Mr. Burnett. She has fallen for him. He promised her things. We think she thought that Mr. Burnett might leave his wife and marry her."

"You didn't believe that this would happen?"

"Not at all. We told her that she was crazy to believe that."

Marks thought about it for a minute. "Do you know if this relationship was still going on?"

Marguerite shook her head. "It ended about a month ago. Mr. Burnett told her it couldn't go on."

"I take it she was upset?"

"She was very upset," Rodrigo said. "He took advantage of her. She's an attractive woman; he is the boss at the company she works for."

"So she told you some things about the relationship and you told her that she was crazy to think anything might come out of it?" Marks said.

"We did," Marguerite said.

"Did you tell her anything else? Did you ever tell her about the comings and goings at the Burnett house? Did you tell her anything about the daily routine of the Burnett family?"

"Wait one second, detective," Rodrigo said loudly. "We advised her on fooling around with Ricky Burnett. Neither one of us ever mentioned anything about the Burnett household. Why would you ask such a question?"

"Where is your sister, Rodrigo?"

"I don't know. I haven't spoken to her for a couple of weeks or so. I don't know where she is right now."

"Know anything about a trip to Mexico?"

Marguerite and Rodrigo looked at each other. Rodrigo spoke. "We don't know anything about that. She never mentioned anything about going to Mexico."

Marks nodded. "The people at the store that she worked at said she was going on vacation to Mexico. A tenant in her apartment building confirmed the same thing. She's saying she was going off to Mexico, but I don't know. She has taken every piece of clothing out of her apartment, including summer and winter wear. I don't think she went to Mexico."

Rodrigo looked at Marks. His look had softened from earlier. "Like I said. She was very upset about Ricky Burnett. She may have gone somewhere to get away for a bit. Where she went, I don't know. We have no idea."

Marks returned his attention to Marguerite. "And you have never mentioned anything to Maria about the Burnett's."

"Never," she said quickly.

"My sister is a good girl," Rodrigo said. "She might not be the smartest one, but she would never be involved in anything like the kidnapping of a little boy."

•   •   •

"So where is Maria Suarez?" Anders asked. They were on their way to the animal hospital.

"Your guess is as good as mine. TH told me the tenant saw her get into a Range Rover with Iowa plates. That doesn't mean she's in Iowa. I'm going to get a check with the airlines for last week, any that went to Mexico, to rule that out."

"Have to probably go out of O'Hare."

"I thought that."

249

"You know, Tammy told me that Ricky and Clay Johnson used to be tight. Maybe he knows something about Ricky and Maria's little romance."

"They were buddies a while ago. Most thought Clay was interested in Ricky's money and cars because it would attract chicks. It probably did, and Clay would be in for that. I don't know that he would know that much about Ricky these days."

"Couldn't hurt to ask."

Marks nodded slightly. "It couldn't."

"Leave no stone unturned, I think you said once."

"Did I? Might make sense, I suppose."

• • •

It was a short drive from the Lopez residence to the Milton Animal Hospital. They parked right in front and walked in. The place didn't look busy. In the lobby of the hospital, they found two young girls looking at a computer screen. They were both giggling. One was Susie; Marks thought the other would be Janie.

"Oh, high Detective Marks," Susie said.

"Hi Susie," Marks said. "Is this Janie?"

The other girl lowered her eyes and stopped giggling. She was about the same age as Susie, but with dark hair. She also wore glasses. "I'm Janie Glassmen," she said.

"This is Detective Hedberg. He is helping me on the case."

"Detective Marks thinks that Buster was the dog of the guy stabbed out by the casino," Susie said.'

"You don't think that the guy who came in here asking about Buster was some sort of a serial killer, do you?" Janie asked. Her eyes were on Marks now and she looked alert.

"Nothing that serious, I don't think," Marks said, "but we would like to ask you a few questions."

"But you're not sure," Janie snapped.

"Relax girls," Anders said. "Nothing bad is going to happen. We just want to see if the person you saw knew anything about how Buster got here. Buster may have been wandering around and this guy might have picked him up and dropped him off. This person may have nothing to do with the crime."

The words coming from the younger detective calmed the girls. Even Janie smiled a bit.

"You got a pretty good look at this guy?" Anders asked Janie.

"Yeah, like real good. He was standing right where you guys are. I talked with him for several minutes."

"Can you describe him?"

"I wish we had a police artist," Marks said.

"I can draw," Anders said. "Do you have a pencil and a clean piece of paper?"

Susie looked through some of the drawers and came up with a pencil and a white piece of paper.

"Describe him," Marks said. "Tall or short?"

Janie tilted her head to one side and closed one eye for a bit. "I'd say tall like you."

"So maybe six-two?" Marks said.

"If that's how tall you are," she said.

"Touche'" Anders said.

"What?" Susie asked.

"Forget it," Marks said. "What was he wearing?"

"That's easy. Jeans and a black shirt, button down. Also had on an old brown, leather jacket."

"Okay, that's good," Marks said. "What about the face?"

Again the head tilt and one closed eye. "Narrow face," she said. "Not much skin to it, kind of pointy. Pointy nose and pointy chin. Eyes caught me off guard. They were a bright blue. His hair was long, hanging down to his shoulders. That and his eyebrows were a muted gray."

"Any other features of his face that you recall?"

She shook her head. "Just the nose and chin. They seem to come to a sharp point, like one of those pairs of pliers."

"A needle nose?" Anders said.

"That's it. He also had some accent that said he wasn't from here. Sounded something like he was from England or maybe up by where all those Kennedys come from. Where is that, like New Hampshire?"

"Massachusetts," Anders said.

"Yeah, something like that."

Anders made a few changes to the sketch and showed it to Janie. "Look anything like this?"

Janie stared at the drawing. Marks moved closer to the counter to get a better look at what Anders had done. He thought the drawing was impressive but got anxious when he saw the scrunched up look on Janie's face. "What is it?" he said.

Janie took a deep breath. "That's the guy. That's the guy that came in here to ask about Buster."

"No doubts?" Anders asked.

She shook her head. "Not one."

"Either of you ever see this guy before?" Marks asked.

They both answered no. Marks nodded. "This guy shows up again, you tell him to wait a second and go into the back room where the animals are held and you call us right away."

"He's not a killer is he?" Susie said.

Anders looked over at Marks. "We don't think so, but maybe he can lead us to someone you committed that murder behind the casino."

•   •   •

They were back at the Burnett home. The FBI had been there and had conducted some preliminary interviews. The mood in the house was tense; there was no real news of where Henry was. There was a distinct possibility that whoever took him meant to keep him. Ricky seemed irritated that Marks and Anders had returned. He led them back to the den.

"I told you guys that it was a stupid mistake, getting involved with Maria. I told you that. I also told you that I ended that relationship. As far as I know, she went to Mexico like she told me."

"Marguerite Lopez and her husband said you promised her some pretty lofty stuff," Marks said.

"I didn't promise her a damn thing," Ricky said, his face reddening. "We were fooling around, period. That was it."

"You ever get together with Clay Johnson while you were with Maria?"

"Clay Johnson?"

"You know who I mean, Ricky," Marks said.

"Okay," he said. "I drove Maria into Dubuque a couple of times. We met up with Clay at a bar or two. We had some drinks, danced a bit. You know."

Marks wasn't sure he knew exactly what Ricky meant. "What did Clay think of Maria?'

Ricky smiled. "What do you think he thought of her? She is gorgeous and that's what Clay thought."

"The last person who saw Maria around here says she got into a black Range Rover with Iowa plates."

Ricky swallowed hard. "Clay drives a black Range Rover."

• • •

They were driving back to headquarters. Marks put in a call to TH Brown. He answered on the first ring. "This Maria Suarez, I think she might have gone up to Iowa with our old friend, Clay Johnson," Marks said.

"You don't say."

"Ricky told us they had gone to Dubuque a couple of times and had hung out with Clay. Clay thought Maria was gorgeous."

"If it wore a skirt, Clay would think it was gorgeous."

"That's true, but we have this connection of Maria getting in a black Range Rover with Iowa plates. Clay drives a black Range Rover."

"That's something. Maybe he drove her to the airport."

"I don't know. Ricky dumped her and suddenly she's driving away in a car that might be Clay's."

"Or might not."

"Can you check? Clay doesn't care for me. He might tell you something."

TH yawned. Coming back to Midwest from California always messed with his sleep. "I'll call him."

"Don't spook him too much."

"You don't think that Clay is somehow involved in taking Henry, do you?"

Somehow involved, Marks thought? "I don't know. The woman is the sister of the Burnett nanny. Ricky Burnett scorns her. She disappears. The kidnapping ring funnels children through Dubuque. Clay Johnson maybe gives her a ride. This is fucked up, but well worth looking into."

"Let me call Clay and see what he knows."

. . .

"Who is this guy? Lou Katz said. They were all in his office looking at the drawing that Anders had made.

"I sent a copy of the picture over to Mike Burke to look at, but he hasn't gotten back to me," Marks said.

"Yeah, but those murders up in Chicago were twelve, thirteen years ago," Lou said.

"Guy could have changed his appearance in all of those years," Anders added. "Face looks tight, like work was done."

"No doubt," Marks said. "Looks a little like an old - fashioned hippie artist."

"It's the best I could do," Anders said. "It's only a depiction, based on what Janie told us. I don't know how accurate it is."

"Don't apologize," Lou said.

Stanley Cooper walked into the room and sipped coffee from a travel mug. He looked at the drawing sitting on Lou's desk.

"Recognize him?" Marks asked.

Stanley peered at the picture and put his reading glasses on. "That's that guy Turley that runs that llama farm west of the town, near Plato."

"Llama farm?" Lou said.

"That's what he raises He's got about fifty of them running around on that little ranch. We went in there one time to look around. Strange guy, but that drawing looks just like him."

Marks looked at Anders. "Guess we should take a ride over there and see this guy."

"What are your thoughts on this Maria Suarez?" Lou said.

"She was sleeping with Ricky Burnett and he squashed that. She may know something about what Lisa was up to during the week, but would she really kidnap Ricky's son to get back at him? Sounds a little farfetched."

"But a witness saw her get into a car with Iowa plates," Anders said.

"Think TH can get anything out of Clay Johnson?" Lou asked.

"I suppose if Clay had any idea that Maria was involved in a crime, he would tell us what he knew," Marks said. "He might think she's a great looking woman if he's involved with her, but he is not going to jeopardize his career over her."

Lou ran his hand through his hair. "Let's see what he tells TH. In the meantime, why don't you and Anders go see the llama guy?"

. . . . . .

The sun was up and it was warming outside. Marks still hadn't heard anything from Tori, but that wasn't that strange. There were times when she got into her "artist mode" that she just worked on a sculpture and nothing else mattered to her. There were days where she didn't check her phone. It pissed Marks off, but he knew she was like that. At least he hoped that was why she hadn't checked in with him.

He had called TH Brown and left a message on his phone. He told TH that he wanted him to check with Clay Johnson about anything that he knew about Maria Suarez as fast as he could. He hoped that TH would get to Clay quickly and they could try and pin down where the Suarez woman went, if Clay knew.

The llama guy was named Lloyd Turley. As Stanley had said, he owned a nice-sized ranch east of town where he raised llamas. As Marks and Anders drove up the long driveway to the house, they could see several of the exotic looking creatures roaming idly in the fields along the way.

"Wonder what he does with them," Anders said.

"We can ask," Marks added as they pulled up to the house.

The house that Lloyd Turley lived in was a two-story, stone structure that looked almost Medieval. It was a beautiful building fronted by several large pine trees. There was a huge wooden front door that had a large brass knocker of a llama's head on it. There was also a conventional doorbell. Marks gave the doorbell a push.

They didn't have to wait long. The door was opened by an older man, gray haired, wearing bifocals. He was dressed in jeans with a denim shirt. His neck was adorned with a red scarf that was tucked into the shirt. He looked over the bifocals at the two detectives. "I saw your car coming up the drive," Lloyd Turley said.

"I'm Detective Marks. This is Anders Hedberg. We'd like to ask you a few questions," Marks said.

Turley still glared over his glasses at them. "I can give you a few minutes. Step into my study."

Turley turned away from them and led them into the house. Anders smiled; Marks shrugged. The first thing they saw was an enormous knight in armor over eight feet tall. This figure guarded the front foyer. Turley led them into a large room, bookshelf lined, that held an old desk and several leather chairs. He walked behind the desk but remained standing. He pointed out two chairs to Marks and Anders.

"Cool house you have here," Marks said.

"I like it. It took a while to build, but it's amazingly comfortable."

Marks nodded. "This is also a nice piece of land, good for your little ranch."

"Not so little, Detective. Twenty acres, perfect for the llamas."

"What do you do with them?"

"The llamas? I raise them. I have over a hundred and twenty as we speak."

"What's the endgame?" Anders asked. "Do people buy them? You can't eat them, can you?"

Turley winced at that comment. "Of course not, unless your starving, I guess. Like lambs, I raise them for their coats. Their hair makes excellent sweaters, coats, hats, and gloves. Very profitable, I might add."

"That's impressive," Anders said.

"How old are you?" Turley said.

"The reason we are here, Mr. Turley," Marks said, "is that we understand that you went by the Milton Animal Hospital and asked about a stray that had been turned in, a mutt called Buster."

"I did, Detective. I was the one who brought Buster into the hospital. I found him wandering along the road out on 20. He looked very scared and cold. I took him over there and tied him to the fence where the help could find him."

"You found him on 20? What night would that have been?"

"That would have been last Sunday night. As I was driving along, I noticed him standing on the side of the road. I slowed and noticed he was wearing a chain and a collar. I let him into the back seat of my truck and drove him to the hospital. I would have taken him home with me, but he smelled God awful. I tied him to the fence post and left him there. I should have done more, but I thought he would have been killed out on 20."

"What time do you think this was?"

"I don't know for sure, but sometime after twelve, maybe near one. I was out at the casino; I have this stupid little thing for penny slots. I lose a hundred or two and then I come home. I go there maybe once or twice a week."

"Did you go with anyone or see anyone you knew out there?" Anders asked.

Turley smiled. "I always go alone and have never seen anyone that I know. It's kind of my private little vice."

"And yesterday," Marks said, "you went to check on how Buster was doing?"

"That was it. I had been terribly busy with the ranch, and I'd almost forgotten about him. I just thought I'd pop in and see that he was okay. I felt bad leaving him tied up out there and I hoped he'd done alright."

"Do you know that Buster belonged to a homeless man who was murdered behind the casino the night you were there?" Marks asked.

Turley's hand went up to his mouth. "My god. I read about that. I had no idea."

"You would have called us had you realized that?"

"Of course. What a terrible crime."

Marks looked at Lloyd Turley for a moment. He got the feeling that he was dealing with an eccentric, llama rancher who had a thing for penny slots who found a stray on Route 20 and turned him into the animal hospital. "I think that should do it," Marks said.

In the car, Anders seemed upset. "You didn't question him much about the murders."

Marks turned quickly to look at him. "What do you mean? I believed what he said about finding Buster. He went to Aces, lost some money, and found him on the side of the road along 20. This was after Herbert had been killed. It made sense to me."

"So, you don't think there's a possibility that he could have killed Herbert and then grabbed Buster?"

"I don't. Plus, we think we might be looking for a woman."

"Okay," Anders said. "The guy was just a little creepy, odd."

"Maybe, but I believed him."

.   .   .

"You'll never guess who we just picked up," Stanley Cooper said. He was standing in the doorway to Marks' office. Marks was trying to reach TH Brown; Anders was thinking about Lloyd Turley.

Marks hung up the phone. "You're not going to really make me guess, are you Stanley?"

"There was a disturbance at The Witches Cauldron. A patron thought one of the witches shortchanged him on a lap dance. He started a bit of a row and got decked by a bigger, badder, bouncer. Turns out the troublemaker is Micky Farrell."

"You don't say?"

"All true. He's cooling his jets downstairs. We've got Kyle James coming by to have a look at him; he was released from the hospital. Maybe he can identify him as the person who kneecapped him."

"That's something, but I need something on Henry Burnett or the killer of homeless people."

"Lloyd Turley is not the killer?"

"Nope. Just a guy who raises llamas and goes to the casino occasionally. Found Buster on the side of the road and took him over to the animal hospital for some help. I don't think he had anything to do with the murders."

"I'm not sure," Anders said.

"Anders thinks he's creepy," Marks said.

"He is creepy and I think he bears looking at further."

"Anything else Stanley?"

"Yeah. One more thing. Micky Farrell wants to talk with you."

"Me?"

"He named you in his request. Said, 'I want to talk with Detective Marks'."

"Set him up in room three with the intercom and one-way. We'll talk to him when Kyle gets here. I want Kyle to see him and hear him."

"No problem," Stanley said.

"Did Micky say why he wanted to talk with me?"

"Not at all. What I told you was what he said."

"Let me know when Kyle gets here."

• • •

Lisa came into the kitchen where Ricky was washing dishes, something he never did. She grabbed a towel and dried a glass that was in the rack. "What did the police want with you in the den?" she asked. "Do they know something more about Henry that they are not telling me. They've talked to you privately a couple of times."

He felt his face go flush. "It's nothing like that. It has to do with an employee of mine. Her name is Maria Suarez. She was supposed to be on vacation in Mexico, but Marks isn't so sure. She is missing."

"Maria Suarez," she said. "That's Marguerite's sister-in-law, I believe. "I've heard that she is very attractive."

Ricky looked right at her. "She is a nice -looking woman."

"I have also heard that you are screwing her."

"What? That's outrageous. She is an employee of mine."

She waved her hand at him. "It's not important. You know that I have been seeing Kyle James and Jack Wheeler, so I guess we are kind of even."

"This is not about being even, Lisa. This is about our little boy. He's out there and he is alone. This is also about our marriage."

Her eyes filled with tears. "I don't know what happened, Ricky, but when Henry got taken it was like I got a wake-up call. I realized for the first time what I was doing. I wasn't trying to recapture my youth like my friends say. I realized that I needed something else."

"So you decided to fuck around with an auto mechanic and a cocaine addict?"

"No. I decided I needed someone and something else. I love Henry when I am with him, but I also love my freedom. I used to love you until I realized that you love your stores more than you love me and Henry, too."

His eyes narrowed. "You used to love me?"

A single tear rolled out of her left eye. "I used to love you, Ricky, but that was a long time ago. Now, I want to get our son back and I want to move on with my life. I have made many awful mistakes in the past, but I know what I want now. I have made that decision." She hung up the towel that she had been using and left the kitchen.

Ricky washed one more coffee cup, scrubbing angrily at a stubborn coffee stain. He placed the cup in the drainer and looked out the window. A goose was waddling across the fairway.

•   •   •

Tammy called Anders while he was still sitting in Marks' office. They were waiting for Kyle James to show up. "I checked with all of the major airlines. There is no record of a Maria Suarez leaving for Mexico in the last week. I also checked with the passport office. Maria Suarez doesn't have a current passport."

Anders shook his head. "That's all great stuff, Tammy."

"See you tonight? she asked.

"Don't think so. I have to keep an eye on someone tonight. I'll be in touch," he said.

"Young love," Marks said. His phone rang before Anders could respond. "Hello," he said.

"It's TH," TH Brown said.

"Good news for me?"

"Clay said that he met Maria a couple of times when Ricky brought her up to Dubuque. They went to a couple of bars, had a few drinks, but that was about it. Said she was a good -looking woman. He said it was a good thing Ricky had money because he could sure bring in the ladies."

"Had no idea about her going to Mexico?"

"Not one. He said he hasn't seen her in a while."

Marks nodded. "Thanks for checking, TH. I'll keep you posted." Marks hung up the phone. "You get all of that?"

"Clay Johnson doesn't know much about Maria Suarez. Tammy told me that no airlines has any record of a Maria Suarez heading to Mexico. She also checked and confirmed that Maria Suarez doesn't have a valid passport."

"So, let me give you some thoughts. Ricky breaks up with Maria. She is upset and tells everyone that she is going to Mexico for a little vacation. Little Henry Burnett is kidnapped. Maria probably knows Lisa Burnett's daily routine better than anyone. Somebody in a black Range Rover with Iowa plates picks up Maria the day she is supposed to be headed for Mexico."

"You think Maria took little Henry to get back at Ricky and is somewhere in Iowa?"

"That's what I think."

"But no ransom demand has been made."

"That's the part I don't get. Maybe she isn't looking for ransom. Maybe she's looking to hold onto Henry permanently. She couldn't have Ricky, but maybe she can have his kid."

"Sounds a little nutty."

"Maybe. Do you have anything better?"

"Nope."

"Let's try and find Maria Suarez. I'm going to put out an APB and also call Clay Johnson. I'm thinking she's in Dubuque. He can find her if anyone can."

· · · ·

Marks asked Anders to leave his office so that he could call Clay Johnson. Anders closed the door behind him. It wasn't that Marks thought that the call would be contentious, but he'd had a bad history with Clay. He wasn't sure how the call would go.

Clay's secretary asked who was calling when Marks called; she said Clay was in a meeting. Marks told her who he was and that the matter was extremely important. Clay picked up the phone moments later. "It must be really important if you called me instead of TH Brown."

"Hello, Clay," Marks said. "I would say it is very important."

There was a sigh from Clay. "What can I do for you, Marks?"

"We are looking for a woman. Her name is Maria Suarez; I can text you a picture of her. We think she might be involved in the kidnapping of Henry Burnett, Ricky's kid. We think she might be in Dubuque. I just ordered an APB on her. I'd like to ask for some special consideration to help find her."

"TH already told me about this woman. I told him I had met her when she was with Ricky. I can't recall exactly when this was, but it was a while ago. I told TH that I don't know more than that."

"We think she might be in your neighborhood."

"Yeah, TH told me about the Black Range Rover with the Iowa plates. That doesn't mean she's in Dubuque. Iowa isn't a small state."

Marks rubbed his eyes. "Look, Clay, I don't know what else I can tell you. I'm trying to find little Henry. This Maria Suarez sounds like a spurned woman who might be looking to get a little revenge on Ricky. That's all we've got that makes any sense. The woman has flown the coop here, taken all of her clothes. Her family knows nothing. I think she's local."

Marks could only hear Clay breathing. "I'll put out an alert for her, Steve. TH already sent me her picture, but I know what she looks like. Nice looking gal. We'll take a look, but there's no way I can promise you much."

"I get that. I'm just trying to find Henry and help Ricky. He is still a friend of yours?"

"He is," Clay said. "I said we'll take a look."

"I heard a compliment about you that nothing happens in Dubuque without you knowing about it."

Clay Johnson smiled. "That's probably true. We'll take a look for Maria Suarez and we'll let you know."

Before Marks could thank Clay or say anything, the line went dead.

• • • •

Kyle James showed up around half an hour later. His injured knee was heavily bandaged and he was using crutches to get around. He was moving slowly and awkwardly.

"You've got the guy that smashed my knee?" Kyle said when he saw Marks.

"I see you're moving around," Marks said.

"If you call this moving. Did you get the guy?"

"Maybe. We're going to talk with him about something else, but you'll be able to get a good look at him and hear him speak."

"I told you guys it was dark when he attacked me. I didn't get the best look at him," Kyle said.

"Try and listen hard to him, Kyle. It might be the best we get if he's the guy."

They rode an elevator down to the lower level and Marks led the way to the area where the interrogation rooms were located. They could see one large pane of glass where a room was lit up. Marks looked into the room. Stanley Cooper was talking with a squat, tough looking guy who Marks figured was Micky Farrell.

"He can't see us?" Kyle asked. "I don't want this fucking guy showing up in my parking lot again."

"Can't see us and can't hear us. Take a good look."

Kyle peered long and hard at Micky Farrell. "This guy has the same square shaped head and the ears stick out enough and they're kind of curled at the tops."

"Like cauliflower ears?"

"Yeah, like what boxers and wrestlers get."

"But you're not sure?"

"Nope. Can I hear him talk?"

"Sure." Marks reached across and flipped a switch on a panel in front of him.

"You know that girl took my money and she danced for like thirty seconds. She totally ripped me off," Micky Farrell said.

"Why didn't you ask to speak to the manager instead of starting a brawl?" Stanley asked.

"Would have ended the same way. All of those fuckin places, they do the same shit, always trying to rip people off."

"That's him," Kyle said. "Sounds like the guy has been smoking since he was ten years old. Sounds like his throat is loaded with chipped glass."

Marks reached over and turned off the sound. "You sure about this, Kyle?"

"Pretty clear on his looks; real clear on the voice. I heard him speak enough. It's him."

Marks thanked Kyle for coming in and walked him back to the elevators. He walked down the other side of the floor and to the room that held Micky Farrell. He rapped on the door twice and entered.

Micky Farrell turned to see him walk into the room. Stanley got up and let Marks have his chair at the table. Micky Farrell had a rugged face, weather beaten with a couple of short scars. His left eye had been blacked, from the encounter with the bouncer. He smiled at Marks. "Detective Marks," Micky said.

"Hello, Micky. I heard you wanted to talk with me."

"I do want to talk with you."

"That's great, but first we have few things to discuss with you. First we have the little altercation at the Witches Cauldron."

"The girl screwed me. She danced for about a half a minute and left."

"She said you grabbed at her," Stanley said.

Micky waved a hand. "That's bullshit. I may have touched her ass, but I didn't grab her."

"The dancer had bruising on her butt and her leg, Steve," Stanley said.

"Wasn't me," Micky said.

"Forget that for a minute. Tell me about Kyle James," Marks said.

"I don't know Kyle James."

"He said he knows you. Says you showed up in his parking lot a couple of days ago and whacked him on the knee with a crowbar. He's done a positive ID on you and is ready to press charges."

Micky Farrell rubbed a hand over his face. Little beads of sweat appeared on his forehead. He wiped them with his sleeve. "You guys know Ricky Burnett?"

"We do," Marks said.

"Ricky asked me to look into something for him that I'm sure will interest you."

"What does this have to do with the Cauldron or Kyle James?" Marks asked.

Micky smiled. "It looks and sounds like I'm a little fucked here, so maybe what I tell you can help me out of this little jam."

"So you tell us something and get you off the hook for these infractions?"

"Yeah, something like that."

"You know I can't do that, Micky. I'm sure we can settle something with the Cauldron, but Kyle's knee is in bad shape. I'm not sure he's ready to just say let's forget it."

"I've got money. I can offer him some money." There was that smile again.

"I can't speak for Kyle, but I can talk with him," Marks said. "Of course it's based on what you tell us and I want to warn you. If you know something about Henry Burnett's disappearance, you'd better tell me, regardless of what happens to you. If you withhold anything from us, I'll make sure you get tagged as an accessory to that crime."

The smile went away and Micky swallowed hard. "About a month ago I was talking with Ricky about other things, bill collections, normal business bullshit. We were at Wheeler's and he'd had a couple of drinks. He asked me if I knew anything about moving a child out of the country."

Marks felt his shoulder and neck muscles tighten. "Move a kid out of the country?"

"I didn't know what he was talking about. I asked him to clarify for me. He then asked if we wanted to move a child out of the US and into a foreign country, maybe to Europe, did I have any idea how to get this done?"

"Ricky Burnett asked you this?"

"Yeah, no shit. I asked him what kid he was talking about and he told me it was a hypothetical situation. I asked if he was talking about snatching some kid, maybe from a bad custody situation and trying to move him or her abroad. He took a big swig of his cocktail and told me to forget it. Said he was trying to help somebody out. I told him I wanted nothing to do with anything like that. Anyway you looked at it, it was kidnapping. He laughed and just told me to forget it."

"When did you say that you had this little conversation?" Marks said.

"Like, a month ago. I forgot all about it until I heard Ricky's kid was gone. I think on that one you'd better take a hard look at Ricky."

"I gotta run, Stanley," Marks said as he started for the door. "I've got to get over to the Burnett's."

"You'll remember what I told you? Won't you, Detective Marks?" Micky Farrell said.

There was no answer from Marks. He was already out of the interrogation room.

• • •

Marks had supervised the interview with Micky Farrell on his own because he had given Anders permission to return to Sterling to have the bad tooth dealt with. Anders hated the dentist, hated the scraping of his teeth with sharp instruments, but he had let the cavity go and now it was reminding him with every bite he took that something was wrong. He asked the dentist, Doctor Beasely, for double Novacaine, but only got a laugh for a response. Whatever it was that Beasely shot into his gums seemed to be doing the trick. Anders felt nothing as the dentist worked to repair the tooth.

In the chair, leaning back with his mouth open and the bright light in his eyes, Anders thought of Lloyd Turley, the llama rancher. He wasn't happy that Marks had given up on Turley so quickly. Turley said he made regular visits to the Aces Casino to quell his urge to gamble. Anders could buy that. What he couldn't understand was why Turley would pick up a stray dog on a freezing night and just tie him to a fence outside of the animal hospital, leaving the poor dog to deal with hours of cold, brutal weather. Obviously, Turley had a love of animals. Wouldn't it make more sense to take the mutt home with him, leave it in the garage for the night, and take it to the animal hospital in the morning? That made more sense to Anders. Then Turley had returned to the hospital to the hospital to check on Buster. Did Turley not want to be associated with the dog, the dog of a murder victim? Something wasn't right about the situation. Anders felt that Lloyd Turley needed further watching. He didn't think Marks would authorize any surveillance, but he could do it on his own. That's what he would do. Once he got out of the damned dentist's office.

• • •

Marks drove as quickly as he could to Ricky Burnett's house. He had called Anders but got no response. He was probably in the dentist's chair. Marks walked up the walkway and into the house without ringing the bell. Donny Briggs got up quickly when Marks entered the house but sat back down when he saw who it was. The family members stared at Marks with worry on their faces as his abrupt entrance signaled that something was wrong.

Marks scanned all of the family members. One was missing. "Where's Ricky?" he asked.

They all were quiet for a moment. Finally, Lisa spoke. "Has something bad happened?"

Marks understood that his bursting in the house gave the impression that something was amiss. "Nothing is wrong, but I need to talk with Ricky."

Ricky's father stood. "Ricky got a call. He said he had to go out for a bit. He left an hour ago."

"Got a call from who? Where did he go?"

The family shared glances with each other, no words. "He didn't say," Lisa said. "He said he had to go out. He left in a hurry."

Marks looked over at Donny Briggs. "That's what he said, Steve. I didn't think too much about it," Donny said.

Marks made his way to the Burnett Furniture store on Main. The store was doing a brisk business. Marks asked at the reception table, but the young lady manning the desk, shrugged and said she hadn't seen Ricky. He hadn't been in all day.

Marks called Ricky on his cell, but the call went right to voicemail. Lisa had called him before Marks had left the house but got the same outcome. Ricky seemed to have gone underground.

Marks called Stanley Cooper. "Stanley, put out an APB for Ricky Burnett. The little shit left his house a while ago. He didn't tell anyone where he was going and he's not answering his cell. We need to find him and figure out what the fuck he was talking to Micky Farrell about."

"Micky wanted to know if you were going to help him," Stanley said.

"He can cool his jets in the cell for a bit."

Marks tried Anders again and got him on the first ring. "How's the tooth, Anders?"

The Novocain was wearing off. The tooth didn't hurt, but the gums were irritated and swollen. "Not so good," Anders mumbled. "I've got some stuff to help the pain."

"Listen," Marks said. "I don't need you to come in right away, but we're looking for Ricky Burnett. He took off from the family house and is not answering his phone. I think he knows something about Henry's disappearance."

"You're kidding," Anders said, a bit of drool running out of the corner of his mouth.

"Not at all. I've got an APB out for him. Now we're looking for him and Maria Suarez. This gets more fucked up by the minute. You get a little rest and I'll keep you posted. Once we find Ricky he's got some answers we need."

Anders hung up. Would Ricky somehow be involved in the kidnapping of his own child? The wife, Lisa, seemed more obvious to want to get away from the parenting life. Anders shook his head. His thoughts turned back to Lloyd Turley. Anders would rest up, but he could rest and keep an eye on Turley. He would head home for a bit, hoped the mouth would feel better, and head out to Turley's ranch as night approached. He just had a hunch.

•   •   •

They kept trying to reach Ricky Burnett on his cell phone; there were no answers. Calls were put into all of the furniture stores. Again, no one had seen or heard from Ricky Burnett. Patrol cars were looking for Ricky's car. There had been no sightings. He had gone into hiding. No one knew for sure why, but Marks figured it had something to do with what he'd heard from Micky Farrell. There were a couple of times that Marks' cell phone rang. He was hoping to hear back from Tori, but that didn't happen. Secondly, he hoped to hear anything on Ricky Burnett. That also resulted in nothing. He checked in with Clay Johnson, but the call went to voicemail and had not been returned. He did get a call from Anders. Since there was nothing new to report on any front, and Anders had the bad tooth, he told him to take the rest of the night off. He told Anders he would get ahold of him if anything changed.

• • •

The dentist told Anders that once the pain killers wore off the area around the bad tooth would hurt. They were trying to save the tooth, but it would be better if the damn thing came out. Anders took a couple of pills and got ready to head out to the Turley llama ranch. It was close to eight o'clock when he got in his car and headed out. He was only out the door a few minutes when his phone rang.

"I'm kind of bored, Anders," Tammy said.

"I'm sorry," he said. "My mouth is swollen and it hurts. I'd be no fun at all tonight."

"You don't sound like you're in your apartment."

He turned down the car radio. "I'm going to go out and check out Turley's place at night. Just curious, but I want to see what goes on when the lights go out."

"Don't do anything stupid out there, Anders. You're on your own out there and Marks doesn't know what you're up to."

His mouth throbbed. He rubbed his jaw. "I know, Tam. I'm just going for a look. I've got this hunch."

"Don't hunch yourself out of a job."

He laughed. "I'll behave and I'll call you later."

"Be careful, Anders."

He smiled and hung up the phone. He drove in the direction of Turley's ranch.

From the top of a small hill, Anders got a pretty good look at the Turley house. There were lights around the house which lit it up where it was viewable from a distance. There didn't seem to be much going on. Anders sat in the car listening to a classic rock station; his mouth throbbed from time to time and he was getting a little tired. The clock on his dashboard said nine-forty-five.

• • •

Marks went to Lifers and ordered a cheeseburger and an IPA. He had a terrible ache in his shoulders that ran up his neck. They hadn't located Ricky Burnett. There were minimal clues in the homeless murders. He hadn't heard a word from Tori. For the first time that he remembered, Marks got the idea in his head that he didn't know what he was doing, not only professionally, but in his private life. He wondered out loud if he was a failure.

• • •

The clock had just edged past ten o'clock and Anders was about ready to call it a night when several lights went on in the back of Turley's house. He sat up straight in his seat and turned the radio off. The lights went off for a minute and Anders relaxed, but soon he saw the shining of headlights coming around the corner of the house.

Turley was on the move and going somewhere. There were two ways towards town and Anders hoped he would take the route away from him so he could follow. Turley's car came down the long drive and took a right turn away from where Anders was. He threw his car into drive and started down the road after him.

· · ·

Marks had taken two bites of his burger when he realized he wasn't really hungry. He didn't have that problem with the beer. He drank half of it in one swallow and quickly ordered another. He pushed his food plate away when his phone buzzed. He immediately thought of Tori, but the number was not one he recognized. It had a 312 area code, Chicago. He answered.

"Steve Marks," he said.

"Detective Marks, sorry for the late call, but I had some running around to do. This is Mike Burke."

Marks remembered he had called the old Chicago cop. "We had a little lead in the case, but I'm thinking that it's not much."

Burke laughed. "A little lead is better than no lead at all."

"True," Marks said. "We had a guy come into the animal hospital and check on Buster, who if you remember, was Herbert's dog. The guy said he picked up Buster along Route 20 after a night at the casino. We went and saw him and he claimed he was just doing the humanitarian thing of leaving the dog by the hospital."

"Doesn't seem like such a bad thing, but I don't blame you for following up. Does this guy have a name?"

"A name? Sure. The guy's name is Lloyd Turley. He runs, believe it or not, a llama ranch just outside of town."

There was silence on the other end of the phone. Marks wondered if the line had disconnected. "You there, Burke?"

"Run that name past me again," Burke said.

"Lloyd Turley. Do anything for you?"

"Lloyd Turley was the husband of Pauline Archer. She never took his last name for professional reasons. Pauline Archer was the sister of Richard Archer, my first victim back in 2008."

Marks could feel his mouth hanging open. "You're kidding."

"Not at all," said Burke. "You should get this guy now."

• • •

There is a place at the far end of town called The Lodge. It has an alley that runs behind it that backs up to a heavily wooded lot. Anders watched as Lloyd Turley parked his car and shut off his car's headlights. He parked behind Turley, about seventy-five yards away. He watched as Turley emerged from his car. Turley was wearing a long black coat. He reached into his car for something and took out a floppy black hat that he placed on his head. Anders could feel his heart rate intensify;

his palms got sweaty. He forgot about his tooth. He got out of his car and drew his gun. He started walking towards Turley. He got within fifty yards and shouted his warning.

"Turley, stop right there. Milton Police!"

Turley coolly turned and looked at Anders. In one quick motion he was back in his car, turning the ignition. Anders was stunned as the car's lights went on and the door was closed. Anders thought for a minute and then fired one shot wildly at the car that was starting to roll. He turned and ran to his car and got back in it. He had left it running so he threw it into gear and stormed after Turley. His phone rang and he saw it was Marks. He answered.

"Anders, Turley is the killer. He was married to Pauline Archer, the sister of Burke's first Chicago victim."

"You're a little late, Steve. I'm on Turley. He just left the alley behind The Lodge and is heading south towards the bridge."

"Shit! Keep in close contact if you can. Keep us posted. I'm with Stanley. We'll make our way towards the bridge."

Anders got within fifty yards of Turley who was not driving particularly fast. Turley got to 20 and turned right towards the massive bridge over the Mississippi. A car cut in front of Anders, but he was able to see Turley's car proceeding towards Iowa. Anders could see that the stop light in front of Turley had gone red, but Turley ran right through it. Anders still had the car in front of him, but weaved past it, onto to the shoulder, and through the light. A car almost clipped him. At the entrance to the bridge, he could see Turley. There was some traffic midway across the bridge. Turley pulled into the emergency lane and hit his break lights. Anders stopped well behind him. He called Marks. "He's in the pull off lane going west. He stopped his car," Anders said.

"Right behind you. Don't do anything stupid," Marks said, echoing what Tammy had said.

Turley got out of his car and stood by it for moment, facing the river. Anders got out of his car and slowly began moving towards him. "Turley, stop," Anders said.

Lloyd Turley turned towards Anders as Stanley and Marks drove by the scene in the middle lane. They pulled off the road about fifty feet in front of Turley's car. They each got out of the car. Turley took five steps towards Anders and raised his right arm. Anders didn't see his gun right away and was too stunned to draw his own. He took a deep breath as Turley fired. The bullet struck Anders in the left collarbone and once it was deflected, it exited through his shoulder. Anders felt the bone snap and the searing heat of the bullet as he was knocked backward onto the street. He hit his head hard on the concrete surface. He only saw the blazing bridge lights high above him before he passed out.

Marks saw Turley shoot Anders and raised his gun to fire, but Turley had gotten behind his own car and Marks' vision was impaired. He cautiously moved forward, wanting to get to Anders, but not wanting to get shot; Stanley Cooper was several feet behind him.

Lloyd Turley tossed his gun into the Mississippi. Then he quickly scaled up on top of the four foot restraining wall, holding tightly to the guide wires. At the top of the wall he turned and faced the traffic. His floppy hat was blown off into the river; his long black coat billowed behind him. His long gray hair was pushed away from his face.

Marks saw what Turley had done and moved out from behind the car. He had Turley trained in his Glock; Stanley came up the other side of the car. "Turley, get down from there right now," Marks said.

Turley laughed, a crazy giggly laugh. "It's too late, Detective. Everything is too late. As they say in sports, the clock is running out."

"Get down," Marks ordered.

"No. Not today. I'm not going to be arrested. It's just too late in the game," Turley said.

Marks didn't take his eye off of him. "Why, Turley? Why kill those men? And why the people in Chicago?"

"The homeless," Turley said. "The dirty fucking homeless. The scum of the earth. They killed Pauline's brother, Richard, and then she vowed to kill them all. Granted, she was killing them one at a time. When Pauline was taken from me, I felt it was my duty to continue her work, but then things got too hot, as you cops like to say, and I had to leave Chicago. I waited a long time, but Milton seemed like a great place to resume my work and to raise my llamas."

"Who did all the killing in Chicago?" Marks asked.

Turley smiled. "Does it matter?"

"Get down, Turley," Marks said, taking a step closer.

Lloyd Turley looked at Marks and let go of the bracing. It might have been the strong wind, but both Marks and Stanley would say that Turley took a perfect, backwards dive off the bridge, tumbling more than a hundred feet into the icy, river waters.

"Jesus Christ," Stanley said, rushing to the edge of the bridge to look over.

Marks holstered his gun and ran to Anders. He knelt by the young cop and felt for a pulse. He got one, but Anders was unconscious. He yelled to Stanley to call 911. He looked at Anders' face; He looked to be sleeping. "Don't go on me, Anders," he said. He took Anders' hand.

•   •   •

They all waited in the waiting room as Anders underwent surgery. Marks was there along with Tammy Glazer, Stanley Cooper, Lou Katz, and Anders' mother. She kept praying out loud, asking that God not take her only son. None of them knew the extent of damage that Anders had endured. One thing was for sure, the loss of blood had been extensive. Damage to any vital organs was unknown when they took him into surgery.

Marks felt especially bad for Tammy and Anders' mother. The two women were trying to console each other but kept falling into fits of tears and hugging each other. Marks wanted to help but felt useless. He decided it was better to stay out of the way. He got some results from the scene on the bridge. Lloyd Turley's gun was somewhere in the river. His car was immaculate, except for a pair of women's high heels in the front seat. A police boat had been put into the river, complete with divers, but there was no sign of Turley's body, dead or alive. Mike Burke had been contacted and started to write up a report for the Chicago Police Department, closing four murders. The original murder of a homeless man, Richard Archer, was still unsolved.

At two-ten AM, a young looking doctor made an appearance in the waiting room. He looked tired, like they all were, and didn't smile. Marks felt his stomach tighten. "I want you all to know that Anders' surgery was a success. The bullet fractured his collarbone and exited the left shoulder. There was some muscle damage, but no organs were injured. The collarbone needed some repairs and, of course, rest will be required. Anders lost a good amount of blood, but that has been replenished. He is sleeping now and I suspect he will be out for some time. I am confident that he will make a full recovery."

The men in the room were all excited, celebrating the news with back slapping and loud exclamations. The two women, Tammy, and Ander's mother, went back to their hugging and crying. Marks made sure to say goodbye to them, but he wasn't sure that they heard him.

He had parked his car in the underground lot and made his way to the elevator. He'd been up almost the whole day and needed a shower and was hungry. He was pretty sure he was going to fall asleep as soon as his head hit the pillow. He got to the elevator and a figure came out from behind a car. Marks had only one thought, "this is when I die."

"Steve, sorry, I didn't mean to startle you," Ricky Burnett said.

Marks didn't know whether to punch him, shoot him or just arrest him. "You took off, Ricky."

"I know. I know. I needed sometime to figure some things out."

"Micky Farrell told me some things about you," Marks said.

Ricky shook his head. "Micky doesn't know anything about this."

Marks let that go for a minute. "Tell me what's going on."

"I made a big mistake," Ricky said. "I had a little fling with Maria Suarez."

"That's not news."

"Well, when I broke it off with her, she was very upset with me. She threatened me and the way she got back at me was through Henry."

"She took Henry?"

"Her and Clay Johnson. Clay met her and became enamored with her, and she liked him. They took Henry and are holding him for ransom."

"But there was no ransom demand."

"It was all done privately with me. They want a million dollars and they will return Henry. I told them I don't have a million dollars, but they persisted."

Marks' neck muscles tightened. "Why didn't you tell us?"

"They said if there was any interference from the police, Clay said he could monitor this, that we would never see Henry again. They said they could move Henry in another direction, up into Canada and then Europe. They said there were buyers for white kids."

"Jesus Christ," Marks said.

"I think I know where they have him," Ricky said. "Clay has a house on Goose Lake, about twenty miles from Dubuque. I was there once. Clay told me he likes to go up there to get away from things, to hide out. It's very secluded."

• • •

The house on Goose Lake was secluded. There was a long drive that wound through thick pine trees to get to the place. The sun was just starting to come up, reflecting off the lake in the distance behind the one story log cabin. Marks and Stanley Cooper made the half hour drive to the house in near silence. They weren't sure what they'd find. Ideally, they hoped for Maria Suarez and Henry. Marks didn't want to deal with Clay Johnson, but he knew he might not have that option.

As they got close to the end of the drive, Marks had Stanley cut the lights on the cruiser. He stared at the house for a minute. There was a light on the outside front of the house, but nothing from the inside. It was just past six o'clock.

"How do you want to play this, Steve?" Stanley asked.

"For some reason, I don't think we should just ring the doorbell. Do you want the front or the back?"

Stanley rubbed his bushy mustache. "I'll take the front. At some point we've got let them know we're here."

Marks felt nervous. They should have bought more men. There was a large oak about twenty feet from the front door. "Get behind that tree. When I text you, yell out that you're with the Milton Police. Get behind that tree. I'll go around in back."

"Weapons drawn?"

"I'm thinking that's a good idea."

They both got out of the car and headed up the remainder of the drive. Stanley peeled off towards the oak; Marks continued around the house on the drive. Behind the house, parked at the end of the drive, stood a black Range Rover. He walked towards it and took cover behind it.

Inside the house, Clay Johnson had heard the vehicle come up the drive. He'd seen the cops turn off their lights and get out of the car with their guns drawn. He saw Stanley Cooper and Steve Marks make their way towards the house. Stanley headed towards the big tree in front of the house. He saw Marks take the drive around towards the back. He thought quickly and figured his only way out of this mess was to take out the two cops and then head out of town. He could get what he wanted out of Ricky Burnett; it didn't matter where he was holed up. He figured Marks to be the tougher of the two cops to take out. He headed for the back of the house.

Marks was about to text Stanley that he was in position when a door in the back of the house opened. Clay Johnson stepped out of the house wearing gray sweatpants and a tee shirt. For a minute, Marks thought how silly he looked. Clay turned and started towards the car. "What the hell are you doing here, Marks?" Clay said.

Marks' hands were down by his side; his gun was pointed squarely at the ground. "Do you have Henry Burnett in that house, Clay?"

"What kind of dumb ass question is that?" Clay said, and he raised his arm and fired a small revolver at Marks.

The bullet struck Marks in the right arm. It hurt like a bee sting. Marks dropped his gun but hit the dirt rolling towards the back of the Range Rover.

With his other arm, Clay Johnson raised a Magnum .45. He fired two shots at Marks, both striking the Rover. "You motherfucker," Clay yelled. "I'm going to kill you."

Whether it was his dislike of Marks or his sudden obsession with killing him, Clay forgot Stanley. Stanley heard the shots and came around the other side of the house behind Clay. He could see him approaching the car. He couldn't see Marks but knew he must be down. Clay was stalking Marks, moving slowly towards the Rover, the .45 out in front of him. Stanley got up pretty close. "Drop the gun, Clay," Stanley said. He had his Navy Colt Revolver pointed at Clay Johnson.

Clay turned slowly towards Stanley Cooper. "Hey Stanley," he said. "You're not going to shoot me because we used to be friends, and I'm about to cut you in on a deal where you can make a ton of money."

Stanley spit on the ground. "We were never friends, Clay, and, I thought you were a pompous asshole. Secondly, I will shoot you if you don't drop that gun."

Clay looked in the direction of Steve Marks but couldn't see him. He turned completely towards Stanley Cooper. The thought of jail popped into his head. An ex-cop in with the cons. If he just gave up, that's what he would have faced. He only had one more chance. He quickly raised his gun hand.

Stanley's bullet hit Clay Johnson just above the sternum. It knocked Clay off his feet and onto his back. His gun went flying. Stanley walked over and looked at Clay. His eyes were open in disbelief. "You fuckin shot me," Clay said.

"You okay, Steve?" Stanley yelled.

Marks got up off the ground and came from behind the Range Rover. The bullet had only grazed his arm, but there was some decent bleeding. He came over to where Stanley was hovering above Clay. "We've got to get him an ambulance."

"Fuck that," Clay Johnson said through blood bubbles coming out of his mouth. "You finally got me, Steve, but not really. Stanley Cooper of the Wild West killed me. Let the record show that. Let it also show that

I kidnapped Henry Burnett and wanted a one million dollar ransom." Clay coughed hard and a lot of blood came up.

"Tough to get a signal," Stanley said.

"On my laptop," Clay managed to choke out. "Find the file named King Henry."

Clay shuddered once and his eyes went blank. There wasn't any need to do anything further. They knew he was dead.

"I've got something in the car for your arm," Stanley said.

"Forget that for now. I'm fine. Let's go get Henry. And Stanley, thanks for saving my life."

"I've never shot a man, but I ain't shamed of the one I did."

They entered the back door; the one Clay had come out of. They both had their guns out again. There wasn't a light on in the house and the sun was just starting to brighten the day. They moved through the kitchen and into the main living area. In a rocking chair sat a beautiful Hispanic woman bouncing a small boy on her knee. The boy had a smile on his face and giggled ever so lightly. The woman had tears running down her face.

"I'm sorry," she said. "I am so sorry for what I have done."

Marks nodded. "Stanley, get what you can for my arm. I'll help Maria gather her stuff and Henry's so we can take him home."

• • •

Henry Burnett was reunited with his family about two hours after the shootout at Goose Lake. At about the same time, the body of Lloyd Turley was fished out of the Mississippi. The body showed no prominent external damage; the initial thought was that he had drowned. Maria Suarez was being held in the jail in the basement of the Milton Police Department basement until she could be officially arraigned. Stanely Cooper, after a bit of a hero's welcome, and processing a full report of the shooting, went to Lifers with his girlfriend and started on vodka tonics. Marks had his arm treated. The wound was superficial but was deep enough to cause some heavy bleeding. Once he was cleaned up and released, and had filed his report, he went and saw Lou Katz. Katz told him to take a few days off. Marks went home, took a shower, and changed clothes. He headed for Ricky Burnett's house.

There was no longer any police presence at the house. There was fresh coffee and blueberry muffins. All of the family members hugged Marks and thanked him. Marks had a cup of coffee and a muffin and found himself laughing at little Henry as he played on the floor with Lisa. Ricky's father smiled broadly; his mother was mostly crying. Marks went into the kitchen for more coffee. Ricky followed him.

"Steve, I really want to thank you for what you did for my family. I don't know what would have happened if we couldn't have gotten Henry back," Ricky said.

Marks sipped the coffee. He was going to wait a day or two to have this conversation, but they were away from the family. "But you had some plans, but they got changed."

Ricky laughed. "What do you mean?"

"Before he died Clay Johnson told us that he had abducted Henry and demanded a ransom of one million dollars from you. He fully admitted to the crime."

"Yeah. That's not surprising, seeing how it's the truth."

Marks took another sip of coffee and placed his cup on the counter. "He also told us about a file that he kept on his laptop titled King Henry."

Marks let that comment sink in. Ricky said nothing.

"In the file there were a couple of email transactions. In one, Clay tells you that a buyer is being arranged for Henry. He says the offer looks to be in the area of $250,000. He asks you to confirm that's okay. You responded okay."

Again, a short laugh. "It's not what you think, Steve."

"Oh, it is, Ricky. You were trying to move Henry through Dubuque to Canada and onto Europe. I'm thinking that you backed out of this at the last moment, you dumped Maria Suarez, and Clay and her decided to double cross you. At one time you asked Micky Farrell if he knew anything about this kidnapping ring. He wanted no part of it, but Clay decided to play the game

293

until you pulled the plug. He had a thing for Maria, they partnered up, she grabbed Henry, and then the game got nasty."

"Steve, you've got to hear me out. Before Henry came along, Lisa and I had the best thing going. It was fantastic. Everything about it was unreal. When Henry came along, everything changed. Life wasn't fun anymore. Lisa changed. Our relationship changed. She was looking for excitement again, but not from me. She started fooling around. I got involved with Maria. It all had to stop. I thought if I moved Henry, we could get back to where we were. I made a terrible mistake."

Marks shook his head. "You are a person that had everything from the day you were born. You ended up with your dad's business, a beautiful wife, and a great little boy. There's always glitches in life, Ricky. You had a few, but you went in the wrong direction to try and fix them. What you did was inexcusable."

"What are you going to do?"

"I'm not going to embarrass you in front of your family today. There is too much joy in this house at this moment to be so cold. I will let you enjoy this day. Tomorrow is different. You can come into headquarters by nine tomorrow and turn yourself in. If you don't show up by then, I will come and arrest you for plotting the kidnapping of Henry."

"Steve, listen, there has to be a way we can work this out."

"Stop while you are ahead, Ricky. Don't make me sick enough where I decide to shoot you."

Marks made his way back to the living room and bade his farewells to the family. He reached down and gave Henry Burnett a little pat on the head. Henry waved at him and said goodbye. Marks gave one more look at Ricky Burnett. He would always remember the look on Ricky's face, total defeat.

• • •

Anders was sitting up in his bed, watching a daytime game show. He smiled when Marks came into the room.

"You look pretty good," Marks said.

"Feeling better, mostly just a little weak. Heard you found Henry Burnett."

"It's a little complicated, but Clay Johnson was working with Ricky to push Henry through to Canada and then into Europe. Ricky got cold feet and backed out on the deal. Clay with Ricky's little girlfriend, Maria Suarez, decided to blackmail Ricky, but Ricky turned us on to them."

"Clay Johnson under wraps?"

"Clay got me in the arm, a minor wound. Stanley shot Clay, not so minor."

"He's dead?"

"Very much so. So is your pal, Lloyd Turley. They fished him out of the river."

"He was killing those men and also the victims up in Chicago?"

"It's a little complicated. We're thinking the ex-wife did the killing in Chicago. Her brother had been Burke's first case, one that was never solved. She went on a vigilante kick."

"Turley's wife?"

"Yep, but she died. Burke came around asking about her and Turley left Chicago. Turley started to continue her quest of killing the homeless, wearing some women's heels. Very bizarre."

Anders shook his head and shifted on the bed. "What about Ricky? What happens to him?"

"Told him to turn himself in tomorrow or I would go get him. I think his life has hit a bad spot."

"Looks like your two big cases have been solved."

"Pretty much wrapped up, but paperwork, but we need you back soon so we can get to work on other stuff. I'd like you to stay with us full time."

Anders' face told the story. "I don't think so, Steve."

"You'll go back to Sterling?"

"Not that either." He closed his eyes for a moment. "I had a long talk with Tammy. There's something there and I don't want to screw that up. I don't want to hurt her. I don't want to end up like my dad, shot by some random nut job. I'm going to move down here with Tammy. I'm going after my master's degree. I'm going to try and teach."

Marks smiled. He thought of passing up the job in Chicago. "No better time to chase your dreams than the present."

"I mean, the cop thing was exciting, but the getting shot part kind of sucked."

Marks felt his arm itch where the bullet had creased it. "Yeah. Just a little."

• • •

Marks found his mother sleeping in her room. She looked peaceful; you wouldn't be able to tell how sick she was. Marks watched for a bit and was amused when he saw a smile cross her face. He wondered what she was thinking or dreaming about. Had she wandered into another long gone relative? He didn't want her to suffer. He hoped that when she did go it would be like this, dreaming and smiling.

"She's had a pretty rough couple of days," a voice behind Marks said. He turned and there was an older nurse in the doorway. "I'm glad that she's able to rest now."

"Sure looks like she's happy."

"And proud, too."

"What do you mean?"

"She is very proud of you. When the news came out that you had stopped the Homeless Killer and found Henry Burnett in one day, she couldn't stop talking about it. She couldn't stop saying that you were her son."

Marks looked again at his mother and felt tears forming in his eyes. For the first time he was glad to have stayed with the Milton PD. "That's nice to hear," he said quietly.

"You should be proud of yourself, Detective Marks. That killer was a horrible person and that poor, Henry

Burnett, out there, all alone. You've done some great things for our little town." She patted Marks on his arm and left the room.

He watched his mother sleep for a while, the slow breathing the only sound. After a while, he left the room.

• • •

Susie was working the counter at the animal hospital when Marks walked through the door. She looked like he had arrived with life -saving goods. "Oh, Detective Marks, I am so glad to see you."

"Hi, Susie. Why are you so glad to see me?"

"The doc wants us to move, Buster. That means we give him to a shelter, and they hang onto him until somebody adopts him or..."

"I get it," Marks said. "You don't have to worry. Get Buster ready. I'm taking him home with me."

They walked back to the caging area. Buster jumped up as soon as he saw Marks and his tail began to wag. Marks could see that he had put on some weight. "He looks pretty good," he said.

"He's a great dog," Susie said. "You are doing a very good thing by taking him home."

Marks smiled. He could get used to all of this adulation. "He deserves a nice home."

• • •

Marks was watching an NBA playoff game in his living room. He had picked up takeout chicken and what was left of the meal was on the table in front of him. Before he got his own food, he stopped and picked up food and other supplies at a pet store for Buster. Susie had given Marks a leash and Buster walked obediently by his side wherever they went. Now, Buster was curled up on the couch beside Marks, dozing on an old blanket.

Marks looked at his new friend and back at the TV; the Warriors were killing the Suns in a less than interesting game. Marks yawned and realized sleep would do him good and soon. He heard a key rattling in the front door. He turned in that direction. Tori came through the door, pulling a medium-sized suitcase behind her.

"Hey," she said.

"Hey," he said.

"Man, you like you're tired."

"I'm thinking that my eyes are going to close any minute now."

She smiled. "I've heard you've been pretty busy and successful."

"A little busy and some good things happened. What happened to Chicago?"

She sighed. "A big city, kind of dirty, and lots of people everywhere. Exciting for a bit, but I kind of miss our view."

"Milton isn't so bad," Marks said.

"Want to stay for a while?"

"I do," he said.

"Me, too," she said. "With you."

Marks smiled. "That's nice to hear."

She moved a little further into the living room and noticed the dog sleeping quietly on her sofa. "Who's your friend?"

"This is Buster. He's going to be staying with us."

She smiled. "He looks like a nice dog."

He patted Buster on the head. "Buster is a great dog."

The End

ABOUT THE AUTHOR

John Sturgeon is the author of the four-book *Levee District* series published by Black Rose Writing. Black Rose has also published his stand alone novel, *The Murder of Fatty Fuller*. The fifth *Levee District* book, *Evil Returns* is due out in early 2023. John is an avid reader and a mediocre golfer. He resides in Wheaton, Illinois and has a winter residence in Sarasota, Florida, where he resides with his wife, Mary.

NOTE FROM THE AUTHOR

Word-of-mouth is crucial for any author to succeed. If you enjoyed *Burn Marks*, please leave a review online—anywhere you are able. Even if it's just a sentence or two. It would make all the difference and would be very much appreciated.

Thanks!
John Sturgeon

We hope you enjoyed reading this title from:

BLACK&ROSE
writing™

CPSIA information can be obtained
at www.ICGtesting.com
Printed in the USA
LVHW090045071022
730138LV00015B/533